Rona carefully closed the lid on the piano and rolled the stool back underneath. When she turned, Anna was still standing in the doorway.

"What's the name of that song?" Anna asked. "I'm not familiar with it."

"'Lover's Dream,'" she replied as she walked to the door. Anna didn't move.

"It's a beautiful song. I'm surprised I've never heard it before," Anna said.

Rona licked her lips and glanced away.

When she didn't reply, Anna asked. "Do you know who wrote it?" Anna stepped toward her.

"Yeah." She took a deep breath and fought the urge to retreat. She started to answer, and the words died as Anna leaned in and kissed her.

Visit

Bella Books

at

BellaBooks.com

or call our toll-free number

1-800-729-4992

When Love finds a Home

MEGAN CARTER

Bella
BOOKS

2005

Bella Books, Inc.
P.O. Box 10543
Tallahassee, FL 32302

Printed in the United States of America on acid-free paper
First Edition

Editor: Christi Cassidy
Cover designer: Sandy Knowles

ISBN 1-59493-041-4

Martha
My home is with you.

Acknowledgments

Martha—Sometimes words aren't enough. Thank you for all you do. Listing everything would be a book unto itself.

PJ—Thanks for taking the time to read the manuscript.

Heather Fitzpatrick—Thanks for explaining plane handlers to me and for your never-failing sense of humor. Stay safe, sailor.

Terry—A woman who will probably never read this book, but who nonetheless inspired it. Wherever you are, please know, I promise never again to look without seeing.

Christi Cassidy—What can I say? There was something better waiting to be brought to light. Thanks for not letting me get away with being lazy.

Becky Arbogast—Thanks for all your hard work.

About the Author

Megan Carter lives in Texas. She enjoys hanging out with friends at the coast and taking long, romantic road trips with her partner. Megan is the author of *On the Wings of Love*.

You may e-mail the author at mcarterbooks@aol.com.

Chapter One

Rona pulled the tattered blanket more securely around herself and Karla, the trembling child she held. The temperature was dropping rapidly. Tiny needles of sleet darted like sparkling schools of minnows through the glow of the security lights that illuminated the side of the building. Today was her thirty-sixth birthday. Had her parents remembered? The child in her arms shivered. All she could do for her was to hold her closer. The enormous cooling unit that looked like something out of a science fiction movie not only allowed them a hiding place, but it also protected them from most of the weather and placed them in a good position for quick access to the rear entry door.

"How much longer?" Tammy whispered.

Rona leaned over until her lips were touching Tammy's ear. They couldn't afford to be caught and chased away by the fat security guard. "It won't be much longer, but we have to be quiet. As soon as I nudge you, grab Katie and follow me. But for God's sake be quiet when you do."

Tammy nodded and hugged the child she was holding closer.

Rona looked from Karla, the young girl in her arms, to her twin sister, Katie. They were only four but had been living on the streets with Tammy, their mother, for over a year. Rona didn't know Tammy's entire story, only that there was an abusive husband hunting her. He had already found her at least once, but she ran away again at the first opportunity. Tammy had told her she was petrified of losing her kids. They were her life.

Rona glanced nervously at the rear door. Something was wrong tonight. There didn't seem to be any activity within the building. Normally, both the security guard's truck and the van used by the cleaning people would be parked behind the building. Tonight, the only vehicle in sight was a light-colored Honda in the side parking lot. She knew the security guard's routine by heart. He would hang around until the cleaning people moved down to the first floor. They always started on the top floor of the four-story complex and worked their way down. When they made it to the first floor, he would go to the second-floor lounge and sleep until it was time for him to make his rounds at midnight. Then he would check the door at the main entrance and the back door before going back to the lounge and sleeping until five. At that point, he would return to the tiny cubicle where he was supposed to spend his nights, fill out a few papers and leave at six. Rona assumed each tenant had a key to open the front door, but a wide-shouldered, gray-haired man was the first one in each morning. He arrived shortly after the security guard left and he always left the front door unlocked. As soon as he disappeared into the elevators, she would walk out the front door and disappear.

Rona had stumbled onto this little goldmine by accident. She had been searching for a place to sleep for a few nights, to avoid being picked up in one of the raids that the San Antonio Police Department were staging in an attempt to clear the homeless out of the downtown area. While slipping through the back parking

2

lot, the alien-looking cooling system caught her attention. She had started crawling among the massive pipes and units, checking out its possibilities as a new home. That's when she noticed that the cleaning people propped the back door open while they rolled their carts filled with garbage bags out to the dumpsters. For a few short minutes, the door was open and unwatched as they emptied the cart. Rona returned to watch the building each night for two weeks. Every night the routine was identical. The security guard would hang around until the four-person cleaning crew came down. He would then get on the elevator and disappear until midnight.

Then one miserably cold, rainy night, she got desperate enough to dash into the building while the door was open. As she raced down the narrow hallway, she caught a glimpse of the tiny cubicle where the security guard was supposed to be and then the elevators. The hallway led to a small lobby that housed two waist-high ficus trees, along with half a dozen chrome and imitation leather chairs. She hid behind one of the chairs and waited until the cleaning crew left. After letting enough time pass to ensure the cleaning crew was not returning, she explored the first floor and found a second hallway that led to an architect's office located across from a lawyer's office. She tested both doors and found them locked. On tiptoes, she climbed the stairs and heard the guard snoring long before she spotted him stretched out on a sofa in the lounge. The lights from the nearby vending machines cast an eerie glow around him.

Careful not to wake him, she slipped back into the stairwell before stealthily exploring each of the four floors. The second and third floors consisted of offices for an insurance company, an investment firm and a financial planner. At the end of the hallway were two doors displaying the names of oil companies. It was the fourth floor that made her smile. A computer software training center took up the entire fourth floor. The main training center was locked like the offices on the other floors, but the restrooms in the hallway were not. The women's restroom contained two chairs that she could pull together and use as a makeshift bed. The following morning she was back in the lobby behind a chair when the security guard came down to fill out his forms and leave.

At first, she had been terrified of being caught by workers coming in, but after the wide-shouldered man arrived and left the door unlocked, she was free to leave with little risk of being seen.

The office complex became her ace in the hole. Only on the worst nights, like this one, would she take the chance. Tonight she was breaking her own golden rule of not bringing someone with her. Over the last several months, she had developed a soft spot for the twins, especially little Karla. When the colder than usual February temperatures started dropping and the city began to hum with the possibility of snow, she went searching for Tammy.

As the time crept by, she began to worry. If the cleaning people weren't there to prop open the door, she wouldn't be able to sneak inside, and tonight was going to be bad. The sleet was coming down much harder now. The parking lot was beginning to take on a shiny gleam. She sensed Tammy's nervous glances. Rona had promised the girls a warm place to sleep tonight and she was beginning to fear it wasn't going to happen.

Tammy touched her arm and nodded toward the parking lot where the one lone car waited. Two men were walking toward it. Even from this distance, Rona recognized them as Harper and Roach. Two homeless men anyone with any sense avoided like the plague. They were both trouble.

Rona cursed under her breath. If they broke into the car, she and Tammy could forget about trying to sneak into the building tonight.

Katie started to giggle when Roach slipped and fell on the icy pavement, but Tammy quickly shushed her.

He got up and the two men made their way to the car, peeking into the windows. As they walked around to the passenger side of the car, the back door to the office complex opened with a loud squeal.

Rona's muscles tensed to dash inside. When she turned, she saw a tall dark-haired woman rather than the cleaning crew she was expecting. Rona's muscles slowly relaxed as a she watched the woman carefully make her way toward the car. She was carrying a large briefcase, and a purse hung from her shoulder. A quick glance back to the parking lot showed Roach and Harper were nowhere in sight. "Where did they go?" she whispered in Tammy's ear.

"They're behind the car."

Rona knew what was about to happen. "We have to get out of here." She clutched Karla to her and started to stand.

"What about her?" Tammy asked and nodded toward the woman gingerly picking her way across the parking lot.

"She'll learn a lesson that she won't soon forget," Rona replied without looking at the woman. She felt bad for her, but there was nothing she could do. Sometimes life handed you a bum deal. She began to make her way around to the other side of the gigantic cooling system.

"Rona, wait," Tammy hissed. "We can't just leave her."

"Are they going to hurt her?" Karla asked as she twisted her head around, trying to see the woman.

"No. They won't hurt her. They're just hiding," Rona murmured.

"That one that fell was Roach," Katie piped in. "He's mean. He tried to hurt Mama."

Rona stopped and looked back at Tammy, but Tammy wouldn't meet her gaze. A scream echoed from the parking lot. *Where was the damn security guard?* This is not my problem, she told herself. They needed to find shelter somewhere else, and she had no idea where that would be. All the best spots would be taken by now. As she turned to leave, Katie began to howl that they were hurting the woman.

"We've got to do something," Tammy said. Rona stopped when she saw the glistening of tears on her cheeks. Tammy was tough. She never cried.

Rona cursed and set Karla down. "Damn it. Wait here." She

started running toward the car. As she left the covered protection of the cooling system and stepped onto the slippery pavement, her feet almost slipped from beneath her. Years of ice-skating as a child in Michigan finally paid off. She used her arms as balance. It looked like she might be too late; the woman was on the pavement and Harper was struggling to yank the purse off her arm. She realized she wasn't going to make it across the icy parking lot in time to stop them. In the hope of buying the woman a little extra time, she began screeching like a wild woman. Maybe if she made enough noise they would run. Both men whirled to face her and took a step away from the woman. For a moment, Rona thought they were going to run, but they stopped and actually took a few steps toward her.

She was on the verge of running back to Tammy and the girls when another screaming ruckus kicked up behind her. *Good old Tammy.* Rona renewed her own shouts. Apparently, Roach and Harper found the second intruder more than they wanted to deal with and ran off into the night.

When Rona reached the woman, she was trying to get up. "Let me help you," Rona said.

The woman screamed and lashed out when Rona touched her arm.

"Where in the hell is that security guard," Rona muttered.

Tammy and the girls were making their way across the lot. Rona decided to wait; seeing the kids might calm her down.

"Get away from me," the woman yelled as she swung her arm.

"Will you stop it," Rona snapped. "You damn fool. I'm trying to help you."

The woman peered at her suspiciously but finally nodded and tried again to stand. This time she allowed Rona to help her.

"Is she okay?" Tammy asked.

"I don't know, but we need to get out of here in case someone called the police." Rona glanced around nervously.

Ignoring her, Tammy stepped closer to the woman. "Did you hurt yourself when you fell?" Tammy asked.

"My head," she answered as she kept swaying.

Tammy ran her hand over the woman's head. "There's a nasty bump on the back of her head."

When Rona released the woman's arm, she almost did another nosedive.

"She needs to get to a hospital," Tammy said as she helped steady the woman.

"She can call for help. I'm sure she has a cell phone. We have to get out of here," Rona insisted.

"We can't leave her," Tammy protested. "She can barely stand. They might come back."

"Please, don't leave me here," the stranger whispered.

Tammy leaned over and picked up a ring of car keys from the ground that Rona hadn't noticed. "Help me get her into the car," Tammy said.

"No. I'm not going to get any more involved than I already am," Rona insisted. "Don't you understand that we have to find a warm place to sleep tonight and her stupidity just cost us the perfect spot." Rona caught Karla's disappointed glance just before the child stepped forward and braced her tiny body against the stranger's legs, as if she could help hold up her upright. Katie immediately rushed to her aid.

"We'll help you, Mama," Karla said.

Rona swallowed the curse that threatened to erupt as she watched the girls temporarily overcome their fear of strangers in order to assist their mom. "Christ in a handbasket," she grumbled as she grabbed the woman's arm. "Open the door first," she said as she gently moved the kids out of the way.

It took some doing, but she and Tammy eventually got the woman buckled safely into the front passenger seat.

"You and the kids get in the car," Rona said as she went back to pick up the woman's purse and briefcase and toss them into the car.

"No. I need to find a place," Tammy said as she continued to stand on the opposite side of the car.

"The hell you do," Rona snapped. "You got me into this mess and you're going with me every step of the way."

"Where are you going?" Tammy asked.

"*We* are taking her to the hospital and dumping her ass there, and then *we* can find a place for the night."

Tammy ushered the kids into the car. "Watch your language. You know I don't like that kind of talk around the girls."

"Don't you think they're going to hear worse in jail?"

"Mama, are we going to jail?" Karla cried out.

"See what you've done," Tammy hissed as she leaned over to comfort Karla. "No, baby, they don't put kids in jail. Rona's just being mean."

"Will they put you in jail, Mama?" Karla sniffed.

"No. I'm not going anywhere. Rona, tell them." Tammy's tone of voice left little doubt that she was pissed.

Rona looked back to find Karla watching her with suspicion clearly written on her face. She rolled her eyes and sighed. "We're not going to jail. I was just teasing. Now, everyone get in the damn—in the car. Please."

Chapter Two

It took Rona a moment to figure out how to turn on the car's headlights. When she accidentally turned on the windshield wipers, Katie piped up from the back.

"Are you sure you know how to drive?"

Rona bit back a retort as she turned on the defroster to help clear away the thin layer of ice forming on the windshield. She was trying to adjust the defroster fan when the woman reached over and did it for her. "You seem okay to me. Are you sure you need to go to a hospital?"

The woman looked at her and seemed rather dazed.

"Rona," Tammy snapped.

"Yeah, yeah," Rona muttered, as she put the car in gear and began to ease her way out of the parking lot.

"Who are you?" the woman asked. "What happened?"

"Shirley Temple," Rona snapped sarcastically. "Two men

attacked you in the parking lot. We're going to drive you to the hospital."

"Thank you, Shirley," the woman said as she pulled her coat tighter around her and began to tremble.

With the woman silent, Rona ignored her and turned her attention to driving. The steering wheel felt odd, yet good, in her hands. She hadn't driven in a long time. She used to love to drive. As she grew more comfortable with the car, she noticed the faint smell of lavender. The scent reminded her of her grandmother's room. Rona was only three when her Grandfather Kirby died and her grandmother came to live with them. She would make lavender sachets and tuck them among the silky handkerchiefs and undergarments in her dresser drawers. As a young girl, Rona would sneak into her grandmother's room to open the drawers and smell the fragrant aroma. She could remember how the beautifully decorated cotton handkerchiefs had felt beneath her hand. She pushed the memory away. A long time had passed since the last time she touched anything soft. In her world, softness equated to weakness. You quickly learned that if you were weak, you didn't survive long on the streets. She had endured the past sixteen months by being tough and ruthless. At first, she was too numb to care about anything. A part of her wanted to die, or at least she thought so at the time. After almost being raped at one of the shelters, the first tiny spark of self-preservation ignited. She started trying to escape the streets, but she quickly discovered no one wanted to hire a homeless woman who possessed only minimal job skills. Even the men who arrived in trucks each morning at the work centers looking for day laborers seldom had work for women. In desperation, she tried to do the one thing she swore she would never do again—music—but no one at the clubs would even let her audition. They took one look at her dirty, ragged clothes and kicked her out. In truth, she didn't have much of a voice. She could play rhythm guitar but so could almost anybody with even the slightest interest in music. Her skills on keyboards were much better, but she had been forced to sell all of her equipment. The only area where she felt she stood out from the tens of thousands of other musicians was her songwriting skills. No one important was going to take the time to listen to someone looking as she did now.

Rona saw the brightly lit hospital sign and followed the directions to the emergency room entrance located at the back of the building. As soon as the car came to a halt, an orderly came rushing out. Rona eased the window down and called out, "She fell and hit her head. She seems to be drifting in and out of consciousness."

A wheelchair appeared and the woman was quickly removed from the car. Before whisking her away, the orderly leaned down and poked his head into the car. He frowned and drew back slightly as he took in her appearance. "Admissions will need to talk to you and get all her information."

Rona nodded. "I'll park the car and then come back." She held her tongue as she drove away. She had no intentions of coming back, but first she needed to get Tammy to agree to her plan.

After parking the car, she turned off the motor and sat listening to the sweet silence. The three in the backseat remained motionless, allowing the silence to intensify. Rona had spent most of her nights on a narrow concrete ledge beneath an overpass—not that she did a lot of sleeping. There was the constant noise of traffic and the fear of someone attacking her for her blanket, shoes or something as small as a slice of bread. Mostly, it was a place to curl up and try to stay warm.

She ran a hand over the smooth leather of the dashboard and smiled as she remembered the battered interior of her ancient Chevy Impala. The car had been a gas-guzzler, but its enormous trunk and backseat were perfect for hauling the band's equipment. For the briefest moment, she saw Mary sitting in the seat next to her smiling. Without thinking, she reached out a hand to her, only to find vacant space—the same vacant space that had been filling her heart since Mary's death.

"We've done all we can. We'd better get out of here," Tammy said.

11

"Wait a minute," Rona said as she twisted in the seat to look at Tammy. "We could stay warm in this car tonight."

"Someone would find us out here," Tammy said as she glanced down at the sleeping kids.

"I didn't say we'd have to stay here." Rona kept her voice low. "There are plenty of places where we could park this car and not be found for a couple of days."

Tammy frowned. "We'd be in a lot of trouble if we got caught."

Rona shrugged. "We're going to be in worse trouble if we can't find a place to stay tonight. It's freezing. Even if we got desperate enough to go to a shelter, by now they'd all be full and they'd turn us away."

Tammy looked at each of the twins and smoothed down their hair.

Rona glanced away and as she did, she noticed the woman's purse. She picked it up and began going through it.

"What are you doing?"

She heard the disapproval in Tammy's voice. "I'm looking for something that will tell me who she is. I'm just curious." She found her wallet and opened it. The driver's license identified the woman as Anastasia Pagonis. The address was not a street she recognized, but that didn't mean much. Unless it was a central downtown address, she wouldn't know it. There was less than thirty dollars in cash in the wallet, but there were two major credit cards along with a few useless department store cards. The major credit cards were safe to use for at least a few hours. She knew of four convenience stores that ignored people using credit cards bearing names that changed from week to week, as long as the amount being charged was under twenty dollars. With the car, she could easily hit all four stores in less than an hour. Eighty bucks would buy several cans of chili and canned meat. For a moment, she let her imagination run wild. They could drive down to Brownsville where it was warmer, or maybe all the way to Florida. A glimmer of guilt tried to worm its way into her conscience, but she quickly squashed it. The woman probably had scads of insurance on these cards and wouldn't be held responsible for any of their charges. Even if she did, eighty dollars wouldn't be that much for someone like her. She probably made more than that before her morning coffee. Rona slipped the cash and the two major credit cards into her sock, being careful to get them below the big ragged hole.

The car would be a different issue. Rona knew that if she took it to any of the areas she was thinking of, it would soon be stripped down to its chassis. She pushed the thought away. Keeping this car could mean the difference in the four of them surviving the night. She and Tammy might be able to make do, but the kids were too small. She looked over the seat at their sleeping faces. Even beneath the blankets, it was obvious that they were painfully thin. They should be tucked into warm beds with nothing more to worry about than whether there would be nursery school tomorrow or not.

Tammy looked up. "Don't steal anything from her," she pleaded.

To avoid waking the girls, Rona forced her voice to stay low. "It's a car. The insurance company will replace it. What's the big fucking deal?"

Tammy shook her head. "I don't know. It just feels wrong."

Rona got a handle on her anger. Tammy never responded well to anger. "Listen," she said calmly. "We have no place to go. That office building she came out of has lawyers, realtors and other professionals. You know she's not hurting for money."

"What if she's just some clerical flunky?" Tammy hissed back. "Maybe that was why she was working so late."

Rona suppressed a groan of frustration. "Look at the car she's driving. It's almost brand new." She was about to say more when she remembered the statement that Katie had made about Roach hurting Tammy. "It's because of Roach isn't it? What did he—"

"Shut up," Tammy snapped so harshly both girls were startled awake.

Rona remembered the guy who tried to rape her at the shelter. It had been too dark to see his face, but from the contact she had with him while fighting him off, she came away with a vague sense of his general physical description—short, not as thin as most, and clean-shaven. For weeks afterward, she would shake with rage every time she saw a homeless man fitting that description. Tammy's empathy for this woman was going to be the death of them.

"Rona, put whatever you took back. We don't need the car. I can't take the chance of being caught. I'd lose them for sure. Please."

Rona gritted her teeth as she pulled the items from her sock and stuffed them back into the wallet. "All right, but if we're going to leave the car here, I'm not taking a chance on someone else stealing it and me getting blamed." She jerked the car door open.

"Where are you going?" Tammy demanded.

"Wait here. I'm going to take her wallet and her keys in and give them to the doctor or someone. As soon as I'm done, I'll come back for you."

"Here, take this or you'll freeze," Tammy said as she tossed Rona's old blanket to her." Too mad to care, Rona wrapped it around her and headed back toward the hospital. She was freezing by the time she had crossed the parking lot, which was much closer to the front entrance than it was to the emergency room. She raced up the salt-covered steps, already anticipating the delicious warmth that would greet her inside. She had barely cleared the front door when a security guard grabbed her by the arm.

"You're not sleeping in here," he said as he spun her around and pushed her toward the door.

"I brought a woman in and I need to give her the keys to her car," Rona said as she tried to control her anger. The son of a bitch wouldn't even listen. Too late, she realized she should have walked back around to the emergency room entrance where people who looked like her were a more common sight. This wasn't the first time some overly zealous security guard had thrown her out of a building.

"Yeah, right. Get out of here before I call the cops and have your ass hauled downtown." He made a slight huffing sound. "Course, that's probably exactly what you want. A night in jail guarantees a free bed and a couple hot meals. I don't know why you bums just don't get a job."

"Who would you have to bully then, you dickless wonder?" Rona snapped.

He shoved her out the door. "If I catch you trying to sneak back in here, I'll give you a taste of this." He patted the nightstick attached to his service belt.

A young couple was heading up the steps. Rona saw them scurrying to the far side of the stairs, getting as far away from her as possible. Embarrassed and angry, she pulled the blanket more securely around her shoulders with as much dignity as she could muster before walking back to the car. She would lock the keys and wallet inside the car. Let Ms. Anastasia Pagonis hire a locksmith.

She strode back to the parking lot and stopped. She couldn't remember where she had parked. No single vehicle stood out in the sea of cars. She wasn't even certain what color the car was. It was a Honda, and she vaguely remembered it was a light color. She walked toward a silver Honda and glanced into the backseat. It was empty. She saw another similar-looking car a couple of rows over and went to check it out. As soon as she leaned over to look through the window, a blinding pain shot through the back of her legs. Her knees buckled under the pain and sent her crashing to the ground. Before she could recover, something cold pulled tightly against her throat.

"Where's that smart mouth now," a voice growled in her ear. "You're about to find out that a few years for grand theft auto won't be as much fun as a quiet night at the county jail."

She managed to get one hand around the nightstick that was crushing her windpipe and relieve enough pressure to speak. "I'm not stealing it," she croaked. "I have keys. I told you—"

He tightened the pressure on her throat before grabbing her other arm and twisting it behind her back. "Save your breath. Anything you've got to say can be said to the police."

"I'm telling you—"

He cut off any further conversation by tightening the pressure on her arm. "Wrong, bitch. You ain't telling me nothing." He shoved her forward while keeping her arm twisted behind her.

Rona tried not to cry out, but each step sent a searing pain through her shoulder. It seemed to take them forever to reach a side door. The security guard fumbled with a large ring of keys for several seconds before he finally found the one he needed. He opened the door and pushed her inside a small room that smelled strongly of sardines. As the door slammed behind him, he fastened the key ring back on his belt.

Rona barely had time to see a metal desk and a long row of filing cabinets before he pushed her to the floor and slapped one end of a handcuff over her wrist. With an ease that led her to suspect he had done this before, he passed the cuffs around the desk leg and snapped the open end around her other wrist. "Will you listen to me?" she tried again.

He slapped the nightstick against the desk near her head without answering and reached for the phone.

She wiggled her body into a more comfortable position and listened to him explain how he had caught her breaking into a car in the parking lot. She closed her eyes and told herself to remain calm. The keys to the car were in her pocket. Hopefully this Anastasia Pagonis wasn't so rattled that she wouldn't remember that Rona had driven her to the emergency room, and all of this would be straightened out as soon as the police arrived.

She forced herself to stay silent. The guy was nuts, and provoking him would only make it worse. If she pushed him too far, there was no telling what he'd do. She kept her eyes closed even when he paced back and forth in front of her, occasionally tapping her shoulder with the stick.

It felt like hours before the police, a tall, handsome African-American woman and a blond man with the physique of a body-builder, finally arrived.

The security guard started his explanation of catching her stealing the car, but the woman cut him off.

"Why is she on the floor handcuffed to that desk?" she asked.

"Do you see a jail cell around here anywhere?" the guard replied, clearly unhappy that he was having to explain himself to a woman.

"Unlock the cuffs," the bodybuilder said in a voice so soft Rona almost missed the order.

The security guard hesitated until the bodybuilder took a step toward him.

As soon as the cuffs were off, Rona pulled herself upright and grimaced as pain shot through her right calf. She was certain there would be a nasty bruise where the guard had struck her with the nightstick.

The policewoman extended a hand to steady her. "Are you okay?"

Rona nodded.

"What's your side of the story?" the woman asked.

"Why you asking her?" the security guard demanded. "You know damn well she's going to lie about what she was doing out there."

The policewoman hooked her thumbs over her belt. "Why don't you sit down somewhere and wait until we need you?" she instructed. Before the security guard could claim the desk chair, the woman pulled it around and motioned for Rona to sit down. The officer perched on the corner of the desk before pulling a notebook from her coat pocket and flipping it open. "Okay, let's hear your story."

Rona had been on the streets long enough to know that you didn't reach into your pockets or make any sudden moves around police officers. She carefully related a somewhat altered version of what had occurred, careful not to mention Tammy. When she had finished, both officers were staring at her.

"So you're saying you have the car keys and wallet that belong to this woman, and she's in the emergency room right now?" the woman asked.

Rona nodded. "The keys and wallet are in my pocket. I can show them to you, if you'd like." She waited until the woman nodded, before reaching two fingers into her pants pocket and slowly pulling out the items.

"She probably stole them too," the security guard complained.

The policewoman turned to her partner. "David, would you go over to the ER and see if you can locate this"—she checked her notes—"Anastasia Pagonis."

"You come with me," David said to the security guard.

As soon as both men were gone, the policewoman began to flip through her notes. The minutes ticked by slowly for Rona. The overheated room made her swelter under the double layer of clothing and blanket she was wearing. She let the blanket fall off her shoulder, but was too embarrassed to remove her top sweater because the one beneath was full of holes. To make matters worse, her unwashed clothes were beginning to give off a stale odor. She tried to bathe whenever she could sneak into the office complex, but it was impossible for her to be able to wash her clothes and get them dry before having to go back out into the cold come morning.

As the minutes ticked away, Rona wondered if Tammy was still waiting for her in the car or if she had gotten scared and run. If Roach and Harper had recognized them, they all might have to leave San Antonio. She considered where she would go to next. Since she no longer had the option of a nice set of wheels to take her somewhere, maybe Corpus Christi would be a possibility. It was a long walk, but it would be warmer. She might even be able to find a vacant spot to claim as her own somewhere near the water. Of course, being near the water would be too cold during the winter. She recalled a conversation she'd had with another homeless woman who had moved from Corpus to San Antonio because of the mosquitoes. During the summer, the pesky insects swarmed without mercy. The thought of black clouds of buzzing mosquitoes made her shudder. Maybe she could hop a freight train to Dallas. She had never hopped a train before, but she had talked to several people who did so regularly. One woman traveled cross-country that way twice a year. As soon as the temperatures started to rise, the woman hopped a freight train headed north and eventually made it all the way to New York. When the first cold snap came, she headed back toward California. Rona had always wanted to see San Francisco. She wondered if she'd have the guts to try to hop a freight train for a journey all the way to San Francisco. Tammy probably wouldn't agree to go with her. If she did, they certainly couldn't be hopping on and off of freight trains with the twins.

At some point in her travel fantasies she dozed, but the door opening woke her. David and the security guard had returned. David was pushing the woman in a wheelchair.

"Her story checks out," David said as he parked the wheelchair to one side.

The policewoman slid off the desk. "Okay, then our business here is done." She turned to Rona. "I'm sorry this happened."

Rona could see the security guard bristling. She shrugged and turned to the woman she now knew as Anastasia Pagonis. She looked much more alert.

"Are you all through here?" Rona wanted to get out of there before anyone started asking more questions.

"No. I need my wallet and insurance card and, by the way, my name is Anna Pagonis. Thank you for helping me." She hesitated a moment. "Wasn't there a woman with kids—"

Rona glanced at the glowering security guard and interrupted. "I'll walk back over there with you to get that taken care of," Rona said as she handed the keys and wallet over to their owner. She didn't want to hang around and give the security guard another chance to use that nightstick.

The paperwork took much longer than Rona would have ever anticipated. As they were getting ready to leave, the nurse turned to Anna and asked, "How are you getting home? You can't drive."

"She'll drive me home," Anastasia said, massaging her temple.

Rona and the nurse stared at her in surprise. The nurse slid a sideways glance at Rona. "You were attacked. Perhaps you should call someone you know and trust. Is there anyone, a family member or a friend, you can spend the night with?" she asked.

"I'll be fine. The doctor said it's nothing more than a nasty bump." She pointed to Rona and continued, "She drove me here." She stopped. "I'm sorry. I didn't mean to assume . . . would you mind driving me home? I'll pay you and of course I'll pay for a cab to take you wherever you need to go."

Humiliated, Rona glared at the nurse. "I'll drive you, and you don't have to pay me."

The nurse shrugged. "Suit yourself, but the hospital is not responsible for your safety once you leave here. Remember, Ms. Pagonis, no driving for at least twenty-four hours, and if the headache persists you'll need to contact your family physician."

It took another twenty minutes to finish the paperwork, but at last they were ready to leave. Rona parked Anna's wheelchair out of the way of the emergency room doors. "I'll go get the car."

"Thanks."

Rona shuffled from foot to foot and played with the keys until Anna finally glanced up. "Is something wrong?"

"I don't remember where I parked it," Rona replied gruffly.

"Once you're out in the parking lot, push that button," Anna said as she pointed to the keyless entry gadget on the key ring. "The lights will start to flash."

Rona walked out into the frigid night. The cold wind cut through the thin blanket and sleet stung her face. She hunched her shoulders against it and headed back around to the general location of where she thought she parked the car. As she walked, she began to berate herself. *This is what you get for trying to be a goody two shoes. From now on, I won't worry about anyone except myself. If I hadn't gone all softheaded and tried to rescue Tammy and the kids, I'd be sleeping in a nice warm chair right now.* She vaguely acknowledged that her assumption didn't ring true because the cleaning people hadn't shown up for work, but it didn't stop her from feeling sorry for herself. She pushed the locator button and gained a small measure of satisfaction in knowing that if Tammy was still in the car, the sudden flashing of the lights would scare the crap out of her. For good measure, she pushed the button again.

Chapter Three

Rona's calculations on the location of the car weren't off by much. When the lights began flashing, she was only two rows away. A small sense of relief rushed through her when she saw that Tammy was still in the car.

"What took you so long?" Tammy asked as soon as Rona got in.

"Same old bull—" Seeing the kids were awake, she cut the curse short. "They made her fill out a dozen forms." She wasn't going to tell anyone about how the security guard or the nurse had humiliated her.

"What are we going to do now?" Tammy asked.

Rona could hear the fear in her voice and experienced a small measure of regret for her earlier pettiness with the lights. "She wants me to drive her home, but not to worry, she'll call a cab to take me home."

Tammy gave a harsh laugh. "That's decent of her."

Rona cranked the car. She knew she didn't have to tell Tammy that they were in trouble. At this time of night, all the best places would be occupied. Maybe just this once they should try to find a shelter or a church that would have room for them, but that was probably a pipe dream too. Those places would already be filled beyond capacity. The best they could hope for now was finding an unlocked car somewhere in Anna's neighborhood, and she wouldn't place money on those odds.

When Rona pulled the car up to the entrance, Anna was standing inside the doorway waiting. She came out before Rona could stop the car. As soon as she climbed inside, she turned to the strangers in her backseat.

Rona watched as Anna slowly assessed the kids. She could almost feel Tammy trying to blend into the car's upholstery.

"I'm Anastasia Pagonis, everyone calls me Anna. Thanks for helping me. I'm sorry you had to sit out in the cold waiting," she said as she smiled at the kids.

"Pagonis? Is that Greek?" Rona asked in an attempt to direct her attention away from Tammy.

It seemed to work as Anna turned around and fastened her seatbelt. "My paternal grandparents came from Lakonia. That's—"

"Part of the Peloponnesus peninsula that forms the southern part of Greece," Rona finished for her.

Anna looked at her and nodded carefully. "Yes. Have you been to Greece?"

"No, but you'd be surprised by the amount of useless knowledge the human brain can store. I used to spend a lot of time at the public library until having to see the 'increasing number of derelicts and misfortunate' began to make the well-meaning citizens of San Antonio uncomfortable."

Anna squirmed in her seat before saying, "I guess everyone is uncomfortable with things they don't know or understand."

Rona chuckled and ran a hand over the dashboard. "I don't know. I've never driven a car this nice, but I don't feel the least bit uncomfortable."

"You know that's not what I meant," Anna replied, giving her a sharp look. "I'm sorry. I don't remember anyone's names?"

23

"I'm Rona." She was surprised when Tammy introduced herself and the girls.

"Take a left out of here," Anna instructed.

The car fishtailed slightly as she made the turn out of the parking lot. Rona eased her foot off the accelerator.

Anna reached over and raised the fan speed on the defroster. "The interstates are probably closed by now, so we'll have to take the long way home." She gave Rona further directions.

"So what happens if it really snows tonight?" Rona asked.

"The city will shut down, basically."

Rona chuckled.

"I take it you're not from here?" Anna asked.

"No. I was born and raised in Port Austin, Michigan. That's located on the tip of the thumb," she replied. "*My* great-great-grandparents were from Norway." She gave Anna a mocking smile and was certain she saw her blush before she turned away.

"Sorry, I guess I got a little carried away with the genealogy," Anna said. "What did you mean by the tip of the thumb?"

"Michigan is shaped like a mitten." Rona held up her hand to demonstrate. "Port Austin is right about here." She wiggled her thumb.

"That's interesting. I'd never noticed that before," Anna admitted.

They rode in silence while Rona struggled to think of something to talk about. She didn't want to give Anna time to dwell on the kids.

Anna spoke first. "I really appreciate you driving me home. I could have called one of my brothers, but they would have read me the riot act for working so late. They mean well, but sometimes they can get overly protective. When we get to the house, I'll call a cab and have it take you home."

Rona couldn't stop the look of disgust she sent Anna's way. This time there was a definite blush.

"Or a shelter," Anna hastened to add.

Rona shook her head and answered without thinking. "Oh no. I'm not spending the night in one of those places."

Anna glanced at her. "It's supposed to drop well below freezing tonight."

Despite the warmth of the car, Rona couldn't stop the shiver that ran up her spine. "There are worse things than freezing to death. I tried staying in one of the shelters in Austin one night, and the men seemed to think all the women were there for their pleasure."

"All the shelters aren't that way, are they?" Anna asked.

"I don't know and I don't intend to find out." Rona said.

"The sleet is getting worse. No one should be out in this tonight." Anna was quiet for several seconds. "You pulled me out of a bad spot back there." She seemed on the verge of saying more when a small sneeze erupted in the backseat.

"Is she sick?" Anna asked.

"No," Tammy replied quickly. "She just sneezed."

Anna continued to look over her shoulder for several seconds. "Are they twins?" she asked.

"I'm Katie and that's Karla."

In the rearview mirror, Rona saw Tammy pull the girls closer to her.

"How old are you?" Anna directed her question to Katie.

Apparently, Tammy had communicated some silent signal to Katie to be quiet. "They're four," Tammy replied reluctantly.

"My youngest brother has twins. They just turned five." She turned around and stared through the windshield.

They rode in silence except for the few times Anna gave directions. The sleet was still falling steadily, but Rona felt completely at ease in driving. It felt good to do something so normal. When she got her life straightened out again, and found a job that offered vacations, her first vacation was going to be a long road trip, all alone on the road, no blaring music, none of those books on tape crap, just the sweet sound of tires on pavement.

"Turn left at the next light."

Rona turned and drove beneath a large stone archway holding a wooden sign for Stone Brook Estates. The bottom of the arch was hidden by a thick stand of shrubs.

Streetlights resembling the old carriage lights lined both sides of the street. The neatly kept homes were tucked away behind expertly trimmed hedges and large oak trees. In this area there were no cars parked on the streets. Reflective signs, tastefully displayed, warned anyone with ill intentions that a neighborhood watch program was in place.

"Take a left and then a quick right at the next block," Anna said.

Rona followed her directions.

"It's the third house on the right." As soon as the car pulled into the driveway, Anna reached up and pressed the remote that was hooked over the sun visor. The garage door began to rise.

Rather than pulling in, Rona sat staring at the house. "How many people live here?" she asked.

"Just me."

Rona looked at her and frowned. "You live in this huge place all alone?"

Anna glanced at the enormous two-story red brick house. "I bought it as an investment. I'm a financial planner," she explained. "This area was undergoing revitalization. In a few years the property should double in value."

Rona remained silent and continued staring at the house.

"I don't intend to stay here forever."

"It's none of my business where you live," Rona said as she drove the car into the garage, killed the engine and reluctantly handed the keys to Anna. There was an awkward moment as they all sat listening to the ticking of the cooling engine. Rona's head jerked up when the garage door began to slide down. "We should be going," she said to Tammy as the door hissed closed. She reached over and pushed the button to reopen the garage door before they started getting out of the car.

"Wait a minute," Anna said over the top of the car. "Let me pay you for your trouble."

Rona shook her head. "We didn't do it for the money." Then an idea came to her. She picked up Karla and bundled her beneath the ratty blanket.

"Where will you go?" Anna asked as she walked to the back of the car. The freezing wind blew through the open door. Anna pulled her coat more snugly around her and folded her arms. "Do you have someplace to go?"

Tammy was busy bundling Katie beneath her blanket.

"We'll be fine," Rona assured her as she deliberately turned Karla's innocent face toward Anna.

"It's freezing out there. If you have somewhere to go, at least let me call a cab."

Rona shook her head. "We're fine."

"Maybe you are, but what about those children?"

Rona heard an edge to Anna's voice that hadn't been there before. She wondered if she had misjudged this woman. They all jumped when the door began to close automatically.

"Come on inside," Anna insisted, "before we catch pneumonia." Without waiting for anyone to respond, she turned and walked to the door that led into the house.

Rona looked at Tammy, who was shaking her head no. She stepped closer. "It's late," she reminded her, "and we're a long way from downtown. I don't know this area. Do you?" She felt certain that Anna's guilt offered them an advantage.

Tammy shook her head again.

"Tammy, maybe we need to think about the kids."

"I always think about my kids," she snapped.

Rona apologized. "I know you do. I'm sorry. All I'm saying is that for now, just this once, maybe we should trust someone. She seems decent enough."

"Mama, I'm cold," Karla whispered.

Rona hugged the child to help ward off the cold but also for her unwitting help.

Tammy blinked rapidly and swallowed before nodding.

When they stepped inside, Rona heard Tammy's breath catch as

27

she gazed around the spotless kitchen of gleaming stainless steel appliances and black granite countertops. Everything seemed to sparkle beneath the overhead light.

"I guess you like to cook," Rona said as she continued to take in the kitchen.

"When I have time," Anna admitted. "Come on in." She led them through the dining room and living room. "I spend most of my time in the den," she said as they entered a medium-sized room that held a slightly battered recliner, a pair of end tables and a couch. Across the room from the couch was an overly ornate fireplace, and across from the recliner was a wide-screen television. The flooring was distressed pine boards that shone warmly in the light. Anna pulled her coat off and draped it over the back of the recliner. "Have a seat," she said and waved her hand toward the couch.

Everything looked too clean to sit on. Rona finally perched on the edge of the couch and held Karla on her lap. Tammy followed her lead and held Katie.

Anna sat in the recliner and leaned forward to talk to them. "Look, I don't know what your situations are and it's none of my business. I feel as though I've somehow made them worse. I don't know you and you don't know me, but I don't think you mean me any harm or you wouldn't have helped me tonight. If you'd like to spend the night here, there are three spare bedrooms upstairs. My room is down here. In fact, I rarely even go upstairs."

Rona practically shouted in glee, but she carried out her act perfectly. She stood so suddenly that Karla must have thought she was falling because she grabbed on to her and gave a small squeal. "We don't need charity," Rona protested.

Anna frowned at her. "I wasn't offering any. I was trying to return a favor." Without waiting for a response, she stood. "Besides, my mother would disown me if I sent company away without a meal." She smiled down at the twins. "Is anyone other than me hungry?"

Rona's feet itched to dance. She held her breath, terrified

Tammy would insist on leaving. Her gut twisted sharply as the girls looked to their mother for some guidance on whether they should accept the food or not. When Tammy turned to her, Rona gave what she hoped sounded like a sigh of resignation.

Anna nodded and turned to leave. "The rooms are at the top of the stairway. If you would like to see them, the food won't be ready for at least twenty minutes. I think you'll find everything you need. If not, there's a supply cabinet at the end of the hallway just outside this door." She pointed toward the den's entryway. As she walked out of the room, she stopped a moment. "Rona, could you help me with something, please."

Rona's heart flew to her throat. Had Anna seen through her? She set Karla down and followed her out into the hallway.

Anna started to speak and as she did, she held her hand up. "Before you yell, it's not charity. I just wanted to let you know that in the big closet at the end of the upstairs hallway, there's a box that has the word . . ." She hesitated and took a deep breath before continuing, "It has the word *bitch* written on the side. In it, you'll find some clothes. If there's anything you or Tammy can use, you're welcome to it." She took off before Rona could reply.

29

Chapter Four

Rona and Tammy stood at the open bedroom door and stared at the vast, sterile space. The walls and ceiling were white, as were the headboard and dresser. The carpet was a darker ivory shade. There were no knickknacks or photos to soften the harsh décor. The room was almost as big as the one-room efficiency Rona had shared with Mary in Austin. She closed her eyes and let her memory take her back to those four short years—the laughter, the love and the music—always the music, Mary's powerful voice accompanied by Lenny's soul-wrenching lead guitar and punctuated by Eric's pounding rhythm and Zac's thumping bass. Rona could almost feel the smooth yellow pencil in her hand scribbling desperately to record the lyrics that had poured so effortlessly from deep within her during those few golden months. The band had been on its way. If only . . .

Her eyes flew open as her body began to topple. Tammy grabbed her and eased her to the floor.

"When was the last time you ate?" Tammy asked.

Rona lowered her head to the floor and waited for the room to stop spinning. "Yesterday morning."

Tammy kept her hand on Rona's shoulder. "Just breathe deep; you'll be okay in a few minutes."

Rona closed her eyes and waited for the dizziness to pass. Normally, she could find enough change, dropped by people in a hurry, to buy a breakfast taco and on good days a cup of coffee. Once she had been able to buy a taco every morning for over a week after finding a ten-dollar bill caught in the debris clinging to a security fence around a construction site. The past week had been rough. No one seemed to be losing money. She and Malcolm, a seven-foot giant of a man who claimed he was from Kenya and had come to this country to play professional basketball, had finally gotten desperate enough to pick a few pockets.

During the first few weeks on the street, she tried to find work and had occasionally found an odd job, but as her appearance and clothes began to deteriorate so did the employment opportunities. At first, she had refused to steal. When the odd jobs disappeared, she had gotten so desperate that she stood on a corner of a busy Austin street and begged. It was the most humiliating experience of her life, and she swore she'd die before she did it again. She still drew the line at physically hurting anyone, but if a woman was careless enough to leave her purse open, she wasn't above lifting a wallet. Tourists were the easiest marks. Most of them were ridiculously careless with their money or shopping bags. Recently, however, times had been tougher than normal. The cold weather was keeping people at home.

After the dizziness passed, Rona sat up.

"Feeling better?" Tammy asked.

Rona nodded.

The girls were wandering around the room. "What do you think about this woman?" Tammy asked in a low voice. "Do you think we can trust her not to call the authorities?"

"She seems okay, but in case there's trouble and the cops show

31

up, I'll do something to cause a ruckus. You grab the girls and try to make your way back downtown. You'll have to be careful, because people in these neighborhoods will notice you fast."

Tammy agreed.

"If you see Malcolm, let him know where you're staying and I'll catch up to you eventually." She stood up. "Let's check this place out."

Together the little band of four slowly walked around the room, careful not to touch anything. She wondered what Anna's real motive was. No one opened their home to strangers. Her resolve wavered. Maybe it would be better to leave now. Even one night within these walls would make returning to the streets harder. She hadn't forgotten those first few days on the street—the gnawing hunger, the humiliation and discomfort of never being able to bathe properly and the constant fear of not finding food, dodging the sporadic police raids, fear of going to sleep and never waking up, or worse, waking up and finding that the nightmare was real.

They stepped into a spacious bathroom that was also completely white—the walls, tiled floor, rugs and linens.

"Isn't it beautiful?" Tammy whispered.

"It doesn't do much for me," Rona said, shivering at the coldness of the room. "Why don't you take this room?"

"Mama, can we take a bath?" Karla asked.

Tammy looked at Rona, who shrugged and said, "She said to make ourselves at home." She suddenly remembered the clothes Anna had mentioned. "I'll be right back."

At the end of the hallway, she found the closet. There, exactly as Anna had described it, was a cardboard box with the word *bitch* spelled out in large black letters.

Rona grinned as she dug through the clothing and wondered what the story was behind it. Inside she found several T-shirts, a few sweatshirts, a bright yellow sweater and two pairs of sweatpants. She pulled out the black sweatpants, a couple of the T-shirts and a faded red Texas Tech sweatshirt. At the bottom of the carton, she found a pair of thick wool socks and added them to her small stack. She returned the remaining items to the box and carried it down the hall to Tammy before leaving to explore the other two doorways. The room next to Tammy's bedroom was much smaller. There was a bed and dresser. The back wall was stacked high with brown moving boxes. Across the hallway, she found another bedroom very different from the white mausoleum. She flipped on the overhead light. This room was much smaller and held a hodgepodge of mismatched furniture. Several gold-framed, brightly colored Fiesta posters softened the white walls. This room was awash with vibrant colors and the fragrant scent of lavender. Everywhere she looked, there was color, from the pink and blue floral comforter to the rich cobalt blue carpet. The faint fresh smell of furniture polish teased her nostrils as she approached the bed. The rich tones of the maple headboard glowed beneath the overhead light. Rona laid the clothes from the box on the bed and prodded the mattress with her fingertips. The bed was soft and warm to the touch, as she remembered a bed being. Across the room, several lively-looking black and white porcelain kittens posed in playful settings across the top of an old scarred dresser. Rona went over to look at them. There were six figurines, each approximately three inches tall. One of them had a small butterfly perched upon the tip of its paw. The expression of sheer pleasure on the kitten's face brought tears to Rona's eyes. She rubbed a shaking, cracked fingertip across the kitten's face and marveled at the uncomplicated beauty of the scene. She tried to remember the last time she'd seen a kitten. Or even a butterfly. Embarrassed by the sudden rush of emotion, she quickly set the figurine down.

Unable to stop herself, Rona looked into the wide mirror above the dresser. On the streets, she was careful never to look at her own reflection in store windows. On the rare occasions she was able to slip into public restrooms, she religiously avoided looking into the tiny mirrors above the sinks. To do so would reveal what she had become, and to see that was to admit all she had lost. She stared at the disheveled woman staring back at her. The once short brown hair was now long and lifeless. She touched a rough fingertip to the dark hollows around her eyes. Mary had called her beautiful. What would she say if she could see her now? She moved away from the mirror.

A doorway beside the dresser led into a small bathroom sporting a seascape motif. She quickly grabbed the clothes from the bed and carried them into the bathroom where she stripped off clothes that had gone far too long without being washed. She rolled the stale-smelling clothes in the smallest wad she could and set them on the light green tile floor before stepping into the shower. She moaned in pleasure as the water poured over her. She had once thought the hardest aspect of poverty would be the lack of food and shelter, but she now knew it was the loss of dignity. It hadn't taken her long to learn that being homeless quickly robbed her of the most basic of human need—privacy. Of all the things she no longer possessed, privacy was the most dear. She ate, slept, bathed and relieved herself in public. During her first few days on the street, she had tried to maintain the same sense of propriety and uphold the social mores instilled in her as a child. She soon learned the streets had an entirely different set of rules.

Determined to enjoy the first real shower she'd had in months, Rona pushed away all thoughts and concentrated on the luxurious pleasure of hot water cascading over her body. She found shampoo, soap and a razor among the items on the shower shelves and took her time putting them all to use. After triple washing every square inch of her body, she reluctantly turned the shower off and wrapped herself in one of the enormous fluffy sea-green bath towels. In the medicine cabinet, she found a small plastic comb, deodorant, a new toothbrush and toothpaste. After combing her hair, she vigorously cleaned her teeth and felt the first shreds of humanity returning.

Before slipping into the new clothes, she meticulously cleaned the shower and left everything as tidy as she had found it. The clothes were meant to fit someone shorter, but they felt wonderful to her.

Chapter Five

Rona tapped on Tammy's door and smiled as a freshly scrubbed Katie opened it. She was wearing a T-shirt from the box. It hung below her knees.

"Mama's still in the bathroom," she announced as she grabbed Rona's hand and pulled her into the room.

Karla was sitting on the floor flipping through a magazine.

Rona sat down beside her. "What have you got?" As she got a closer look, she realized it was a flower seed catalog.

Karla scrunched over closer to her. "A book with pretty flowers." She thrust the catalog into Rona's hands. "Read it to me."

"Well, it's not really a reading book. It's a catalog that you order flower seeds from."

"But there's words." She pointed with her tiny finger. "Read this part here to me."

A fine sweat broke out along Rona's hairline. She had completed high school, but reading had never been easy for her, not like reading music, which seemed as natural as breathing. The numerous hours she'd spent reading at the library since she'd been on the streets had helped improve her reading skills, but she still wasn't comfortable reading aloud. Knowing Karla wouldn't know the difference, she read the words she knew and made up words for the ones she didn't recognize. She was saved from her misery when Tammy came out of the bathroom wearing a dark green sweatshirt and the gray sweatpants.

Rona jumped up. "Are you ready?"

Tammy looked up, a surprised expression on her face. "You seem awful eager to get back down there." She smiled teasingly. "Has something or someone caught your attention?"

Rona felt the blush run up her neck and across her face. Tammy knew she was a lesbian, but she had never made mention of it before. "I don't know what you're talking about," she sputtered.

Tammy chuckled. "Okay. You're just hungry."

"You bet I am," Rona said, stuffing her hands deep into the pockets of the sweatpants.

Tammy moved closer to Rona and slightly lowered her voice. "Check out the magnets on her refrigerator. You'll probably find a couple of them interesting." She gave Rona a wry grin. "Katie, put your shoes back on."

"I don't want to. I like the way the floor feels," Katie said as she dug her toes into the carpet.

"Well, I would like for you to put your shoes on," Tammy replied.

Katie gave a great heaving sigh as she plopped down and put her tennis shoes back on.

They walked back to the kitchen together. As soon as Rona picked up the smell of food, her stomach began a wild churning rumble. When Tammy's hand flew to her own stomach, Rona knew they were all as hungry as she was. It took every ounce of her willpower not to bolt into the kitchen.

Anna was setting the table when they entered the room. "Oh, your timing is perfect," she said. "I was about to take the soup off the stove. I hope everyone likes tomato soup. Since it's so late, I didn't want to fix anything too heavy, so I made some tomato soup and grilled cheese sandwiches." She waved to the kitchen table where plates and bowls waited. "Please, sit down."

"You don't have to feed us," Rona protested as they sat. A sharp pain radiated up her shin as Tammy kicked her.

"I told you. I'm Greek. It's in my blood to want to feed you. Entire cemeteries filled with my Pagonis ancestors would spin in their graves if I didn't feed you." She began to ladle soup into the bowls. "Of course, they'd also be spinning over what I'm serving."

"How's your head?" Tammy asked.

"A little headache." Anna returned the pot to the stove, grabbed the plate of sandwiches and sat down. "I guess they scared me more than they hurt me. They came out of nowhere. I mean, one minute I'm in the parking lot alone, and the next, they were right there beside me."

Rona's stomach grumbled loudly. Karla, who was sitting at the opposite end of the table, grinned. Rona didn't know if she had heard her or was just being sweet. She almost shouted with joy when Anna finally stopped talking and passed the plate of sandwiches to Tammy.

For the next few minutes, conversation was at a minimum as everyone, Anna included, dug into their food with relish. Rona couldn't remember a grilled cheese sandwich tasting so good. When the last of the plates were pushed away, they all leaned back with a contented collective sigh.

"That was a fine meal. Thank you, Anna," Tammy said.

Anna smiled. "I just wish my brothers could have heard you say that. They are forever giving me grief over my lack of cooking skills."

"My mama cooks good," Katie said as she gave a large yawn.

"I think someone's about tuckered out," Anna said as she glanced at the clock. "My gosh, it's almost one-thirty, no wonder she's so tired."

Tammy stood and started stacking the dishes.

"I'll do that," Anna said. "You all go on to bed. You must be exhausted."

Rona took the bowl from Tammy's hand. "Go ahead. I'll stay and help her." She didn't miss the mischievous smile Tammy sent her way. It was then that she remembered to check out the magnets on the refrigerator. Two were rainbow-colored. The one she could see well enough to read was for the San Antonio Gay and Lesbian Task Force.

After Tammy and the kids left, Rona and Anna moved quietly around the table gathering dishes. Rona found herself watching Anna. Did Tammy think she was attracted to her simply because she might be gay? Anna was tall with dark hair, and those dark eyes were nice, but she wasn't Rona's type. *As if I have a type*, she thought as she gave a small grunt. She carried the dishes to the counter while Anna loaded them into the dishwasher.

"That's everything," Anna said as she closed the dishwasher door and turned it on. They stood staring at it for a moment. "Would you like a beer or a glass of wine?" Anna asked and then waved her hand. "I'm sorry. I'm sure you're exhausted."

"A beer would be great," Rona replied.

Anna smiled. "Thank you. I'm sure you're just being nice." She removed two beers from the refrigerator and twisted the caps off before handing one to Rona. They sat down at the table. Anna traced the pattern on the tablecloth with her finger.

"Are you okay?" Rona asked.

Anna gave a small false laugh. "I know I'm being silly, but I can't stop thinking about how those men just appeared out of nowhere. I thought I was being vigilant, but I didn't even see them until they grabbed me." The bottle in her hand began to shake. She set it down and folded her hands on her lap.

Rona weighed the pros and cons of explaining what had happened. She couldn't see the harm in telling. After tonight, security at the office complex was sure to be increased and she wouldn't be able to sneak in again. "They saw you come out of the building and hid behind your car."

Anna looked at her. "How do you know?"

"Tammy and I were hiding behind that big cooling system thing behind the building. Those guys showed up just before you came out. They were looking for something to steal from your car. They heard you when you came out the door. It makes a loud screeching noise whenever it's pushed open. They heard it and hid." She stopped and shrugged. "They came around the other side of the car and then up behind you. You couldn't see them because they kept the car between you and them."

"That's when one of you came out screaming? I remember hearing someone screaming."

Rona nodded. "I didn't think they were going to leave at first, but when Tammy came charging toward them, they tucked their tails and ran."

"I'll never be able to thank you both for all you did tonight." She picked up her beer. "I'm sorry about the way they treated you at the hospital."

Embarrassed, Rona looked away. "It doesn't matter."

"It does to me," Anna said as she started to take a sip of her beer. The bottle stopped halfway to her lips. "Did you tell me your name was Shirley?"

"Sorry about that. I was being an ass." She looked up to find Anna watching her. For a moment, their gazes held until Rona shifted in her seat and cleared her throat.

"Where will you all go tomorrow?" Anna asked.

"Does it matter?"

"Of course it does. It would matter if it were just you and Tammy, but with the twins—" She stopped. "Aren't there some kind of programs out there to help her?"

"I suppose, but she won't go."

"Why not?" Anna asked.

Rona hesitated. She shouldn't be talking about Tammy's business, but recently she had begun to worry about the kids. Both were too skinny. They needed a home, with hot meals and warm clothes. They should have a bed to sleep in rather than some cardboard box in a vacant lot. They should be in nursery school. If Tammy didn't get them off the street soon, there was no telling what might happen to them. Besides, it might make Anna even more determined to try to *save them*. "She's running from an abusive husband."

"I know there are organizations that help battered women," Anna said. "My sister-in-law Lupie volunteers at one of them."

Rona shook her head. "You don't understand. She's terrified of him. He's already found her once and she ran off again. She usually avoids people. The only reason she was with me tonight was the weather. She knows people tend to remember the twins. I think that's how her husband found her before."

"I could call Lupie in the morning and ask her to come by after work. She could explain all the services that are available."

Rona swallowed her exasperation. This was not going the way she wanted it to go. "You don't get it," she said as she leaned toward Anna. "It doesn't matter what organizations are out there. Tammy is scared in ways that neither of us will ever understand. You don't know how hard it was for her to come here tonight. She's terrified that you'll call someone and that her kids will be taken away from her."

"I would never do that," Anna protested, clearly shocked by the suggestion.

Rona studied her for a moment. "No. I don't think you would, but then those aren't my kids. If they were, I might be a lot less trusting."

"There has to be something we can do."

Rona forced herself to remain calm. This was going to be easier than she thought. She leaned back and sipped her beer. "Why do you care what happens to us?"

Anna seemed to consider the question for a minute before she answered. "I don't honestly know. I mean, there's the obvious thing that no one should be homeless, and certainly not a woman with children." She stopped. "I guess it scares me. That whole there-but-for-the-grace-of-God-go-I thing."

Her answer surprised Rona. They drank their beer in silence until Rona finally stood. "I'm going to turn in. Will you be all right?"

Anna nodded. "There are extra blankets in the hall closet if you need them."

Rona left the room. Anna had no way of knowing that this was the warmest any of them had been in many days. As she walked up the stairs, she smiled. Her birthday had turned out pretty well after all.

Chapter Six

The smell of coffee and bacon pulled Rona from her dream. Mary was fixing breakfast. She stretched and opened her eyes. A moment of panic seized her as she stared around the strange room. As realization took hold, the smell of coffee and bacon began to lose some of its appeal. She glanced at the bedside clock and saw it was already after eight. She couldn't remember the last time she'd slept this late.

She quickly pulled on the clothes she had worn the previous night and wondered if she should try to wash her old clothes or whether they would simply disintegrate in the washer. She made the bed and went to brush her teeth.

On the way down, she saw that the door to the bedroom where Tammy and the girls had slept was open, but they were nowhere around. She found everyone in the kitchen. They had already eaten. Tammy and the girls were still dressed in the clothes Anna gave them the previous night.

"Good morning," Rona said as she smiled at the girls. "I guess I was a sleepyhead this morning."

"Would you like some coffee?" Anna asked.

Rona nodded. "I'll get it," she said as she went over to the pot. She sipped the black coffee on the way back to the table. It was a strong dark roast, just the way she liked it. "How's your head?" she asked as she sat down.

"It's sore, but the headache is gone." She walked over to the stove. "There's still some bacon," she said. "How would you like your eggs?"

There was a basket covered with a yellow cloth on the table. Rona flipped up the cloth and saw biscuits. "No eggs. I'll take that bacon and one of these biscuits and make myself a sandwich," she said as she winked at Karla.

Anna placed a dish with bacon on it in front of Rona before she began to pick up the dirty plates.

Tammy reached over and stopped her. "No, I'll do that. You sit down and drink your coffee."

Rona ate as Tammy moved around the kitchen, clearing the table and loading the dishwasher with an easy confidence, as if she were in her own kitchen. Tammy couldn't be more than twenty-five, although she looked younger with her long, slightly curly light brown hair pulled back and caught in a rubber band. Other than being painfully thin, she was somewhat pretty. A knot on the bridge of her nose gave it a slightly off-kilter look. Rona suspected the knot was the result of a broken nose. She was almost finished with her bacon sandwich when she realized everyone seemed to be waiting on her. "What's going on?" she asked as she looked around.

"It snowed," Katie said.

The biscuit she had eaten suddenly seemed very heavy in her stomach. She walked over to the small front kitchen window. The light reflecting off the snow made her squint. She pushed the kitchen curtains all the way open and wondered if Malcolm had found a warm place to sleep.

"Let's go into the living room," Anna said. "We'll be able to see the snow better." Together they made their way into the living room where Anna drew back the drapes on the large bay window. The front lawn was pristine. "Isn't it beautiful?"

Rona stared out at the cold white blanket. From this side of the window it was beautiful, but from the other side it wouldn't look quite so pretty.

"According to the radio, four inches fell and they're predicting we may get even more today," Anna said. "They've closed all the interstates and most of the city is shut down."

Tammy and Rona exchanged worried glances. As the small group continued to stare out the window, Tammy suddenly pointed, and in her soft Southern accent said, "Will you look at that? There's a man out there on skis." They all watched as the man glided down the street toward them.

He was almost to the house when Anna started laughing. "That's Julian, my silly baby brother," she said as they watched Julian's slender form ski up the driveway.

Anna went to the kitchen and raised the garage door for him. A moment later, he burst into the kitchen wearing an electric blue ski suit.

"Annie Bella, grab your boots. We're going to build a snowman." He stopped suddenly when he realized there were others in the room.

Rona saw his gaze take in the girls' clothing, but to his credit, he didn't miss a beat.

"I'm sorry. I didn't realize you had company." He yanked off the matching wool cap from his head as he walked over to the women and shook their hands. "I'm Julian. Anna's handsome brother," he said as he knelt down before the girls. "And who are these cuties?" He tweaked their noses.

"I'm Katie and this is Karla," she said and giggled.

"What's so funny?" he asked.

"Your hair is dancing," she replied.

"Dancing?" he glanced up at Tammy.

"Static electricity," she said.

44

"Ah." He reached up to smooth his hair. "I thought maybe it was doing the robot." He made a series of slow jerky movements that sent Katie into a new series of giggles.

Karla continued to cling to her mother's leg.

"I have a set of twins at home," Julian continued talking to Katie. "But one of them is a boy. He's not nearly as cute as you two are. Can I trade him for you?"

Katie shook her head and moved over to stand by Karla, who had hid her face against her mother's leg.

Julian tousled their hair and stood. "I'm sorry I barged in. I wanted an excuse to play in the snow, so I insisted on coming over to invite you to the house to help us build a snowman. Gina called the rest of the clan, and they'll be there."

"Julian and Gina and their five children live a couple of streets over," Anna explained.

Julian nodded to Rona and Tammy. "If you'd like to come, everyone's welcome."

Rona saw Tammy tense.

"I think we'll just stay in and drink hot chocolate today," Anna said quickly.

Julian nodded and winked at Katie. "Well, I'd best be on my way." He turned back to Rona and Tammy. "It was nice to meet you." They nodded as he headed toward the door.

"I wanna build a snowman."

Rona looked down to see little Karla staring at Julian.

He stopped at the door and turned back.

"Not today," Tammy said stroking Karla's hair.

"But there might not be no snow tomorrow," Karla insisted.

"Bring them on over," Julian said, unaware of the situation. "My twins are about their age. We have three more that are nine, seven and three, and then there's Hector's and Pietro's rascals, so there will be plenty of kids for them to play with."

Anna stepped forward. "Tammy's an old friend of mine from Miami. She didn't anticipate this cold weather and didn't bring clothes warm enough for the kids to be outside in this."

Julian nodded. "The same thing happened to us two years ago

45

when we went to Colorado to visit Gina's parents. There was a late snowstorm and as soon as we went out and bought coats, the temperature started warming up." He stopped a moment, and then turned to Tammy. "I'm sure Gina still has the twins' coats from last year. If you don't mind, the girls are welcome to use them for as long as you'd like. It would certainly be better than having to go out and buy one for just the time you're here." He looked at Katie and winked. "Although one of the coats is a *boy's* coat." He gave an exaggerated grimace that caused the child to smile.

Anna linked arms with her brother.

"Can we?" Katie whispered.

Tammy quickly brushed her hands over her face to wipe away the tears as she nodded.

"Wonderful. I'll go back to the house and get those coats. Annie Bella, come and help me get my skis back on, please." He waved again before they stepped out into the garage and closed the door behind them.

"Are you okay?" Rona asked as the girls ran to the window to wait for Julian to reappear.

Tammy nodded. "We should get out of here. These people scare me."

Surprised, Rona stared at her. "Why? They seem like nice people."

"They are," Tammy hissed. "That's the problem."

"How's that a problem?"

Tammy looked at her daughters. "It's harder to leave nice people, and"—she stared at Rona—"I know you're planning something. I don't want you to do anything to hurt them."

Shocked, Rona stared at her. "I would never hurt anyone."

"You don't have to hit someone to hurt them," Tammy said.

Rona was saved from replying by Katie's shout.

"There he goes."

Rona and Tammy went to the window to watch the young man. As he skied out of the driveway bundled in his expensive ski suit, Rona couldn't help but wonder about how much his outfit must have cost. She was going to have to be more careful around

46

Tammy; she was starting to know her too well. They were still at the living room window watching Julian disappear down the street when Anna returned. She was holding her briefcase.

"Well, since the entire city is shut down and the mayor is asking all non-essential personnel to stay off the streets, I guess I have no choice but to declare a holiday and keep the office closed." She nodded to them. "Make yourself at home. There's a television in the den. I'll only be a few minutes; I just need to reschedule a few appointments."

As soon as she was gone, Tammy turned to Rona. "When are we leaving?"

Rona gazed out at the snow as a sense of dread began to squeeze her stomach. They had a good thing here. Why couldn't Tammy see that?

"Rona." Tammy took her arm. "I think we should leave before she comes back."

"And go where?" she asked in harsh whisper. "If we leave here, we'll have to go to a shelter. Are you willing to do that?" She leaned closer to Tammy. "How long do you think those babies will survive in this weather?" She scrubbed the heels of her hands against her eyes. "Let's just go with the flow for now."

Tammy gazed at her closely.

"I'm not going to do anything," she snapped.

"You better not," she warned.

Taken aback by Tammy's sudden protectiveness toward Anna, Rona motioned toward the den. "Let's go see what they're saying about the weather on television. Maybe something will come to me."

The four of them sat on the couch as Rona turned on the television and found a local channel. As she suspected, the weather was the big news. The news crews had filmed endless shots of laughing kids and adults sledding down slopes on everything from an occasional real sled to large pieces of cardboard. Then the anchorwoman's voice turned serious as she began to explain the film footage of lines of homeless people waiting to get into shelters. When she announced that two people had already died because of

47

the freezing temperatures, Tammy reached over and clutched her arm. They were still glued to the news when Anna came in wearing neatly pressed jeans and a gray and white sweater pulled over a long-sleeved gray turtleneck. A pair of sturdy hiking boots encased her feet. She perched on the edge of the recliner.

"I need to talk to you both," she said.

Tammy glanced nervously from Anna to the girls.

Rona tried to read Anna's expression but couldn't. Was she about to ask them to leave? Maybe her brother's invitation to a family event had shaken her up.

Anna walked to a bookcase beside the television. "Do you girls like"—she glanced at the DVD in her hand—"*Dora the Explorer*?"

The girls looked at each other and shrugged.

"My niece loves this show. She'll watch it for hours." She popped the disc in before turning to Rona and Tammy. "Maybe we could talk in the kitchen while the girls watch television."

A look of concern crossed Karla's face and she started to stand. Tammy leaned over and patted her shoulder. "It's okay. I'll be in the kitchen." She kept her hand on Karla's back until the child nodded and sat back down. As if by some silent mutual agreement, the three adults remained in the room until the kids were engrossed in the cartoon. Karla barely gave them a glance as they slipped out of the room.

The women sat down at the kitchen table. Without preamble, Anna began, "I was watching the weather while I was dressing and it appears this arctic front, as they describe it, is going to be around for a few days. They're predicting more snow tonight and below freezing temperatures for the rest of the week."

"Please, don't call anyone. We'll go to a shelter," Tammy promised.

Anna looked at her for a long moment. "Maybe so, but you won't be able to get in. Because you have the kids, someone might be able to pull some strings and get you in somewhere, but I have another idea. You can stay here."

Rona wanted to jump up and continue her sham of outrage, but her knees were too weak. It was really going to happen. She had spent her last night on the street. They were both looking at her. "I can't take your charity." If the words came out as weak as they sounded to her, no one seemed to notice.

Anna glared at her. "Fine. Walk outside and see how long your pride keeps you warm. You know Tammy won't stay unless you do. Is your silly macho dignity worth one of those kids getting sick and maybe dying?"

Rona saw Tammy blanch.

"Well, is it?" Anna demanded.

"Tammy doesn't need me here. She can stay," Rona said. Anna's righteousness was starting to piss her off. Without realizing what she was doing, she stood.

Tammy reached out and grabbed her arm. "No. You can't leave. She's right."

Both Rona and Anna looked at Tammy in surprise as she squared her shoulders and turned back to Anna. "We thank you for your offer, but we have to help out where we can. I can cook and clean." She turned to Rona and asked, "What can you do?"

Rona's face burned under the scrutiny of the other women. She hadn't expected this. "I don't know . . . I mowed yards one summer. I can shovel snow and help clean." As they continued to watch her, she wanted to shout that she could shoplift and was a fair hand at picking pockets.

Anna leaned back in her chair. "Can you type?" she asked Rona.

"Yeah, some. I learned in high school and worked in an auto parts warehouse for a while. My job was to track inventory. I had to input new products into the system." *What the hell! Was she being interviewed?*

"Speed isn't so important, but accuracy is," Anna explained. "I was planning on hiring a temp to set up a mailing list and to help with the mail-out of an advertising campaign. It's only for a couple of weeks at most, but it should help to keep your pride intact," she said with a touch of sarcasm.

Tammy nudged Rona.

"I guess it would be okay," Rona replied.

Anna nodded. "Good. Now, for salaries—"

"Hold it," Rona cried. "I thought this was an even swap. You let us stay here while we work for you."

Anna frowned. "I can't charge you that much for staying here. It's not as though it's going to cost me anything. I'd heat the entire house whether you're here or not," she said with a shrug. "The water bill might be a little more."

"It'll cost you more to feed us," Tammy said.

Anna shook her head. "You're right, but it won't be that much."

"We should do something," Rona protested.

"I should contribute more, since there are three of us," Tammy said.

Anna rubbed her forehead. "This is getting too complicated. Rona, the temp position is going to pay six-fifty an hour. You'll be saving me money because the temp agency would cost more. Tammy, I'm currently paying a cleaning service one hundred dollars to clean once a week. I'll cancel the service. You take over the housecleaning as well as most of the cooking during the week. I'll increase the weekly salary to two hundred dollars and I'll cook on the weekends to give you a break. I'll take care of the household bills. You two take care of your personal items and anything extra you want." Anna stood. "Is it a deal?"

Tammy slowly nodded.

Rona wasn't certain how long she should pretend to protest. She decided to give one last weak protest. "I don't see what you're gaining here."

Anna gazed at her. "Are you this stubborn about everything? If it makes you feel better, your salary is tax-deductible." The phone rang before Rona could respond.

As Anna went to answer the phone, Rona turned to find Tammy watching her. "What's wrong with you?"

Tammy shook her head. "You promised me. I'm going to be watching you."

"I think I'll go see how the kids are doing," Rona snapped as she stomped out of the kitchen.

Chapter Seven

An hour later, Rona stood by the bedroom window gazing out at the snow-covered roofs. The overcast sky and snow reminded her of Michigan. It had been nearly fifteen years since she lived there. In rare, unguarded moments, she would still be overtaken by a sense of longing for those cold crisp mornings when she would wake in a warm bed to the smell of her mother's freshly baked cranberry tarts.

She heard the muffled laughter of the kids across the hallway. Anna's brother had returned in his SUV with a large cardboard box marked GOODWILL and some lame story about the kids' coats being packed away in it. He left the box with Anna so she could take it to the women's shelter, which was supposedly near her office.

After he left, Rona helped Tammy carry the box upstairs. The girls opened it and immediately began to pull out more clothes than they could possibly ever remember. At the bottom of the box were a few women's sweatshirts, two pullover sweaters and three pairs of jeans. The jeans were a little big in the waist, but they were wearable. While the girls were digging through their new wardrobes, Rona mentioned to Tammy that Anna must have told Julian the truth while she was helping him with his skis. The clothes had been given to them in such a way as to allow them to retain as much of their dignity as possible. When Rona made a comment about charity, Tammy scolded her and told her to accept the gesture in the spirit it was given.

The clothes in the box Anna had given them the night before were a much better fit for Tammy, since she was a few inches shorter. The pants from the box Julian brought over were still too short for Rona, but they fit better in the waist since she was heavier than Tammy. By mixing and matching the clothes from both boxes, the women were able to put together a wardrobe that certainly wouldn't fool anyone, but at least it wouldn't be blatantly obvious they were both dressed entirely in hand-me-down clothing.

As Rona pulled on a turtleneck, she was again grateful she didn't have big breasts and could go braless. It was one thing to wear someone else's shirt, but she sure as hell wasn't going to wear a used bra or underwear. She pulled a gray sweatshirt on over the blue turtleneck. Looking in the mirror, she tucked her hair back behind her ears. Except for the dark circles under her eyes, she looked like a normal person.

She found herself wondering about Anna. The clothes in the box with the word *bitch* written on the side might belong to Anna, but she didn't think so. Her rainbow magnets were a good indicator, but having a rainbow magnet didn't necessarily mean she was gay. The woman was such a contradiction. At first, she'd pegged her as one of those do-gooders, but she didn't really seem to fit the mold. And there had been a couple occasions when Anna's temper had surfaced.

There was a light tapping on her door. She opened it to find Tammy wearing the bright yellow sweater from Anna's box over a navy blue shirt and navy blue sweatpants. She could see the twins sitting on the floor at the foot of the bed talking.

"You look nice," Rona said. She needed to get back on Tammy's good side.

Tammy blushed and pushed a thin lock of hair behind her ear. "What are we supposed to do?"

"Build a snowman," Rona whispered, mimicking Karla.

"How long do you think she'll let us stay?" Tammy persisted. "I mean, is it for the two weeks that she'll have work for you or what?"

Rona shrugged. "I don't know. I don't think she would cancel her other cleaning service if she only intended to let us stay for two weeks. Maybe she wants to see how it goes. I think she'll let us stay until it starts getting warm."

Tammy gnawed on her thumbnail. "Why is she doing this? You don't think she's trying to trick us into staying until the authorities come, do you? I mean, with the snow and the city being shut down, maybe they weren't able to come out right away." She seemed genuinely worried.

"I think if they were coming, they would have already been here."

"Maybe the snow has slowed them down. You heard what they said on the television. The entire city has shut down except for emergency personnel."

"Why are you worrying? I thought you had become Anna Pagonis's number one defender."

Tammy wrapped her arms around her thin waist, hugging herself tightly. "Stop it. I don't want my girls to get hurt. You know how hard it is to go back out there."

"Then let's make sure they never have to go back."

"What do you mean?"

Rona pulled her deeper into the room. "It's simple. She's giving us jobs. We'll have an address, a place to wash our clothes and ourselves. We could start looking for real jobs. If we can stay here long enough for one of us to find a decent job, then we'll be able to find a small place of our own. You have to start thinking about getting the girls into a school. We could work different shifts so that one of us is always there to take care of them. We can get ourselves off the street."

"How long would it take? Do you think she'd let us stay that long?"

Rona was tempted to reveal her plan, but Tammy had become so protective of Anna that she decided against it. The only thing she knew for certain was that she was not going back to the streets. This house was full of things that could be taken to a pawnshop. One way or another, when she left here she was moving into a place of her own.

At that moment, the girls came running over to join them. Karla was wearing a pair of pink pants and a matching top with a cuddly bear on the front. Katie was in a bright blue sweater and jeans. The blue brought out the color of her eyes.

Rona forced a smile. "Everywhere I look I see beautiful little girls. Who are they?"

"It's us," Katie said and rolled her eyes.

"Where are your coats?" Tammy asked.

Katie pointed back toward the bedroom.

"Well, go get them." Tammy was silent until the girls were out of sight. "I'm kind of nervous about meeting these people. What if they start asking questions?"

Rona shook her head. "Don't worry about it. If they do, just tell them whatever you want them to know. You don't have to explain yourself to anyone." She eyed Tammy and suggested something she had always suspected. "Besides, I have a feeling you'll be in your element."

Tammy's head snapped up as she stared at her. Rona could see the suspicion and fear in her eyes. "What do you mean by that?"

Before Rona could respond, the girls reappeared clutching their new hooded coats. Katie's was obviously a boy's coat, but she didn't seem to notice.

"Can we go build a snowman, now?" Karla asked as she tugged on Tammy's pant leg.

Rona swung her up into her arms. "Only if you promise to let me help you build it."

"Okay. Can Mama help too?"

"Of course she can."

"I don't know how to build a snowman," Katie admitted as Tammy picked her up.

"I do," Rona said. "I grew up building snowmen."

"Did you really?" the twins cried in unison.

"I remember one year it snowed so much, it was almost to the roof of the house," Rona exaggerated.

"It can't snow that much. Can it, Mama?" Katie asked.

"I don't know. Rona said it did."

"What did you do?" Katie asked.

"I rolled all of the snow up into a humongous snowman that was so tall I used the clouds to make his hair," Rona replied as they started down the stairs with the kids shouting their disbelief.

Anna was at the foot of the stairs when they came down. Rona did a double take at the tall olive-skinned woman. Why hadn't she noticed how dark Anna's eyes were? Still dressed in the jeans, thick wool sweater and hiking boots, Anna radiated health and energy. A slight nudge from Tammy reminded her to close her mouth and to quit staring. Anna didn't seem to notice the effect she had on her.

"I wondered what happened to everyone," Anna said. "I thought you all had left without me."

"We couldn't. We don't know where we're going," Katie said.

"That's true," Anna agreed. "Are you ready to go?"

The twins nodded vigorously.

"Then let's get these coats on," Rona said as she helped Karla with her coat and the mittens that hung from a long cord threaded through the sleeves.

As they stepped out into the cold garage, Anna turned to them. "I should warn you that when my family gets together, it's usually the entire clan. There will be a full house. They're sweet people," she added in a rush. "It's just that you might find them a little overwhelming at first."

Tammy glanced at Rona nervously.

"In that case we may have to build two snowmen," Rona said, trying to sound as cheerful as possible. She wasn't going to do anything to screw up this opportunity.

Chapter Eight

"Judging from the cars in front of Julian's house," Anna said as she eased down the snow-covered road, "it looks like the entire family has already arrived." She parked behind a green truck.

As they made their way up the carefully cleared driveway, a chorus of screams and shouts floated out from behind the house.

"It sounds like the party has already started in the backyard," Anna said. She led them through a side gate. As she came around the side of the house, a snowball hit her squarely on the chest. "What the heck?"

"Be careful, Nick," Pietro yelled. "Your Aunt Anna is getting old."

"Yeah," Julian piped in. "Her bones are getting brittle."

Anna scooped up a handful of snow and hurled it in the general direction of her brothers. The snowball fell several feet short. They added further insult to her by not even bothering to dodge.

"Is that the best you've got?" Pietro sneered as he turned and waggled his butt at her.

"Oh, you are so going to get it," she cried as she carefully made her way toward him.

He mocked her by tiptoeing around in a circle and calling, "I'm so scared."

For the next several minutes, snowballs filled the air. The four newcomers were quickly pulled into the battle.

"I thought we were going to build a snowman," Anna shouted and ducked behind a tree to avoid a new volley of snowballs.

"Yeah," Julian replied.

"I don't know how to build a snowman," Trevor, Julian's seven-year-old son, said.

"There's nothing to it," Rona replied from across the yard. "I've built dozens of them. Let me show you." If family meant so much to Anna Pagonis, she could play along.

She showed them how to pack the snow into a tight ball and roll it into a larger ball. By the time Anna's mother, Helen, poked her head out the door to inform them the food was ready, the group had completed a snowman and a rather busty version of a snowwoman. They were trying to decide whether they should use a Spurs cap or a Cowboys cap as headgear for the snowman. The Spurs cap finally won out. Laughing and brushing one another off, the gang tromped toward the house. Tammy's twins were chattering nonstop with the younger Pagonis children.

Rona caught Tammy's gaze and smiled. It felt good to hear the twins enjoying themselves.

As they were making their way across the yard, Rona watched as Anna's ten-year-old nephew, Adam, grabbed Anna's arm. Without really meaning to eavesdrop, she listened to them talking.

"Where's your dad?" Anna asked.

Rona tried to remember the hierarchy of the Pagonis family. Anna had explained who all might be here, but Rona wasn't sure how much she remembered.

"He had to go to the hospital," Adam replied. "With the snow, there's a bazillion accidents."

She remembered now. Hector was a doctor on staff at St. Luke's Hospital. He and his wife, Polly, had three kids. Adam was the oldest.

"Will you talk to Dad for me?" Adam asked.

"What about?" Anna brushed the snow from his dark hair.

"He won't let me get a tattoo."

Rona tried not to grimace. She hated seeing tattoos on kids.

"What does your mom say?" Anna asked.

His long-suffering sigh floated back to Rona. "You know she always agrees with him."

"I guess I can try to talk to him. I'm not sure my recommendation will carry much weight."

"Yeah, it will. He likes you. Besides, they know you got one."

Anna laughed. "He likes you too, and he wasn't happy when he heard about my tattoo."

Rona was so engrossed in their conversation that she almost tripped over the kitchen threshold as she stepped inside. Had she heard correctly? Anna had a tattoo.

The noise from the other family members was making it difficult for her to hear so she eased closer to them in time to hear Anna say, "Secretly, I wish he had been there to talk me out of it."

"Why?" Adam asked, clearly appalled.

"Don't tell anyone I told you so, but it hurt."

His eyes widened slightly. "My friend Sean got one and he said it didn't hurt," he protested.

Anna shrugged. "Well, sure he's going to say it didn't hurt. If you got one and it hurt, would you tell your friends?"

"No way." He shook his head vigorously. "They'd think I was a wimp."

Rona almost laughed aloud at his energetic denial. Was she ever that young?

Anna squeezed his arm. "That's exactly why your friend Sean

didn't tell you," she said before relenting. "I'll talk to Hector if he comes to dinner on Sunday."

Adam nodded as his brow creased in thought. "Maybe I should wait for a while. You know, until I bulk up. Sean and I are planning to start lifting weights this summer."

Anna looked completely serious as she nodded and said, "That's probably a good idea. You wouldn't want to get a tattoo and then bulk up. It might stretch it all out of proportion."

"Yeah." He nodded his head in short bobs. "Thanks, Aunt Anna. You're the coolest." He darted into the living room, yelling for his older cousin Nick.

Anna turned and almost stepped on Rona. "Oh, there you are," she said.

Tammy joined them. She was holding the twins' hands.

"How are you all doing?" Anna said. "I hope my wild family hasn't scared you too much."

"We held our own," Rona said as she reached down and mussed Karla's hair. "I didn't realize Karla had such a pitching arm. Did you see her throw? This girl has some serious muscle." With her thumb and forefinger, she squeezed the child's upper arm through the coat. Karla grinned and hid her face against Tammy's leg.

"As soon as Mom makes all of us savages sit down, I'll properly introduce you to everyone."

"Why are you doing this?" Tammy blurted out.

The question stopped Anna short. "I don't know," she replied. "I want to help if I can. My parents worked so hard to make things easier for me and my brothers." They stood staring at each other until Anna's mom called them into the dining room.

"Come on, come on. The food is getting cold and those babies need to eat," Mrs. Pagonis scolded.

Anna smiled. "I should have warned you. Mom loves to feed people. I guess it comes from all those years of working at the restaurant."

"Your mom works at a restaurant?" Tammy asked.

"Actually they own it. You may have heard of it—Athenians. It's near Ingram Park Mall. We practically grew up in the restaurant."

All of the kids, except for the two sets of twins and Julian's three-year-old daughter, Ellen, disappeared to other rooms. The adults began to crowd around the long table. The three highchairs lined up against the wall were carried to the table.

"Julian," Gina called. "Go to the pantry and get two more high-chairs for these babies."

"We can hold them," Tammy replied.

Gina waved off the protest. "We have plenty. If there's one thing this family has plenty of, it's baby items. It will be more comfortable for you and the girls."

"This family has been blessed with many grandchildren," Mrs. Pagonis added.

Julian and Pietro went for the chairs and placed one on either side of Tammy. With much chair shuffling and good-natured banter, the Pagonis adults and their guests were soon seated.

"Children, it's time," Mr. Pagonis's voice boomed. The sound of running feet filled the house.

"Don't run," Mrs. Pagonis and her three daughters-in-law called out at once.

Anna leaned over to Rona, who was sitting to her right, and murmured, "They've yelled it so many times, they don't even realize they do it anymore."

The children positioned themselves randomly around the table and the Pagonis family members and their guests joined hands.

Rona tried to block out her own father's voice as Mr. Pagonis's deep clear voice said grace. Even though they were at Gina and Julian's, it was obvious to Rona that the elder Pagonises still ruled over their brood. After a hearty chorus of amens, the children disappeared into the kitchen where they would eat.

Chapter Nine

As Anna's family settled down to the table, Rona tried to remember the names of those she had already met. There were so many names she wasn't sure she'd be able to remember them all. To her right was Karla's highchair, then Tammy with Katie to her right. Rona watched as Tammy's twins tried to absorb all the activity going on around them. Watching them and listening to their laughter while they worked on the snowman only served to reinforce her determination that none of them would ever have to return to the streets.

She glanced at Anna. She appeared to be a decent person. In fact, the entire family seemed like good people. Rona found herself hoping that she and Tammy could find full-time work and it would not be necessary for her to steal from Anna or anyone else.

Anna started the introductions and Rona set about committing them to memory. At the foot of the table sat Julian's wife, Gina. Her twins were perched in highchairs on either side of her. She was short with blond hair and robin's-egg blue eyes. A little farther down on her right sat the muscular Pietro and then his wife, Lupie, whose high cheekbones and aristocratic nose suggested her ancestors might have walked among the ancient Aztec tribes. Next to Lupie sat the patriarch of the boisterous family, Stefano Pagonis. Rona had seen men like him around the fishing docks when her mother would take them with her on her occasional trips to purchase fresh fish for one of the many meals she prepared for her husband's business associates. They were hearty men who worked hard, always striving to make life better for their children.

She estimated Anna's father to be in his mid-sixties. His hair was completely silvery-gray. Even with the slight thickening around the middle, which she surmised hadn't been there during his prime, he was still an imposing figure. Beside him was Mrs. Pagonis, a robust woman with salt-and-pepper hair. It didn't require much intuitiveness to understand that here was the heart of the family. Next was Polly, wife of the missing eldest son, Hector. There were already touches of gray in her short brown hair. When Polly smiled and welcomed them, Rona felt an underlying sense of gentleness about the otherwise rather plain woman. At the head of the table between Polly and Anna was the wiry Julian. He had the highchair of his youngest daughter, Ellen, next to him. Like his siblings, he possessed warm olive skin and ebony hair.

When the introductions were completed, there was a new flurry of activity as lids were lifted from the two blue-on-white tureens that sat at each end of the table. As the steam rose up from the large bowls, the air filled with the fragrant aroma of lamb stew. The table looked as if it had been prepared to feed a hungry army. In between the tureens sat large platters of bread and chunks of cheese and bowls of olives. Mr. and Mrs. Pagonis began filling bowls with the savory-smelling stew.

"We hope you like lamb stew," Mr. Pagonis said as he passed bowls over to Tammy and Rona.

"It smells delicious," Rona said as she inhaled deeply.

"It's the perfect day for it," Tammy agreed as she helped the twins with their bowls.

"How old are your twins?" Gina asked. "Jason and Susan just turned five." She nodded to the children on either side of her.

"They're four," Tammy answered as she brushed a hand over Katie's towhead. "How old is your youngest?" She nodded to the chattering Ellen, who sat perched in a highchair beside Julian.

"She's three and getting to be quite a handful."

Rona blocked out the conversation as she added bread and cheese to her plate. A bowl of almond-shaped olives was passed to her. They were a dark eggplant color, not the black olives she was accustomed to eating. She glanced at Anna's plate and saw she had taken six or eight. Unsure about them, she took two from the bowl and passed it to Tammy. She tasted the stew and could barely suppress a moan of pleasure. She had grown up on thick hearty fish stews and soups. After a tentative taste of the sharp, salty olive, she regretted not taking more.

"What kind of olives are these?" she asked Anna.

"Aren't they delicious? They're Calamata olives. I love to eat them with salads or with bread and cheese."

"Where are you girls from?" Mrs. Pagonis asked.

"Michigan. Miami. San Antonio," Rona, Anna and Tammy piped in unison.

Rona cringed as the entire room grew still and all eyes turned toward them. Without missing a beat, Tammy spoke up.

"Rona is from Michigan. I was born in San Antonio and then moved to Miami several years ago."

Rona noticed Mrs. Pagonis watching Anna, who was concentrating on her food.

"Gina, this is a really great batch of stew," Julian said as he helped Ellen tear her bread.

"It's Mother Pagonis's recipe," Gina replied.

Several times during the meal, Rona glanced up to find Pietro watching them.

After dinner the men disappeared into another room as the women worked together to clear both the dining room and kitchen tables where the older kids had eaten. Julian's twins whisked off Katie and Karla.

As Rona had suspected, Tammy seemed completely at ease with these women. It was almost as though she had known them her entire life. Even after the tables were cleared and the dishes washed and put away, they continued to stand in the kitchen and talk about their kids.

"They'll be there all night," Anna mumbled at Rona's shoulder.

"We do seem to be out of the loop," Rona admitted.

"I'm going to show Rona the rest of the house," Anna called out. Gina smiled and gave a slight wave; the rest continued discussing the woes of childbirth.

As they left the kitchen, Anna turned to her. "Do you really want to see the rest of the house?"

She shook her head. "Not really."

"Do you play pool?"

"A little." Rona smiled and rubbed her hands together.

Anna stopped and glanced back at her. "Why do I feel like I'm about to be hustled?"

"I can't imagine what you mean."

Anna led her to a huge game room. Besides a regulation-size pool table, there was a lengthy bar running along the side. A pinball machine sat in one corner, and what she thought was an air hockey table sat across from it. In addition, there were four card tables with chairs in the area between.

Anna began to rack the balls. Four pool cues were in a stand in the corner. Rona hefted each of them and chose the heaviest one.

"I saw that," Anna called from the table.

Rona shrugged. "I just wanted to see if they were all the same."

"Yeah. Sure."

"To prove to you that I play fair, I'll let you break," she offered.

Anna eyed her. "That doesn't make me feel any better."

She stood back from the table as Anna leaned down to break. She was so busy admiring the way the jeans stretched over Anna's rear that she was caught off guard when Anna stood suddenly and turned around.

"Your turn."

She had to look at the table before she realized Anna had

already broken the racked balls. At least, she had made an attempt. The cue ball was caught up in the center of the cluster created by the horrible break. Rona had spent much of her teenage years sneaking over to play pool in a small family-oriented café and sports bar. It was one of few things that her father had never discovered and put an end to. "You didn't leave me much." After walking around the table to review possible shots, she quickly sank the two, four and five balls in three consecutive shots.

"I knew it," Anna said. "I knew you were hustling me."

"It's only hustling if we place a wager on the game."

"You have a point there. Isn't that what you were leading up to?"

Before she could reply, Julian came in, followed by his father and Pietro.

"Annie Bella, shame on you. I don't believe you were trying to hustle our guest," Julian called out.

"To think I raised a daughter who hustles pool," Mr. Pagonis said as he seated himself on a barstool.

Rona turned and found Anna looking a little shamed-faced. "You were hustling me?" Rona asked, dumbfounded.

Julian patted Rona's shoulder. "My sister put herself through college hustling pool."

"I did not," Anna protested. "Dad, tell them."

Mr. Pagonis looked at Rona and shrugged. "All right, I won't say my daughter is a pool shark; however, I gave all my children the same amount of money to go to college. Anna must have been very good at budgeting her money. With her two-hundred-dollar monthly allowance, she was able to buy a stereo, a car and a small house."

"Dad!" Anna exclaimed. "You're being horrible. I never did any such thing."

"Exactly how good are you?" Rona asked.

Anna looked at her and smiled before proceeding to clear the table.

Chapter Ten

Rona and Mr. Pagonis were in the middle of an extremely close pool game. Ever the diplomat, Julian was cheering on both players. Anna walked to the bar and took a bottle of water from the small refrigerator. Pietro was leaning against the end of the bar.

"Dad, can I get you something?" Anna called as she took the stool at the end of the bar. "A bottle of water, a beer, pool lessons maybe," she teased.

"You keep laughing," he called back. "Any moment now, I'm going to stop showing her mercy."

"In that case," Rona called over to him as she sank the seven ball. "I'd better start playing with my eyes open."

"I do believe the gauntlet has been thrown," Julian crowed.

Rona pretended not to notice as Pietro casually strolled over to sit beside Anna. At first she could hear them talking about a house Pietro was building, but their voices quickly became too low for her to hear. By the covert glances Pietro kept throwing her way, she was certain their conversation involved her. She was so busy trying to hear their conversation that she missed the next shot.

"Now, it is my turn," Mr. Pagonis chortled. He quickly proved that his talent could stand up to his bragging. He was about to lay up an easy shot on the eight ball when Pietro's voice cut through the room.

"Are you out of your mind?"

The three at the pool table stopped to look at them.

"Pietro, you almost made me miss my shot. What are you and your sister fussing about?"

"Nothing," Pietro replied. "Anna's just being stubborn, as usual."

Anna glanced at Rona before quickly looking away.

"Don't make me send you two off to your rooms," Mr. Pagonis teased as he made the shot and won the game.

"Pietro," Julian called. "Stop tormenting Annie Bella. It's your turn."

"You take my turn. I'll play after you," Pietro called.

"Oh, come on. You know I'm no match for Dad." He looked at Rona and grimaced. "I barely win when I play the kids." He took a cue. "The only good thing about playing as bad as I do is that the misery doesn't last long."

Rona stood on the opposite side of the room from where Anna and Pietro were. It was obvious that they were having a serious discussion. She saw Mr. Pagonis watching them as their whispered conversation became more animated.

"Mind your own damn business!" Anna suddenly shouted.

"Anna, your language," her father called sharply. "Pietro, what are you doing to your sister?"

The rest of the women chose that moment to walk in. "Pietro," Lupie said, "are you picking on Anna?"

Pietro was struggling for something to say when Anna came to his rescue. "He's disagreeing about a stock I want to invest in."

"We're having too much fun to be thinking about work," her mother scolded. "Who wants to play canasta?"

"Come on, Pietro," his wife called. "And stop picking on your sister. It's her money. Let her spend it as she wants."

Julian and his dad continued playing pool as the rest of the group hunkered around the tables to either play or watch the games. Rona walked to the end of the bar to join Anna. "Everything okay?" she murmured.

"Yes. My big brother is just being a big brother." She rolled her eyes.

"Does it have anything to do with me and Tammy?"

"Not really." Anna began to trace a pattern in the condensation on the bottle.

"I'm sure he's only worried about your safety," Rona said. "Taking in two homeless women might not be considered a safe thing to do by most people." She decided to prod a little. "Do your brothers always tell you how to run your business?"

"God, no!" Anna yelped and quickly clasped a hand over her mouth.

"Anna, your language," her parents called out together.

Rona chuckled.

"What?"

"Maybe we should find something safer for you to talk about before they really do send you to your room."

Anna watched her family and Tammy, who were now fully engrossed with the card game. "This might be a good time for me to hear your story."

"What story?" Rona hedged.

"Okay, if you're not ready, I'll wait."

"Why are you doing this?"

"I'm curious about how you got where you were."

"I mean, why are you letting us stay in your house. That's what your brother was upset about, wasn't it?"

She tossed the empty water bottle into the trash receptacle beneath the bar. "You helped me last night when I needed help. For the most part, I've been blessed. I have a wonderful family. My childhood was great. I was one of those lucky kids who didn't have to work hard to make good grades. I was able to go to college without having to hold down two or three jobs like a lot of my friends did."

"Plus you were a great pool hustler," Rona interjected.

Anna laughed softly. "Well, yeah. There was that." She glanced at her family. "My point is. I've always been blessed. I guess maybe I just wanted to pass some of that on to someone else."

"And now your brother is upset with you."

"Not upset really. He's worried."

"He should be."

Anna glanced at her sharply. "What do you mean?"

"What you did was pretty stupid."

She started to protest but stopped when Rona held her hand up.

"You don't know either one of us. Tammy and I don't even know each other that well. I mean, she has told me how she came to be here, but I have no way of knowing if she's telling the truth. We both could be lying to you."

"Are you?"

Rona looked into her eyes. "That's a futile question. If I were lying to you, do you think I'd hesitate to lie to you now?"

"Then tell me your story. I don't even know your last name."

Rona decided to tell her enough to satisfy her curiosity. "My last name is Kirby. I grew up in a middle-class family, but I never was quite good enough. I barely made it through high school. For some reason, I couldn't get a grasp on the whole school routine. Something about it just never worked for me." She stopped and shrugged. "Maybe I was too busy rebelling. Most of what I know is self-taught. I was serious when I told you that after finding myself on the streets, I spent a lot of time at the library. They wouldn't let you just sit around doing nothing. So, I pretended to read. After a while, I got tired of pretending and started to actually read." She gave a small disparaging chuckle. "I would get books from the young adult section and take them over to where the books on religion were. There weren't as many people in that area. I was doing pretty well, and then they started cracking down on us coming in and sitting around all day. It didn't matter if we were reading. If any of the other patrons started complaining about the way we looked or smelled, one of the librarians would call the security guard and we'd have to leave."

She suddenly realized what she was saying and stopped, embarrassed that she had just admitted to Anna that she had difficulty reading. There was a look in Anna's eyes, but before she could determine what it meant, a loud cheer rang out from the card table, and Anna turned to see what was happening. Rona looked over also to see what the ruckus was. Mrs. Pagonis was laughing and patting Tammy's shoulder.

"Rona, Anna," Julian called from the pool table. "I need help. Dad is whipping my butt. Please, someone come and rescue me."

"Rona," Mr. Pagonis called. "Come on and play. I can't beat that pool-hustling daughter of mine. She's too good."

She glanced at Anna and clucked her tongue. "You should be ashamed, hustling your own father."

There was that look in Anna's eyes again. "I'll wager I'm not the only hustler here," she said before slipping off the stool and going to stand by her mother.

Chapter Eleven

Later that night, Anna and Rona were sitting in Anna's den watching the fire blazing in the gas fireplace. Tammy was upstairs putting the girls to bed. Rona was still leery of Anna's comment about hustlers. No further references had been made and there were no visible signs that she might be upset. In fact, she, Tammy and the kids had laughed and joked all the way home. Now, she seemed mesmerized by the fire. Rona was beginning to wonder if she had imagined the entire episode.

"Are you two awake?"

Rona turned quickly; she hadn't heard Tammy come down the stairs.

"We were just enjoying the fire," Anna said.

Tammy sat on the end of the couch and tucked her bare feet beneath her. They sat in silence. "Anna," Tammy said finally. "Thanks for inviting us to join your family today. The girls were still whispering and giggling when I left the room. It's been a long time since—" Her voice broke. She covered it with a cough.

"We enjoyed having you there," Anna said. "You're such a great canasta player, Mom may adopt you. Dad has already challenged Rona to a rematch on Sunday. It's not often anyone besides me beats him at pool."

"It was a lucky shot." Rona tried to look as sincere as she sounded. She had played the game carefully, watching Anna's dad to see if losing would bother him or if he was the kind of man who always needed to win. When it became obvious that he relished a challenge, she gave it to him. She could have just as easily missed the shot if the situation had called for it.

"I don't understand why you're doing this," Tammy blurted. "I'm sorry," she said as her hands flew to her cheeks. "I don't mean to sound ungrateful, but you must admit that opening your home to complete strangers is unusual by anyone's standards."

Anna ran a finger over her eyebrow several times before responding. "Initially, I felt compelled to repay you for helping me. Then there was the weather. It was so horrible I couldn't stand the thought of anyone being out in it, especially the twins. I kept thinking about Julian's twins, Jason and Susan, and how I would feel if it were them out there." Anna took a moment before continuing. "And, I felt guilty for all the times I've walked by someone homeless without bothering to see them."

"It's nice to know we aren't just the stray-of-the-week," Rona replied, not bothering to conceal her scorn.

"Oh, hush." Tammy swatted her leg. "That's not what she's saying, so don't go all butch on us." She gasped and looked at Anna. "I didn't mean to insinuate—"

"Oh, please," Rona interjected. "I'm gay and I'm not crawling back into a closet for anyone."

Anna didn't hesitate before replying. "I'm a lesbian, so don't worry about it."

"Well, I'm not, and hopefully no one will hold that against me," Tammy said with a slight grin.

Anna chuckled, and what could have been an awkward situation was avoided. A set of wind chimes clanked frantically as the wind began to increase.

Rona walked to the window and peeked through the blinds. With the aid of the security light from the house behind Anna's, she could see the swirling snow. "It's snowing again," she told them. She stood watching the swirling flakes, wondering where Malcolm was.

A moment later, Anna excused herself and left the room.

As soon as she was gone, Tammy turned to Rona. "I'm sorry. I spoke without thinking."

Rona waved off her concerns and walked back to the couch. "Don't worry about it. She didn't seem bothered by the conversation, and I certainly wasn't." In fact, Rona was already wondering how she could twist this new information to her advantage.

Anna reappeared with a tray holding a bottle of brandy and three glasses. "My grandfather lived to be ninety-seven. He attributed his longevity to his nightly shot of brandy."

Rona watched as Anna poured. She liked the way the light danced through the amber liquid. The sound of the brandy pouring into the glass brought to mind the lively melody of a xylophone. They relaxed and enjoyed the brandy as they sat in comfortable silence watching the flickering firelight.

After several minutes, Tammy pulled her knees to her. "Anna, if I'm going to be staying here, there's something I think you should know," she began.

Rona wished she could reach over and clamp her hand over Tammy's mouth. She didn't want her true confessions messing up anything. Of course, she had already hinted at Tammy's situation and Anna didn't shy away; maybe it wouldn't make any difference.

"My husband, Wayne Daniels," Tammy went on, "is what my dad used to call a big fish in a little pond." She stopped and seemed uncertain how to proceed. "I'm an only child. My parents both taught at the University of Georgia. They had long since given up on ever having a baby when Mom became pregnant with me. She was forty-two. I grew up in a loving household, but there was no extended family. Dad never talked about his family much, and Mom's parents died long before I was born. She had a brother living somewhere out in California, but she never really talked about him much. They were overly protective of me and tried to shelter me from what they called the uglier side of life. I understand that their intentions were good, but I was very naïve." She took a taste of her brandy before continuing.

"My parents were killed in a car accident when I was nineteen. I was attending UGA at the time. After the accident, I felt like I had to leave. Go somewhere new, where no one knew my parents or me, and start my life over. There were too many memories. My folks weren't rich, but with their savings and life insurance, I had enough to put myself through college and to live comfortably for a while. I transferred to the University of Tennessee. Three months later, I met Wayne. He was ten years older than I was, handsome, and he paid a lot of attention to me. His father had made a small fortune in the salvage business. When he died, he left it all to Wayne and his sister." She hugged her knees tighter. "We had only been dating for a couple of months when I discovered I was pregnant. As soon as Wayne found out, he insisted I get an abortion. He had plans for his future, and kids weren't part of the package. He kept pressuring me. I couldn't go through with it. Then one night he got angry and I saw a different side of him, one that I didn't like. As soon as he left, I packed my bags and hopped on the first available bus. I ended up in Fresno." She ran her thumbnail over the knee of her sweats.

"I wasn't very smart about it. I used a credit card to buy the ticket, and to rent a motel room. I had been in Fresno less than two weeks when Wayne knocked on the door. He'd conned my roommate at school into giving him my credit card bill and then bribed the kid in the motel office to give him my room number. Within twenty-four hours, he was knocking on my door. He told me he was sorry, that he had nearly gone crazy worrying about me and the baby. He said he had given it a lot of thought and he was ready for a family." She shook her head and leaned her head against the back of the couch. "Like a fool, I believed him. We went back to Knoxville and were married the following week."

"Weren't you concerned about his anger?" Anna asked.

Tammy smiled sadly. "I wanted a father for my baby. I believed him when he said it would never happen again. That it was just the stress of running the business and my news that took him by surprise."

Rona knew that after living on the streets, Tammy would never be so gullible about anything again.

Tammy went on with her story. "A few days after we were married he convinced me to add his name to all my assets and gave me a stack of papers that were supposed to be adding my name to everything that was his." She looked up at them and grimaced. "Like the fool I was, I didn't read the papers. When we discovered I was having twins, he started drinking more." She took a deep breath. "One night, he came home drunk. He started talking about how easily he could kill me. He finally passed out on the sofa. The following day I received a statement from the bank telling me my account was overdrawn. When I called to clear up the mistake, I discovered he had withdrawn everything. All we had was a couple of hundred dollars in the household account. When he came home that night I confronted him with the statement and demanded he give me my money back." She touched her nose. "He broke my nose. I had a restraining order issued against him, but it didn't stop him from breaking in a few weeks later." She stopped and drew her arms tightly around her stomach. "I knew the police wouldn't be able to protect me, so after he left, I packed a suitcase and took off again. I was five months pregnant. On the way out of town, I withdrew all the money in the household account and headed to St. Louis where I managed to get a job working as a waitress." She stopped suddenly. "I'm sorry. I've been rambling on."

Anna set her empty glass back on the tray. "No, not at all."

Rona felt compelled to say something supportive. "Sometimes it helps to get everything out." Her face began to burn when she glanced over and saw Anna looking at her with that strange mocking expression.

"If it helps, please, continue," Anna said.

76

Tammy nodded and continued with her story. "When I took the job as a waitress, I didn't realize the place was on the verge of closing, which it did two months later. By that time, I was seven months pregnant and no one was in any hurry to hire me. I was able to buy food with the small unemployment check I received. When the girls were born, I owed the landlord three months' back rent. I came home from the county hospital to find a lock on my door. He let me take my clothes, but he kept the few pieces of furniture I had bought to help recoup his money. I stayed with a friend from the restaurant for a little while, but she was having her own problems, and two hungry babies in the house only made things worse for her. Then one day, I took the girls and walked to the store for milk. When I got back to the house, I saw Wayne. He was sitting in a car across from the house watching it. I turned around and started walking. A trucker gave us a lift to Boise, Idaho. I managed to get odd jobs here and there and finally secured a position as a receptionist for a small trucking company. It didn't pay much, but Homer and Sophie, the old couple who owned it, had a garage apartment behind their house and let me live in it rent-free. They didn't have any grandchildren and they sort of adopted the girls. Sophie watched the twins for me while I was at work." She traced aimless patterns onto the couch arm with her thumb. "It took Wayne almost three years to find me, but he finally did. I was using my maiden name. Pretty stupid, huh?" She tried to smile, but it got lost in the effort. "He grabbed me one evening as I was coming back from taking the girls to the park. He threw us in the car. I pretended to be happy about going back. I kept whining and crying about how hard it had been trying to make a living on my own. He got careless in Kansas. He left us in the car alone while he went to the restroom. I stole the car and drove until I saw a truck stop. There was an old abandoned barn about a mile away and I hid the car in it. When it got dark, we walked across the fields to the truck stop and managed to hitch a ride all the way to San Antonio."

"You can't keep running forever," Rona said. This time it was

Tammy who gave her an odd look. "All I meant was that the girls are getting older."

"I know. I'm just so scared of what he'll do when he finds us."

"Have you talked to a lawyer? Or considered divorcing him?" Anna asked. "I'm not very familiar with these kinds of situations, but I would think there are legal steps you could take. At the very least, you should be able to have him arrested on assault charges."

"If she serves him with divorce papers won't that tell him where she is?" Rona asked.

"Probably," Anna answered as she rubbed a finger over her lower lip. "But if she has a restraining order against him and he tries anything, she can have him arrested."

Tammy looked at Anna and shook her head. "I'm afraid he's going to punish me by taking my girls."

"Why? He wanted you to have an abortion. He obviously didn't want them," Rona protested.

"That doesn't matter. He knows it's the only way he can truly hurt me. He'll tell the court I'm an unfit mother and—" Her voice broke. "I'll lose them."

Rona tried to find a spark of hope. "So much time has passed. Maybe he'll give up on finding you."

Tammy shook her head and said, "I know him. He won't stop looking until he finds me."

Rona held her breath as she watched Anna digest the last statement.

"You're telling me this because you're afraid he might show up here, aren't you?" Anna asked.

Tammy nodded. "He won't give up until he makes me pay for running away. It may take him a while, but I know someday, somewhere, he'll step out and grab me."

"San Antonio is a big place," Anna reminded her.

"Not big enough." She stood suddenly. "I'm tired. I'm going to bed."

As she started off, Anna stopped her. "Why did you tell us this, now?"

78

Tammy stopped and gazed down at her. "I'm tired of hiding. Being with your family today made me realize the full extent of what I'm doing to my girls. I know it's time for me to stop acting like a coward, but I'm not sure I'm brave enough to do it on my own." Tammy left the room, leaving Rona and Anna staring thoughtfully into the fire.

Chapter Twelve

Rona said good night shortly after Tammy's departure. She wasn't concerned about Tammy's husband showing up. From what she had told them tonight, it had been at least a year since she last saw him, and San Antonio was big enough for a person to get lost in if they chose to. He no longer seemed a viable threat.

A more pressing issue to her was the need to get her personal belongings from the abandoned building. When she decided to make her move, things would start happening quickly. She wouldn't have time to be running across town to pick up the cheap fake leather bag, which contained a dozen carefully folded sheets of music and Mary's ring. As soon as the weather improved, she'd find a way downtown to retrieve the items.

She walked to the dresser and picked up each of the six porcelain kittens. She gazed at the one with the butterfly on its paw. It was strange how something so small could be so beautiful. She wondered if Anna even remembered the figurines were up here.

Had Anna bought the collection, or had someone given them to her? Maybe they were simply something a decorator had added, but this room didn't have the feel or look of being professionally decorated. She suspected this room held the remnants of Anna's childhood furniture. The twin-sized maple bed seemed much newer than the scarred dresser. She let her finger trail along a deep scratch across the dresser top. The obvious craftsmanship that had gone into building the dresser made the scar in the wood seem hideous. She felt an overpowering urge to buff the wound away and restore the battered old dresser to its original luster. She pulled her hand away from the scratch. Anna was obviously happy with it the way it was—hidden away out of sight.

She turned her attention back to the figurine she was holding and tried to recall her own carefree days when the band had been doing well and Mary was still healthy and vibrant. So much had happened in the sixteen months since Mary's death. A faint, painful tingling began deep within her chest. She set the figurine down and flipped out the light before going over to the window.

After opening the shades, she stood looking out over the houses along the street. Some were dark, while others were brightly lit. She thought about a few of the people she had met while living on the street—Malcolm, Tammy, Roach and Harper. They were like those houses. Somehow, Malcolm and Tammy had managed to retain a spark of humanity, refusing to allow it to be extinguished no matter how hard life punched them down, while Roach and Harper had succumbed to the darker ugliness of humanity's baser instincts. She wondered where she would fit in her analogy.

On the distant horizon was the faint glow that marked downtown. Hidden in the shadows of that artificial glow were thousands of men, women and children whose American dream had turned into a nightmare.

She wondered where Malcolm was and how he was getting along. She needed to go find him. Survival was easier if you worked in pairs.

Brief glimpses of the day's events flashed through her memory.

Anna's family was nice. An atmosphere of love and respect existed within the family that she had never experienced within her own. Her parents weren't physically or emotionally responsive people. Maybe it was because they gave so much of their love and devotion to God and the nondenominational Church of God's Love that they had nothing left over for anything else. It was as if she and her siblings had been under contract. Their parents provided all the material things they required to survive; in exchange, the children were supposed to repay that support with perfection. Their part in the contract was to make good grades in school, avoid all unpleasant matters that might embarrass their parents, marry well and provide them with cookie-cutter grandchildren. Where her older siblings, Walt and Kimberly, excelled at these things, she failed miserably. She had been a mediocre student. The only time her photo ever appeared in the local paper was in connection with a botched attempt to hold a Gay Pride parade. That had been the final straw for her father. When she refused to beg God for forgiveness for her wicked thoughts, he kicked her out of the house. She tried to contact them once after the band was beginning to gain some public exposure, but as soon as she mentioned the band, her mother hung up on her. She occasionally wondered how Walt and Kim were doing, but she was afraid to call. If she didn't give them a chance to reject her, she could hold on to the fantasy that someone out there still cared if she were dead or alive.

She closed the shade and stretched out across the bed on her stomach. She wondered what Anna was doing. Had she gone to bed or was she still sitting in the den? Several times during the day, she had caught herself watching Anna. She liked the easy manner in which she moved. The way her eyes sparkled when she laughed. It had been a long time since she'd felt anything for anyone. On a couple occasions, she had wanted to reach over and smooth away the small crease that appeared between Anna's eyebrows when she concentrated. Then there was the way her jeans stretched so deliciously across her hips when she bent over the pool table. A small ember of desire began to make itself known.

She rolled over on her back and tucked her hands beneath her head. It made sense that she felt some inkling of desire for Anna. After all, it had been almost two years since she'd made love to anyone. She was young and healthy. Why shouldn't she feel desire? *Lust*, she told herself. She intended to keep a vow she made to herself after her parents disowned her and Mary died. It was all right to think and lust after Anna Pagonis, but it could never go beyond a fantasy. In the darkened bedroom, she slipped her sweatpants off and opened her legs as an imaginary Anna slowly trailed her fingers down Rona's stomach. She pulled a pillow over her face as the fingers parted her swollen lips and began to stroke their way through the creamy wetness. A whimper of pleasure escaped her as fingers slipped inside and eased back out. As the first inklings of orgasm began, she rolled over onto her stomach, straining against the fingers until escalating pressure melted into a mediocre release of tension.

Afterward, feeling lonely and dissatisfied, she lay in bed staring at the ceiling. It was a long while before she fell asleep.

Rona didn't know what time it was when something jarred her awake. It took her a moment to remember that she was no longer on the streets but in the relative safety of a home. Her pounding heart began to slow as she tried to pinpoint what had disturbed her sleep. After several seconds of careful listening, she realized that it was a dream rather than a noise. She couldn't remember the details of the dream, but there was the vaguest image of Anna being involved.

The following morning, Rona was in the kitchen drinking coffee when Anna came in wearing expensive-looking black slacks and a matching black and tan fitted jacket. The white sneakers on her feet seemed out of place.

"Good morning," Anna said as she hung the black nylon bag that she was carrying over the knob of the door leading to the garage. "Are you always such an early bird?"

"I hope I didn't wake you," she said as she filled a cup for Anna.

"No. I normally try to be at the office by six-thirty. That's when I catch up on paperwork." She took the proffered cup of coffee. "Thank you. It smells good."

"Do you normally work on Saturday?" Rona asked as she sat back down to her own coffee.

"It's not a regularly scheduled day, but I usually go in most Saturdays. I meet with clients who have problems scheduling appointments during the week."

"You mentioned you did something with investments, but I don't remember which company you're with."

Anna sipped her coffee. "I'm a Certified Financial Planner, or C.F.P., but I'm no longer associated with a bank. I used to work for Bank of America, but a little over a year ago, I decided to go out on my own."

"What does a C.F.P. do?"

"I help clients with their investment portfolios and basically provide advice on all aspects of their financial picture."

Rona had never possessed enough money to worry about investing it. Not knowing how to respond, she changed the subject. "It looks like the roads are worse today. It snowed again last night."

Anna grimaced. "I know, but this client I have the meeting with is one of those self-made old ranchers who doesn't believe in letting anything get in his way. He made millions in the oil business back in its heyday and was smart enough to sell out fast when things started going sour. I called him yesterday to reschedule, but he insisted that we meet today. He'll be flying down in his helicopter."

"Where does he live?" Rona blurted out when she heard he was flying over.

Anna chuckled. "His ranch is north of Midland."

"Wow. How did he find you?" She stopped, embarrassed by the rudeness of her question. "What I meant is—"

Anna waved her off. "While I was still with Bank of America, I received a referral for a woman who had bank accounts with us but had her investments elsewhere. She was unhappy with her current advisor and was looking for someone else. While glancing over her portfolio, I noticed that almost half of her investments were in Enron stock. I recommended that she balance her portfolio by diversifying into several different sectors. She mentioned my suggestion to her father, who also followed my advice. All of this occurred a few months before the whole Enron fiasco. By diversifying, they didn't lose their shirts. When I left the bank to go out on my own, they transferred their accounts to my new firm." Anna peered out the kitchen window. "I dread driving in that mess."

"It won't be so bad. Traffic will be light. Take your time and don't make any sudden turns or stops. If you start to slide, remember to tap your brakes and steer into the slide," Rona automatically repeated all the warnings her father would issue to her mother with each new snowfall. She took a sip of coffee, disturbed that she had actually sounded like him.

"It sounds as though you know what you're doing."

Rona shrugged. "I grew up in Michigan."

Anna joined her at the table. "How would you like to start that temp job a couple days early?"

"You really don't want to drive, do you? You did fine yesterday."

Anna shook her head. "I was just driving the few streets over to Julian's, and I was petrified the car was going to slide into something. The thought of driving all the way downtown . . ." She shuddered.

Rona chuckled. "All the way downtown is only about thirty minutes away."

"There's a big difference between thirty minutes of smooth driving and thirty minutes of slipping and sliding," Anna pointed out. "Besides, it's not just the road conditions that concern me. I'm worried about getting hit by all those other drivers who will be driving as badly as I am."

Rona shook her head. "Everyone will be as scared as you are. They'll all be driving like little old ladies on a Sunday afternoon."

"So, you'll drive?" Anna asked, looking at her hopefully.

Rona couldn't keep from grinning. "Yes, I'll drive," she agreed.

They jotted a note to Tammy and left the house as soon as Anna finished her coffee. Since the interstates were still closed, they were forced to take the side streets into the city. By the time Rona finally pulled into the parking lot of Anna's office building, her central nervous system felt as though it had been run through a blender. There weren't many cars on the road, but unfortunately, people who had little or no experience in navigating on icy roads were driving them. Twice they narrowly missed being hit by drivers who seemed to believe that poor road conditions were no reason to reduce their speed. She could feel her insides trembling when she handed the keys over to Anna.

"If I wasn't afraid my lips would stick to the pavement, I'd get out and kiss the ground," Anna said as she took the keys.

A sudden image of such a scene made Rona laugh aloud. She stopped when she saw Anna watching her.

"You have a nice laugh," Anna said as she gazed at her.

Rona quickly opened the car door. The trembling in her stomach now had nothing to do with bad drivers.

Chapter Thirteen

Rona followed Anna to the front entrance of the building she'd once had to sneak into through the back door. How ironic that she was actually going to be working here. She turned her back to the cold wind as she waited for Anna to unlock the door. The jacket Anna loaned her wasn't thick enough to block the frigid wind. After they stepped into the warm interior, it surprised her to see Anna lock the door behind them. She was grateful that the wide-shouldered man who was usually the first one in wasn't as conscious about security as Anna was, or her first stay here could have ended very differently.

Her long stride took her to the elevators a step ahead of Anna. She pushed the button and was slightly surprised that the doors opened immediately. She stepped in and selected the third floor. They rode in silence. When the doors opened, Anna was busy digging in her purse. Rona stepped out of the elevator and automatically turned to the right. She knew from her previous visits that the investment firm was the second door to the right.

"You seem to know your way around here pretty well," Anna said as she came over to unlock the door.

Stunned by her own stupidity Rona could only stare at her.

"How did you manage to avoid the security guard?" Anna asked as she unlocked the door and stepped inside.

Since she didn't ever intend to have to sneak into another building, she saw no harm in telling. "Each night after the cleaning people left, he went to the lounge and slept. He would set his watch to wake him up at midnight and again at five in the morning."

Anna nodded. "Where did you stay? I thought all the offices were locked."

"There's a restroom on the fourth floor. It's outside the training center. I guess that's why they never bothered to lock it."

"So, how many people sleep here each night?"

"As far as I know it's just me. I found the place by accident. The night we met you was the first time I brought anyone with me."

Anna led her through a reception area to what looked like a small conference room. "This is where you'll be working. Two other people work here, but neither of them will be in today. Sharon is my admin specialist and Neal is a sales assistant. He's working at getting his master's in finance. As soon as he does, and he acquires his certification, I'll make him a junior associate." She pointed to a room across from where they were standing. "That's his office." She motioned for Rona to follow her into a room that looked like a small kitchen. There was a microwave and a coffeepot on the counter and an apartment-sized refrigerator. Cabinets filled the space above and below the counters. "This is our *everything* room. We use it as a break room, a coffee shop and supply room. My office is at the end of the hallway. The restroom is down the main hall to the left."

Rona nodded. She knew where it was.

Anna was fumbling with the thermostat on the wall. "I don't know why I bother. I don't think this thing is connected to anything. We complain that it's too cold and the building manager eventually sends someone out who swings this little gadget around in the air and swears it's seventy-two degrees in here, but I don't think it is."

"Do you want it warmer now?" Rona asked.

Anna looked at her. "Don't you think it's cold in here? Sharon keeps a lap robe at her desk."

"I need something with a sharp point," Rona said.

Anna pulled open a drawer. "Like this?" she asked as she held up a fork.

"No. I need something with a single point." She moved to stand beside Anna as she opened another drawer. There was a small black plastic box. Rona picked it up.

"I think those are screwdrivers," Anna replied as she continued to dig.

Rona opened the case. Anna was right. The box contained screwdrivers, but they were too large for what she needed. She was about to close the case when she noticed it also contained three small metal punches. She took the middle one. "I think this will do." After carefully removing the plastic cover of the thermostat, she inserted the punch into the small hole on the bottom. As she turned the punch, the thermostat issued a slight hissing sound.

Anna watched her nervously. "You don't seem concerned about that noise, so I'm guessing this is something you've done before?"

Rona nodded. "When I was a teenager, I would sometimes have to baby-sit the infants whenever special events were held at church. It was always too cold in the room and a friend of mine showed me how to do this." She could feel Anna watching as she replaced the cover. "I didn't raise it very much. It'll be about thirty minutes before you to start noticing a difference in the temperature."

"If you can make this office warmer, you're going to become Sharon's heroine." She started removing her coat. "Let me put my stuff away and I'll get you started on the database." She stopped suddenly. "Crap."

"What?"

"I wasn't expecting to hire anyone until next week or later. I intended to rent a computer to use." She rubbed her forehead. "Why don't you use Sharon's computer today, and I'll have her make arrangements to get you one Monday morning." She nodded as if agreeing with her decision. "Actually that will work out well. Sharon has a template for mailing labels."

Rona went back to the reception area and waited for Anna to hang up her coat. As she came back down the hall, Rona noticed that Anna was no longer wearing sneakers. She had changed into a pair of black pumps. She found herself wondering what Anna's legs looked like. It was obvious that most of Anna's height was from the waist down. She imagined her legs to be long and shapely.

"Are you ready?"

It took Rona a moment to tear herself away from her fantasy.

"Is everything okay?" Anna asked glancing down at her pants. "Do I have mud on me or something?"

Rona turned away to hide the blush creeping up her neck. "No, everything's fine. I was just noticing that you changed your shoes."

"Oh, yeah. I usually wear tennis shoes until I get to the office. Sometimes, Sharon has to remind me to change." She sat down and turned on the computer. As it was booting up, she reached beneath the desk. When her hand emerged, she was holding a small ring of keys. She saw Rona watching. "Tight security, huh?" She unlocked the lap drawer of Sharon's desk and pushed aside a small tray holding pencils. "Pretend like you don't see me doing this. I know they say you should never write your passwords down, but there are too many to remember."

Rona had no interest in Sharon's computer passwords. There was nothing in the computer that could benefit her. She turned away and pretended to study a painting of a waterfall.

After the computer was up and running, Anna locked the desk and returned the keys to their original position. She spent several minutes looking through Sharon's files for the template. After locating the file, it took even longer for them to figure out how it worked. By the time she left to go to her office, Rona was feeling comfortable with the task. Alone at Sharon's desk, she flipped through the stack of papers with the names and addresses she was supposed to be inputting. It was a much shorter one than she had anticipated, only about five hundred names. She started typing the information slowly. Her typing wasn't very fast, but at least it was accurate. After typing for several minutes, she slowly got up and peeked down the hallway. Anna's door was open, but the only thing visible through it was a large walnut table. Rona typed a few more entries before she reached beneath the desk and felt along its side until she located the key ring. She unlocked the desk and eased the lap drawer open. Inside she found the usual supplies, along with a package of gum and one of breath mints. She softly closed it and typed a few more entries before moving to the top side drawer. Here she found what she was looking for, the petty cash box. A tiny lock secured the small wooden box. The box and lock were so flimsy that either could easily be smashed open with a hammer. Rona eased the drawer closed and typed a few more entries before searching through the keys until she found a small flat one. She reached into the drawer and inserted the key into the lock on the box. It popped open. Inside she found thirty-eight dollars and some change. Not as much as she had hoped for, but every little bit helped. She locked the box, careful to leave everything as she had found it. After locking the desk, she returned the keys to their hiding place. She hadn't taken any of the money. For now, she was content with simply knowing where it was. When the time was right, she would have to be able to get to it quickly. She picked up the list to find the next name.

"How's it going?"

The voice startled Rona so, she almost screamed. She spun in the chair to find Anna standing at the doorway. How long had she been standing there? Had she heard something, maybe the desk drawer opening or closing?

"I'm sorry," Anna said. "I didn't mean to sneak up on you."

"Did you need something?" Rona managed to ask.

"No. It's almost nine."

Rona stared at her blankly.

"It's almost time for Mr. Tanner, my nine-thirty appointment from Midland, to arrive. I'm going down to unlock the lobby doors."

Rona stood. "I can do it for you."

Anna shook her head. "I don't want to interrupt you. Besides, I'm going to wait for him and bring him up. This is his first time here. I flew to Midland for our initial visit and since then everything has been handled over the phone and overnight mail. I started a pot of coffee if you want some."

As soon as she left, Rona collapsed against the back of the chair. That had been close. She wondered again if Anna could have seen or heard something. She went to stand in the same spot where Anna was and slowly stepped back. Anna would have had a clear view of the desk long before she reached the end of the hallway. Shaken, Rona went back to the desk and tried to remember how much time had passed between her replacing the keys under the desk and Anna speaking. She couldn't be certain of the exact amount, but it couldn't have been but a few seconds. There was a strong possibility Anna saw her putting the keys back.

Rona sat staring at the computer screen. If she saw her, why hadn't she said anything? *I would have seen her*, she reassured herself as she turned in the chair and looked at the doorway. *If she had been standing there, I would have seen her.*

Several minutes later, she was busy typing when the door opened and Anna came in with a man who looked like one of those wooden caricatures of a cowboy. He was tall and thin. His face was craggy and sun-baked. Work-roughened hands with arthritic knuckles swollen to twice their normal size cradled a professionally blocked, black Stetson. Beneath the unbuttoned sheepskin jacket, Rona could see the front of a white Western dress shirt and a silver medallion bolo tie. Black jeans encased legs bowed from years of being on horseback. An expensive pair of calfskin boots polished to a brilliant luster completed his outfit. His steel-blue eyes held her attention. It was hard to look away from them. She found herself thinking about something her father had once said about God being able to see directly into one's soul.

"Mr. Tanner, this is Rona Kirby. She's going to be helping us out for a while."

He stepped forward and extended his hand. "Mornin', ma'am. I'm Ethan Tanner."

Rona shook his hand, surprised by the gentleness of his voice. "It's nice to meet you, Mr. Tanner. Would you like a cup of coffee? There's a fresh pot."

He smiled and nodded. "I surely would, but that crackpot of a doctor my daughter insists I see has cut me back to one cup a day. Since I gave my word, I'll have to pass, but I thank you kindly for the offer."

"My office is this way," Anna said, gesturing.

Mr. Tanner nodded. "It was a pleasure to meet you, Ms. Kirby. If you're ever in Midland, look us up and we'll throw another steak on the grill."

His offer sounded so genuine that she found herself smiling and agreeing to do so.

Chapter Fourteen

Anna's meeting with Tanner lasted over two hours. Anna walked him out. As soon as they left the office, Rona raced down the hall to Anna's office. The room was sparsely furnished with gray modular furniture. A quick search of the desk drawers and overhead bins revealed nothing of value. She tried the file cabinets but found them locked. Disappointed, she rushed back down the hall to Neal's office but found his door locked as well. She trotted back to Sharon's desk and grabbed the keys. The first one she tried didn't work; the second one did. His desk wasn't locked, but the only thing she found was seventy-five cents in change. She ignored it and quickly left his office.

By the time Anna returned, Rona was busy typing.

"How did it go?" she asked as Anna came in.

"Good. He liked the proposals I showed him." She sat in the side chair. "He has invited us all up for his annual Easter barbecue. If the investments I set up for him do well, he could send other clients our way."

Rona nodded. "Sounds like a productive morning."

"How are you doing?" Anna asked.

"Okay. I know I'm slow."

Anna rubbed a finger over her eyebrow. Rona had come to recognize the gesture as one she made when she was thinking. "This is only the first week in February. How long do you think it will take you?"

Rona counted the number of entries she had completed in the last two and a half hours and did some quick calculations. Each entry was taking a little more than a minute. "I can probably finish inputting the addresses in about six or seven hours."

Anna nodded. "Good. I'm hoping to have them in the mail by the end of the week."

Rona swallowed her disappointment. Anna had said the job would be for a couple of weeks. It looked like she might have to move faster than she had anticipated.

"Did you notice the sun is shining?" Anna asked.

Rona turned to look out the window. "The snow won't last long now."

"It's already starting to turn slushy." She stood. "I need to do a couple of more things before I'm ready to leave. If you get hungry, there are some chips and things in the cabinets above the microwave. Just help yourself."

"I'm fine, thanks."

As Anna walked away, Rona thought about the money in the petty cash box. If she finished the mail-out before the end of the week, she probably wouldn't have a chance to grab the money without Sharon being around. She might be able to take it now and it wouldn't be noticed until after she was gone, but with no way of knowing how often Sharon opened the box she was afraid to take the chance. Her salary for a week's work would be much more that the pittance in the petty cash fund. She wasn't going to do anything to risk losing the salary. If she was able to grab the cash on the way out, great, and if not, she'd have to live without it.

She pushed away the thoughts of the money and turned her attention to the mailing list. By the time Anna was finally ready to leave, several more names and addresses had been inserted into the database.

Anna helped her log off the computer before handing her an envelope.

"What's this?" Rona asked. She noticed that Anna was once more wearing her tennis shoes.

"It's your pay for the morning. If I pay you today, you'll start with a clean slate on Monday and be able to work a full forty hours."

Rona took the envelope and experienced a strange sense of pride and confusion. Unable to comprehend her feelings she folded the envelope and slipped it into her pocket unopened. "Thanks," she muttered.

"I hope you don't mind, but I paid you in cash. Since you only worked five hours, I didn't withhold anything." Before Rona could respond, Anna waved her toward the door. "Let's go home. I'm hungry."

As they left, Anna was careful to lock the office door as well as the door at the front entrance.

The drastic increase in the temperature from earlier that morning surprised Rona. "It must be in the forties already," she said as they made their way to the car. The snow was quickly disappearing.

Anna handed Rona the keys. "I think I'd still rather wait until a lot more of it has melted before I try driving."

Rona took the keys.

"Do you mind if we stop by the grocery store?" Anna asked as she fastened her seatbelt. "I noticed we were low on a few things."

"No. I don't mind," Rona said as she cranked the car and eased it out of the parking lot. Her back ached from sitting all day. She was accustomed to being on her feet most of the time.

Anna gave her directions to the store she wanted to go to, then reached over and switched on the radio.

Rona's breath caught as music flooded through the car's interior and brought with it a rush of painful memories. She struggled to close her ears and block the burning riffs of the lead guitar, but it was persistent and continued until it found a weak seam and little by little plucked away her defenses. Slowly the rhythm took over her body, causing her fingers and feet to move in time. She could almost feel the cold ivory piano keys kiss her fingertips, first as individual notes and then stretching her hands to encompass whole chords. She was powerless to stop the chords from reinserting themselves into her muscle memory. Her fingers began to move in unison with those notes and chords pouring from the radio. Unbidden lyrics crowded together at the back of her throat begging to be set free. The vague smell of stale beer and cigarettes intertwined with the music to send her spiraling back to those glorious nights. She squinted her eyes against the searing stage lights, as her heart pounded in time with the thumping rock bass line. Her blood pulsed in time with the gyrations of hot, sweaty dancers. The plywood stage shook in time to Eric's booming bass drum. Zac's bass guitar plucked at her heart. Lenny's lead guitar made her body hum like tightly drawn wires, and afterward when they were at last alone at home, there were Mary's hands and hungry kisses to release that tension and send her spiraling into another dimension of pleasure. Abrupt silence snatched the dream away and sent it swirling into a cesspool of disappointment and heartache.

Anna's hand was on her shoulder. Her mouth was moving. It took Rona a moment to clear the memory of the music from her head.

"What's wrong?" Anna said.

Rona looked around her. Somehow, even while daydreaming, she had driven them to the grocery store parking lot. This couldn't be right. The images of the band and Mary had been so real. Where had they gone? She sniffed, searching for the stale beer and cigarette smell that had been so prominent only a moment ago. All she could detect now was the vague scent of lavender.

"Are you all right?"

Rona nodded. "I'm just tired." She threw the car door open and let the cold air clear the dying strains of music from her mind. Those days were gone and could never be recaptured. Mary was dead. Zac, Lenny and Eric had moved on with their lives. It was time she did the same. She had a temporary job and, come Monday, she would start looking for a full-time position. Music no longer meant anything to her.

Anna grabbed a grocery cart from the long chain lined up outside the door.

As the made their way down the aisle, Rona ignored the lyrics that popped into her head to accompany the rhythmic clunk of the wheels on the grocery cart. There were only a handful of shoppers in the store, so they were able to move quickly through the aisles.

"Do you like seafood?" Anna asked as she studied the selections of fresh fish.

"Yeah, as long as it's fresh. I can't stand canned tuna. Even as a kid, I wouldn't eat it. For some reason, I always associated it with cat food."

"Don't put that thought in my head," Anna said as she wrinkled her nose. "I like tuna casserole. When I was a teenager, my father would leave the house whenever I'd make it." She ordered some shrimp and a large salmon filet. "I love grilled salmon." She placed the items in the cart. "We need milk and eggs," she stated, turning the cart toward the back of the store. Afterward as they made their way to the checkout counter, Anna stopped and picked up a bag of cookies. "Do you think I should get these for the kids?"

"No," Rona answered seriously. "Tammy only lets them eat Oreos."

"Oh." Anna replaced the bag and reached for the Oreos. "Why only these?"

Rona hid her smile by walking away.

"I think I was just conned," Anna said as she began to unload the groceries at the checkout. "Why am I getting the feeling that it's you who likes Oreos?"

Rona gave an exaggerated shrug and tried to look innocent.

"That's what I thought." She stopped abruptly.

"What's wrong?"

"I forgot to get a red onion."

"I'll get it," Rona said and raced off. By the time she returned, the rest of the groceries were bagged and the cashier was waiting for her.

As they were leaving the store, they passed a young man sweeping the sidewalk. Rona watched him as the *swish, swish, swish* of the broom produced a perfect counterpoint to the cart's clunking wheels. She stepped off the sidewalk and almost fell. Feeling silly, she rushed to catch up with Anna.

"I'll hold the eggs and bread," Anna said as they put the last of the bags into the trunk of her car. She turned to Rona. "You seem tired. Would you like for me to drive?"

Rona shook her head. "I'm fine," she reassured her, grabbing the empty cart and pushing it over to a holding stall. The cold wind made her rush back. She squirmed under Anna's watchful gaze as she cranked the car and drove out of the parking lot. When she was safely on the road, Anna reached into the grocery bag containing the eggs and removed something.

"Here, I thought you might like these."

Rona glanced over to see a small individual-sized package of Oreos and was surprised by the strong emotions that raced through her. She realized Anna must have gotten them from the display shelf at the checkout counter while she was going after the onion.

"I really did forget the onion," she said as if reading Rona's thoughts. "Shall I open these for you?"

Rona could only nod.

"I've never eaten many store-bought cookies."

Rona made a face before repeating the phrase. "Store-bought cookies?"

"Yeah," Anna said with a chuckle. "That's what Pietro used to call cookies that you bought at the store."

"Where did you get your cookies?"

"From the restaurant."

Rona frowned. "You never bought cookies from the store?"

"Why should we when fresh-baked goodies were delivered to the restaurant three times a week?" She handed Rona a cookie.

Rona bit into it and savored the sweet flavor of chocolate. "Well, I was raised on these and I can't imagine anything tasting better." She nodded toward the Oreos. "You should try one."

Anna glanced down at the package in her hand before reluctantly biting into the cookie. She chewed it slowly.

Rona found her herself watching Anna's lips more than she was observing the road.

"It's not bad," Anna admitted.

"You can't truly appreciate them without a cold glass of milk," Rona insisted.

Anna shook her head. "Sorry, the milk is in the trunk." She smiled before taking another bite of cookie.

"How long have your parents owned the restaurant?" she asked to divert her attention away from Anna's lips.

"They opened it when I was a year old, so almost thirty-six years."

"Wow, they've owned it your entire life, practically."

Anna made a murmuring sound of agreement as she handed Rona another cookie. "There's a small room in the back of the restaurant and we played in there when we weren't in school. We would go there after school, do our homework, eat dinner and then play until it was time to close. Later, when we were older, we would work there every summer. I still eat dinner there a couple of times a week. Of course, I won't have to now that Tammy's started cooking."

"That's amazing," Rona said as she declined the next cookie. "You would think that after all these years they'd be ready to retire."

"They've cut back some. They stopped doing the cooking about twelve years ago and they're starting to talk about hiring a manager." She shook her head. "But I don't see that happening anytime soon. It's going to be hard for them to let go of the reins."

"Were they upset that none of the kids were interested in taking over the place?"

"They never pressured us to keep working there, but I think it must have bothered them some," Anna said. Without warning, she changed the subject. "What about your parents? What do they do?"

"Mom was a housewife and Dad was president of the North Division of Groggins." At the blank look on Anna's face, she explained, "Groggins manufactures paper products and then sells them to companies who put their own brand names on them."

"Was?" Anna asked.

Rona glanced at her.

"You said your mom was a housewife and your dad was president of the company. Are your parents deceased?"

"Not unless they've died in the last two years," she replied sharply. She saw Anna's shocked look. "We all didn't grow up with June and Ward Cleaver." She didn't add that as far as she was concerned, they might as well be dead.

Anna folded the wrapper over the Oreos and placed them back in the plastic bag. "I'm sorry. I had no business prying."

Rona regretted her outburst and wished she could take it back. She wanted Anna to smile again but didn't know how to make it happen. They rode the rest of the way back in silence.

It was almost three by the time Rona and Anna returned home. As they opened the kitchen door, a wave of delicious scents rushed out to greet them. "Something smells good," Anna called out.

Tammy and the girls came from the direction of the den. "I thought a bowl of chili might taste good for lunch," Tammy said as she headed out into the garage to help bring in the groceries.

"I should have thought to call and let you know when we'd be home," Anna apologized. "The meeting with Mr. Tanner took longer than I had anticipated and then we stopped at the store."

"Don't worry about it," Tammy said as she put the milk in the refrigerator. "Chili always tastes better after it has set for a while." She walked to the stove and turned on the oven. "I waited to put the corn bread on, because I didn't want it to be cold."

Rona saw a large rectangular pan sitting on the counter beside the stove.

Anna removed her coat and draped it over the back of a chair.

"Good, that'll give me time to put the groceries away and change clothes before we eat."

"Go ahead and change," Rona said. "I'll put the groceries away."

"Are you sure?" Anna asked.

"If I can't find where it goes, Tammy will show me," Rona said. "Go get comfortable."

After Anna left the room, Tammy put the corn bread into the oven then helped Rona put away the groceries.

"You girls go watch television until I call you to eat," Tammy said.

"Can we have a cookie?" Katie asked as she spied the Oreos.

"Not until you eat. Now scoot." As soon as the girls left, she turned to Rona. "How did it go today?"

"Okay. I type slower than anyone she would have hired, but it didn't seem to bother her." She put several small containers of yogurt in the refrigerator. "How did you do today?"

Tammy smiled as she talked about dusting and vacuuming as if it were some grand entertainment. She saw Rona staring at her and blushed. "I know I sound silly, but it's so wonderful to be able to do things like a regular person."

Rona nodded. "I understand what you mean." She took out the opened packet of Oreos and stood staring at them.

"You two are worse than the kids. No wonder you aren't starving."

"We only had a couple," Anna protested.

They turned to find her standing in the doorway wearing sweats and a pair of old house shoes.

Tammy rolled her eyes. "You even sound like the kids."

While they were teasing each other, Rona slipped the Oreos into her jacket pocket. It wasn't the cookies so much as just wanting to hold onto the package. It had been a long time since anyone had bought her anything. She told herself it was a good thing that Tammy hadn't seen her snatch the cookies or she would have been sent to her room without supper.

Chapter Fifteen

The following morning, Rona slept late and stayed in bed for a long while after waking. The house was quiet, but she could smell a vague scent of coffee. Rona glanced at the clock beside the bed. It was a little after ten. By now, Anna would have already left for church. The previous night, she tried to persuade Tammy and Rona to join her family for dinner. She offered to pick them up after church, but they both declined.

Rona lay in bed enjoying the beams of sunshine that crept through the blinds and danced across the room. She finally forced herself to get up and take a long hot shower before getting dressed. As she was pulling on her jeans, she heard a crackling sound. The envelope with the money Anna paid her was still in her pocket. She removed it and tore it open. Inside was thirty-three dollars. She smoothed out the blanket and carefully spread the three tens and three ones out on the bed. It had been a long time since she'd had this much money at one time. She took one of the tens and put it in her front pocket before placing the remaining twenty-three dollars back into the envelope and hiding it under the mattress.

After gathering her handful of dirty clothes, she headed downstairs. The house was empty. She started a pot of coffee then put her dirty clothes in the washer. The utility room was down the hallway, past the den. A second short hallway led to Anna's room. Curious, she walked toward it. The door was open. A wide wallpaper border of red and gray swirling lines topped pale pink walls. Several colorful rugs softened the dark hardwood floor. The headboard and dresser were a dark wood. A small table and rocking chair sat in front of a wall of windows. Through the opened blinds, she could see a portion of Anna's backyard. A large jewelry box sat on the dresser. Rona eyed the jewelry box. She knew she should check it to see if there was anything that might be useful to her but found she couldn't make herself enter the room. As she continued to stand in the doorway, she heard the front door open. As quietly as possible, she ran back to the main hallway and tried to appear calm as she made her way back to the kitchen. She met Tammy and the girls as she neared the kitchen.

Tammy looked up, clearly surprised. "I thought you were still sleeping."

"No. I've been up for a while. I was putting my clothes in the washer."

Tammy seemed to be studying her.

She tried not to fidget. "I made a fresh pot of coffee if you'd like some," she offered.

Tammy nodded.

Rona noticed the girls were not as talkative as usual. "What's wrong?" she asked them, eager to turn Tammy's attention away from her.

Karla hung her head, but Katie finally answered. "Karla wanted to build a snowman, but the snow won't work."

"It's too warm and most of the snow has melted," Rona told them. "That's why you have to build it right after it snows."

104

"I wanted to build one here, so I could see it," Karla whimpered.

"Karla," Tammy implored. "I've told you there's not enough snow. Besides, it won't stick together anymore. You tried and it kept falling apart." She helped the girls remove their coats.

Karla turned and walked toward the den. Katie followed. A moment later, they heard the television.

Tammy sighed and ran her hand over her ponytail. "That child is so stubborn. You should have seen her. We went for a walk to a neighborhood park where there's still snow piled up beneath the trees." She followed Rona into the kitchen while talking. "She must have spent fifteen minutes trying to make a snowball."

Rona poured the coffee and carried it to the table. "I can't imagine where she gets that stubborn streak," she said as she set the cup down.

Tammy made a face at her as she hung the girls' coats on the back of a chair. "Hush."

They drank their coffee accompanied by the distant sound of cartoons.

"What are you doing today?" Tammy asked.

Rona thought about it for a moment before answering. "I don't know. It's been so long since I had anything to do. I'll finish my laundry. Maybe I'll go for a walk later, if it isn't too cold."

"It's not bad at all," Tammy assured her. "If you don't have plans, would you like to go shopping with me?"

"Shopping?" Rona asked, surprised.

"Anna gave me half of my salary for the first week in advance. I thought I'd try to find a Wal-Mart or maybe a Dollar Store. I need to buy the girls some socks and underwear. Maybe some shoes. Katie's are too small for her. She's starting to complain about them hurting her feet."

"Sure, I'll go with you. I saw a thrift store yesterday when we were coming home. It's not too far from here. Not more than a thirty-minute walk."

"Have you eaten breakfast?" Tammy asked.

"No, but I'm not hungry. I'll be ready as soon as I have another cup of coffee."

Tammy nodded. "I'm going to go talk to Karla. See if I can't cheer her up."

Rona had finished her coffee and was rinsing the cup when Tammy and the girls came back into the kitchen. Karla didn't seem to be any happier.

"The washer kicked off, so I threw your clothes in the dryer," Tammy said as she began to put the girls' coats back on them.

"Thanks. Just let me run upstairs and grab my jacket." She started toward the stairs.

"Rona, wait a minute," Tammy called. "There's something I've wanted to do for a long time and couldn't."

Rona took an involuntary step back.

Tammy burst out laughing. "Lord, you should have seen the look on your face. You need a haircut. I want to cut your hair. I found a great pair of scissors while I was cleaning." She put her hands on her hips. "What did you think I meant?"

"I don't know," Rona mumbled and shrugged. "Do you know how to cut hair?"

"I used to cut my dad's all the time. Unless his hair was cut a certain way, he'd have a horrible cowlick."

Rona ran a hand over her thick mass of hair. More than two years had passed since her last haircut. It hung over her shoulder in uneven clumps.

"Come on, you're starting a new job tomorrow. You don't want to be looking all scruffy."

"Okay, but don't do anything weird to it."

Tammy tilted her head sideways and smiled. "Heck, here I was thinking how cute you'd look with a mohawk and a blond stripe right down the center."

"Okay, okay. Where are we going to do this?"

"Upstairs in my bathroom. I can raise the shade and the light will be perfect. Go on up and I'll go get the scissors." She placed their empty cups in the sink.

106

When Tammy arrived, she was carrying the scissors and a straight-back chair. She placed the chair by the bathroom window and raised the shade.

"Stop looking so scared," she scolded as she motioned for Rona to sit down.

"Are you sure you know what you're doing?"

"Trust me."

"I hate it when people say that," Rona groused as she sat down. She told herself to relax as Tammy began to comb her hair. She couldn't see into either of the mirrors from where she sat. Tammy combed part of her hair down over her face.

"Relax," Tammy told her. "If you don't like it, you won't have to leave a tip."

Rona chuckled and closed her eyes. As Tammy began to work, she could feel long tendrils of hair hit her arm before slipping to the floor.

"Your hair is so thick. I'll try to thin it some."

"Just don't leave big bald spots all over my head."

"Oh, ye of little faith."

The steady clipping of the scissors along with the comb running gently through her hair soon lulled her into a comfortable trance.

"Okay, I'm finished."

Rona opened her eyes. "You've already finished?"

"What do you mean *already*? It took me nearly thirty minutes. Look at that mess on the floor."

Rona looked at the floor around her. Hair was everywhere. Her hand flew to her head and after being reassured that plenty still remained there she relaxed. "Wow. That's a lot of hair."

"I'll say. I had an English setter that had less hair than that," Tammy said. "Well, get up and look at yourself. Tell me what you think."

Rona walked to the mirror and did a double take. She looked like a different person. She ran a hand through her hair and liked the way it sprang back into place. "I like it," she admitted. "You did a great job. Thank you."

107

Tammy reached over and rearranged the back of Rona's hair. "You look a lot different. Do you have any money?"

Rona nodded. Tammy's occasional bluntness no longer bothered her. "She paid me for working yesterday."

"Good. While we're out shopping today, we need to find you some decent clothes."

Rona glanced at herself in the mirror. "What's wrong with these?"

"Nothing if you were fifteen pounds heavier and four inches shorter."

Rona hitched up her pants and stared at her bare ankles. "They're perfect for walking in the snow. Besides, I don't want to spend all my money on clothes."

"That's fine, but if you're going to look for work you need at least two nice outfits. Think of it as an investment in your future."

Rona nodded. "I guess you're right."

"Of course I am. Now help me clean up this mess."

After sweeping the hair up off the bathroom floor, Tammy went to get the girls while Rona went to her room to get her jacket. Alone, she looked at herself in the mirror, amazed at the difference a simple haircut could make. She turned to leave and at the last moment, she removed the money from the envelope. Tammy was right. If she intended to start hunting for a job, she would need something to wear. She stuffed it in her pocket and pulled on the jacket.

It wasn't until they were leaving that she noticed Tammy had a key. "You found a key to the house?" she asked.

"No. Anna gave it to me in case the girls and I wanted to go out during the day."

Rona couldn't help but wonder why Anna hadn't given her a key. She tried telling herself that it was because they rode to work together or maybe Anna assumed she would borrow Tammy's if she needed one any other time.

"Don't ever try to make a living playing poker," Tammy said as they walked down the sidewalk with the girls racing a few steps ahead.

"What do you mean?"

"Your face always gives you away. Every emotion you're feeling is right there."

"You're so full of . . . stuffing," she replied, remembering to clean up her language.

"No, I'm not. When I told you Anna gave me a key, you were jealous that I had one and you didn't. When I came in from the park"—she lowered her voice—"you were up to no good. Rona, you promised me you wouldn't steal from Anna."

"I've not stolen anything," Rona snapped.

Tammy was watching her. "Maybe not yet, but I know you're planning something."

"There's a sign for a bus stop up ahead," Rona said, changing the subject. "We need to remember it in case we want to take the bus back."

Tammy didn't pursue the argument, but Rona was beginning to think that when it was time to leave she couldn't tell Tammy. She would have to leave her behind. As they continued to walk, a sense of loneliness settled over her.

The walk to the thrift store took them almost an hour. The girls got so excited about buying clothes, Karla temporarily forgot about building a snowman.

Rona left them digging through a bin of kid's shoes and went to see if she could find something nice to wear. She hated shopping for clothes. It was such a pain in the butt trying to match everything, and her mother always used to make her try everything on. She skipped the dressing room by simply holding the clothes up to her. With that method, she finally settled on a pair of brown slacks with an elastic waist and a white short-sleeved blouse. Both items were marked a dollar each. She found a tan shirt for fifty cents and added it to her pile. Satisfied with her selections she went to find Tammy and the girls. She finally located them in the back, looking at children's books.

Tammy looked up as Rona joined them. "I promised them each a book if they wouldn't wander off while we were shopping," she said and winked. Both girls were sitting on the floor surrounded by a dozen or more books. "They can't make up their minds which ones they want."

Rona glanced at the sign announcing the books were ten cents each. She watched as the girls pulled a stack of books from the shelves and went through them, before returning those to the shelf and pulling out another handful to go through. At this rate, she thought, they might be in school before they decided on a single book.

Tammy began to show her the numerous items of clothing she had chosen for the girls. "Let me see what you've picked out," Tammy said as she reached for Rona's things. "Good Lord, Rona," she scolded.

"What?"

"These look like they belong to someone's grandmother." She giggled. "Heck, they probably did." She draped the clothes over the cart. "Girls, hurry up. We need to help Rona find some clothes."

That's all it took for them to make a decision. Katie chose a book about a kitten and Karla found one with something that looked like a dancing mushroom on the cover.

"There's nothing wrong with these clothes," Rona grumbled.

"Did you even try them on?"

"No, but I held them up to me and they looked fine."

"Rona, when are you going to learn that there's fine and then there's *fine*?"

"I'm only wearing them to look for a job. They don't have to be *fine*." She mimicked Tammy's long drawn-out enunciation.

Without waiting to see if she intended to follow, Tammy and the girls took off toward the women's clothing.

Rona picked up the books the twins had left and waited in stubborn defiance. Finally, she slapped her leg in frustration. "There's nothing wrong with those clothes," she grumbled as she went after Tammy. By the time she caught up with them, the clothes she had picked out were no longer in sight. In their place was a growing pile. "I can't afford all those clothes," she hissed.

"You're not going to buy all these clothes," Tammy hissed back. "These are the ones you're going to try on."

"No." She groaned. "I don't want to try them on."

Tammy stared at her. "I swear you're worse than a kid. How do you expect to get clothes that look decent on you if you don't try them on?"

Rona grabbed a blouse from the rack and pointed to the tag. "I expect to read this and buy a size fourteen."

"Fourteen!"

Rona cringed as three older women turned to stare at them. "Yes," she replied in a lower tone.

"I don't know when you last wore a size fourteen, but take my word for it, that's no longer the case." Tammy grabbed her arm. "Come on. Try these on."

Rona allowed herself to be dragged across the store like a child. Sometimes it was just easier to keep quiet and show them. When her butt didn't fit into those tiny little pants Tammy had picked out then she could go back and find the clothes she had wanted originally.

They found an empty dressing room. Tammy handed her a shirt and a pair of pants. "Try these on."

Rona snapped her heels together and saluted, which caused the twins to start laughing. As she stripped her clothes off in the dressing room she became a little self-conscious that she wasn't wearing any underwear. As she quickly pulled on the clothes, she glanced nervously at the mirror across the back of the dressing room and hoped it wasn't a two-way mirror with a security person behind it. She had heard that some stores used them in an attempt to curtail shoplifting. Once she had the clothes on, she checked herself in the mirror. They didn't look so bad.

"Are you dressed yet?" Tammy asked.

"Yeah, these are fine."

"Let me see."

The curtain flew open before she could protest. From the look of exasperation on Tammy's face, Rona assumed they weren't fine.

111

"The pants are too big and that blouse looks horrible," Tammy insisted as she handed Rona more clothes. "Take those off and try these."

So began a vicious circle that continued until Rona was on the verge of collapsing. She no longer bothered even to look in the mirror. She simply put the clothes on and opened the curtain time after time, until finally Tammy spoke the golden words.

"I think you have enough."

Out of what felt like dozens of outfits she'd tried on, the final selections were narrowed down to a pair of black tapered slacks and a pair of forest green belted slacks. The tops included a long-sleeved white blouse with black piping along either side of the buttonholes, a short-sleeved cotton blouse with a subdued pattern of pale green banana leaves, a white turtleneck short-sleeved pullover, the same turtleneck in green, plus a black blazer. Tammy had also chosen two nice pullover sweaters and a pair of black denim jeans.

When Rona stumbled out of the dressing room, she stared at the mound of clothing. "I can't afford all those clothes."

"So far your total is sixteen dollars plus tax. I've been keeping a tally for you. Everything except the long-sleeved blouse has a green tag. That means they're thirty percent off."

Rona nodded. "Okay. I can handle that. She paid me thirty-three dollars."

Tammy looked at her and smiled. "Good, because you still need to buy shoes."

Rona draped herself over the cart. "No," she whimpered. "I can't take any more."

"You can't wear tennis shoes to a job interview." She pushed Rona off the shopping cart. "Stop whining, shoes are easy," Tammy assured her. "Let's go."

Too tired to argue, Rona trailed behind her.

True to her word, selecting shoes was much easier. Rona simply sat on the short stool and put on the shoes handed to her. Tammy finally settled on a pair of black loafers that looked brand new and a pair of low-cut boots.

"These boots look horrible," Rona protested.

"They just need to be polished," Tammy replied as she put them in the cart.

"How much are they?"

Tammy looked at the tags. "The loafers are five dollars but they're good shoes. The boots are only three dollars. They aren't as good quality, but they still have a lot of wear left in them."

Twenty-four dollars was more than Rona had intended to spend.

"An investment," Tammy reminded her as if she were reading her thoughts.

Rona nodded. "Can I quit now?" she implored.

Tammy ruffled her hair as she would the kids. "Yes, you can quit now."

As they walked toward the counter, Rona suddenly reached out, grabbed the shopping cart and brought it to a stop.

"What's wrong?" Tammy asked as Rona pawed through the contents.

"There's nothing in here for you," Rona said as she turned to stare at Tammy.

"I don't need anything," Tammy replied. "I can make do with the things I have."

"I thought you were going to start looking for a job."

"I am. I can add little things to make do with what I have."

"I don't think so. Girls, let's go help your mom find some pretty clothes."

After trying on several outfits, Tammy finally chose a sand-colored linen pantsuit and a long-sleeved cobalt blue blouse. The only shoes she could find to fit were a pair of brown pumps.

"I don't know," Tammy hedged as she continued to stare at the shoes. "The backs are sort of rough looking."

"They're not that bad," Rona argued. "The pants are long enough to cover the worst of the wear." She put her hands on her hips and tried to mimic Tammy's earlier tone. "Besides, you can't wear your tennis shoes with you new clothes."

Tammy continued to stare at the shoes.

"Take the shoes and let's go," Rona said. "It's already after four and we have a long walk back."

Tammy reluctantly put the shoes in her cart.

On the way to the register, Rona found a large bin with new socks. She added a package of black ones to her stack. She ignored Tammy's sigh. By the time the socks and tax were added to Rona's purchases, she was left with five dollars and some change.

"Investment," Tammy whispered in her ear as she began to unload her items onto the counter. Since most of the kids' clothes were either a dime or a quarter, Tammy's total purchase was only slightly more than half of Rona's.

"Why was my investment so much more than yours was?" she groused as they left the store.

Tammy laughed and ignored her grumbling.

A short distance from the thrift store they came across a bus stop. A young Hispanic woman helped them choose the bus they needed to get back to Anna's neighborhood.

Chapter Sixteen

Rona heard the television when they stepped into the living room. Anna must be back from her parents' house already, she thought as she took Tammy's bags. "I'll take this stuff upstairs for you."

"No, that's okay. I want to wash everything," Tammy said. "Give me your things and I'll wash them for you, so you'll have them for tomorrow."

"You don't have to do that."

"I know I don't, but you only have a few pieces, so give them here."

Rona handed the bags over.

"It looks like someone has been shopping," Anna called as she walked out of the den. Before anyone could respond, she called out, "You got your hair cut."

Rona's hand flew to her hair. "Tammy cut it for me."

"It looks great. You look so different." Anna came closer for a better look. "You did a wonderful job, Tammy."

"Thanks. I used to cut my dad's hair."

"Turn around and let me see the back," Anna instructed.

Rona did so with as much grace as she could. She jumped when Anna ran her hand lightly over the back of her head. It seemed to her that the room had suddenly gotten deadly quiet.

Katie broke the awkward moment. "We got new clothes and books," she announced proudly.

"You have new books," Anna said as she stepped away from Rona. "Will you read one to me? I love books."

"I can't read. You'll have to read it to me," Katie replied. "But I can do my ABCs."

"Well, I guess that's only fair," Anna agreed.

Rona turned to find Tammy watching her and giving her that little shit-eating grin.

Katie turned to Tammy. "Can I have my book now?"

Tammy dug through the bags and pulled out both books.

Rona excused herself, pleading exhaustion, and raced up the stairs. In her room, she sat on the foot of the bed and recalled the way Anna's fingers had felt in her hair. Before she could decide how she felt about it, there was a knock on her door. She went to open it.

"Are you okay?" Tammy asked.

"Yeah, I just wanted to rest a while."

"If you're not too tired, Mrs. Pagonis sent us food."

"That sounds good. I'm starved."

"Well," Tammy scolded playfully, "if you hadn't slept until ten o'clock, you could have had breakfast with us."

After they ate, Tammy and Rona cleaned the kitchen. The twins were in the den with Anna. Tammy had just turned on the dishwasher when the three of them came into the kitchen. "What's up?" Tammy asked when she saw the twins smiling.

"We're going to make a snowman," Karla announced.

"Karla, I've told you there's not enough snow to make a snowman."

116

"We're not going to make it out of snow this time," Anna informed them as she began to pull items from the pantry. "This snowman is going to be edible."

Rona and Tammy took seats behind the table and watched as the twins, standing on chairs, helped Anna make a white cake batter.

As Anna dug through the cabinets for cake pans, Rona asked, "Exactly how does this cake become a snowman?"

"Ah, here they are." She came back to the table with a set of three pans, each slightly smaller. "Here's the magic part," Anna said as she arranged the pans smallest to largest.

Rona nodded. "Okay, I got you."

They all pitched in to help pour the batter into the pans. As soon as the batter-filled pans were in the oven, Anna began to clean up their mess. The twins helped by putting spoons and spatulas in the dishwasher. After several minutes, the timer dinged.

"Are they done?" Katie asked.

"Let's check and see," Anna said as she handed each child a toothpick.

Rona watched as the twins carefully inserted the toothpicks into the center of the largest cake, then held them up for Anna to examine.

"They're done. We need to let them cool," Anna said as she placed the cakes on racks.

While they waited, she and the girls whipped up a thick white frosting. As soon as the cakes were cool, she placed them on a large cookie sheet.

"I think we should all help build this snowman," Anna declared as she passed out butter knives to everyone to help frost the cake. To finish off their masterpiece, Anna produced a jar of gumdrops. She let the twins choose the colors for the snowman's eyes, nose and mouth. With the last gumdrop in place, she and Rona moved it to the middle of the kitchen table.

"I've never seen a prettier snowman," Rona said.

"Do you like this snowman, Karla?" Tammy asked.

Karla nodded her head vigorously and smiled. "We can eat this one," she said with a giggle.

A new surge of activity erupted as plates and silverware were gathered. Glasses of ice-cold milk appeared. Soon the clank of silverware and an occasional sigh of contentment were the only sounds in the kitchen.

Afterward the twins disappeared to the den to watch the *Dora the Explorer* DVD for the tenth time, and the women began to clean the kitchen again.

"That was sweet of you to do that," Tammy told Anna.

"Thanks, but I enjoyed it as much as they did," Anna said.

Rona rubbed her tummy. "I think we all enjoyed it."

After the kitchen was clean, they sat back down at the kitchen table.

"Why is it that women always end up sitting around the kitchen table?" Tammy asked.

Anna shook her head. "I don't know, but it always seems to happen. Some of the most important decisions in my life were made at Mom and Dad's kitchen table."

"What kind of decisions?" Rona asked. She wanted to know what the story was behind the box with the word *bitch* on it. She was sure it was a romance gone sour but couldn't ask outright. Maybe she could lead the conversation around to it.

Anna ran a finger over her lip. "We were sitting at the table when we decided which college I would attend and, again, when I decided to change my major from pre-med to finance. My entire family was at the table when I came out to them," she said and rolled her eyes.

"How did they handle that?" Tammy asked.

"It was sort of shock," Anna said. "I was afraid my father might have problems accepting it, but he didn't. It was Julian."

"He seems so easy-going," Tammy said as she moved her chair into a more comfortable position.

"Julian and I rebelled at about the same time. He went through a short period where everything had to revolve around him." Anna leaned back in her chair. "If it didn't concern him, he wasn't interested in it. At this same time, he became fixated with image. He

118

didn't want people to know his family owned a restaurant. He started hanging around with a group of kids whose parents were doctors, lawyers or corporate CEOs. He wanted to be seen at the right places, wearing the right clothes and hanging with the right people. At that time, having a lesbian sister wasn't exactly considered chic." She went to the wine cooler and came back with a bottle of red wine and three glasses. She poured the wine before continuing. "I went through something similar, but my thing was to shout to the world that I was a lesbian." She grimaced. "I do mean shout. I plastered gay and lesbian pride bumper stickers on my parents' car. I wore T-shirts and buttons announcing I was a lesbian. Everything I owned had either a rainbow or a pink triangle on it."

"How old were you?" Tammy asked.

"I was eighteen or nineteen, and Julian is three years younger than me."

"Did you catch a lot of crap from strangers?" Rona asked.

Anna nodded. "I would get a lot of nasty looks or comments from strangers. I can't tell you how many times my poor parents had their car egged before Hector explained what the rainbow triangle on their bumper meant."

"How did your parents handle it?" Tammy asked.

"You taking notes for the future?" Rona teased.

Tammy made a face at Rona and turned back to Anna.

"My parents believe in family, community, country and God. Dad says if you do right by the first three then you've already honored God. They also believe hard work will cure anything. We were always active in the church and community, but when Julian and I went on our tear, my parents decided it was time for us to start thinking more about other people. They saw to it that whenever we weren't working at the restaurant we were doing volunteer work for either the community or the church and they were right there beside us working. They volunteered us to work with underprivileged kids, with the battered women's shelter and with AIDS patients. Somewhere in all that Julian and I both realized that

119

material possessions and sexual orientation aren't the defining factors of a person's worth."

"It's always easier to overlook material possessions when you have plenty of them," Rona challenged. She despised those men and women who showed up to work at the soup kitchen in their fancy clothes and jewelry.

A spark of anger flashed in Anna's eyes. "My family received help when they needed it, but they also worked hard and earned what they have now."

Rona wasn't interested in a Pagonis history lesson, but she sensed she was about to get one.

"I told you that my grandparents, Nicholas and Damara Pagonis, were from Lakonia," Anna said as poured them more wine. "They came to this country in nineteen thirty-seven with three children. The oldest was six and my father, the youngest, was two. They were going to Chicago, where my grandfather's cousin lived. Grandfather was a carpenter and his cousin had a job waiting for him, but on the trip over, my grandfather got very sick. As soon as the ship docked in New York, he was hospitalized. He spent almost a month there and then another three months regaining his strength. They didn't have much money, and my grandmother had to locate a place for her and the kids to live and then find a way to feed them. She met an old woman who rented out her bedroom. The old woman slept in the living room. She helped Grandmother get a job taking in sewing. It was actually embroidering. They paid Grandmother by the piece. At some point during all this the cousin in Chicago was contacted, and he informed them that he could only hold the job two more weeks." She sipped her wine and shrugged. "Of course, there was no way Grandfather could travel, much less work. The sewing Grandmother took in didn't provide enough to buy food for them. She didn't want to worry my grandfather and tried to hide the fact that she was broke, but things became so bad she finally had to tell him when the old woman threatened to make her move out. Apparently, someone who volunteered at the hospital overheard the conversation. She helped my grandparents get in touch with an Orthodox Greek church that found them a place to stay rent-free and helped with groceries until Grandfather was on his feet. The church helped him find work on a construction crew afterward."

Rona wanted to interrupt, but Anna was clearly not finished.

"My dad never finished high school. He went to work in construction when he was sixteen. When he was nineteen, he came to San Antonio to live with an uncle. Two years later, he met Mom."

A rich rose tint warmed Anna's cheeks. Rona wasn't sure if it was the wine or Anna's passionate feelings causing the glow.

"My mom's family owned a small bakery, but it was her dream to open a restaurant." Anna stopped suddenly and took a deep breath. "I'm sorry. I got carried away. It's just that I'm so proud of my family and all they've achieved."

Tammy patted Anna's hand. "As you should be," she said as she gave Rona a sharp look. They sat in silence until Tammy finally stood. "It's getting late. I need to get the girls to bed." She took the empty glasses and rinsed them as Anna re-corked the wine.

Rona stood. She didn't want to be alone with Anna. "I have some things to take care of too. What time will you be leaving tomorrow morning?"

"I usually leave around six-thirty," Anna said as she fiddled with the wine bottle.

"I'll be ready." Rona hurried out of the room. As she climbed the stairs, she realized she still hadn't learned anything about the woman associated with the box of clothes.

Chapter Seventeen

Rona glanced at the clock. It was ten minutes until five. The alarm was set to go off at five, because she didn't like to rush in the morning. She turned it off and sat on the side of the bed. A fluttering of butterflies tickled her stomach when she thought about meeting her new co-workers. With Sharon at her desk, there wouldn't be a computer available for her to use, and she wondered what she would be doing all day. She hoped she wouldn't have to sit at the front desk while Sharon got to work in the back. The thought of having to greet people when they came in made her feel ill. A grin teased her lips as she recalled her grandmother telling her, "There is no need to be afraid of anything until it happens, and once it happens it is over with and time to move on." She wasn't sure she always agreed with her grandmother's motto, but it seemed to fit today. With one last glance at the clock, she went to shower.

She took her time showering. When she came back into the

bedroom, she flipped the light on and noticed the clothes she had purchased the day before hanging on the back of the door. Tammy must have washed them and then slipped in and left them during the night. A lump formed in her throat when she saw the boots and loafers on the floor by the dresser. The boots gleamed with a new coat of polish. She chose the black slacks, long-sleeved white shirt with black piping and the boots. She made the bed and quickly straightened the room before carefully combing her hair. With nothing left to do, she picked up the black blazer and headed downstairs.

There was a light on in the kitchen and the smell of coffee filled the air. She walked in expecting to find Anna but found Tammy instead. She was mixing something in a bowl.

"What are you doing up so early?" Rona asked as she waited for Tammy to say something about her new clothes.

"I'm making breakfast," Tammy said, stating the obvious. "I made you a lunch. I didn't figure you'd feel comfortable going out with them somewhere. It's in the refrigerator, so don't forget it."

Rona was again touched by her thoughtfulness. "Thanks. You didn't have to do that. Thanks for washing the clothes and cleaning up the shoes. You were right about the boots. They almost look new." When Tammy didn't immediately respond, Rona went to pour herself a cup of coffee.

"I didn't do it because I had to," Tammy replied tersely.

Surprised, Rona stared at her. "What's got you in such a pissy mood?

Tammy shook her head. "I'm afraid you're going to do something stupid."

Rona waved her free hand. "I've told you I wouldn't."

"Then why did you have to smart off about Anna's family last night."

"I didn't 'smart off.' When she kept bragging about what all her family has done, I simply stated it was easier—"

"I know what you said," Tammy said, interrupting her. "I don't think she was bragging." She stopped beating whatever was in the

123

bowl and turned her attention to Rona. "Don't you see that's why Anna is helping us? It's the way she was raised. My parents were good people, but it never would have occurred to them to volunteer somewhere. For them, helping others meant you fed someone's dog while they were on vacation or if one of their students was struggling they would help him find a tutor." She went back to mixing the contents of the bowl. "Anna has every right to be proud of her family."

"Damn, when did you become a one-person Anna Pagonis cheering squad?"

Tammy slammed the bowl down onto the counter and glared at Rona. "The minute my girls started smiling and sleeping in a warm bed."

They both fell silent as Anna walked into the room.

"Good morning," Anna said as she went to the coffeepot.

Rona mumbled a greeting and sat at the table. She stole a glance toward Anna. She must have heard them arguing.

"Morning," Tammy replied. "Breakfast will be ready in a few minutes."

Anna walked over and peeked in the bowl Tammy was holding.

"It's what my mom called breakfast hash," Tammy explained. "It has a little of this and a little of that thrown in with some eggs. I used yesterday's chili."

"Can I help?" Anna asked.

"No, thanks. I've got it."

Anna brought her coffee to the table and sat down. "You look especially nice this morning." Before Rona could respond, Anna rushed on, "I've been thinking that since we don't have a computer for you to use today, maybe you could help Sharon with something." She stopped and took a sip of coffee. "I'm hoping if Sharon calls the rental company this morning, they can have the computer delivered and set up this afternoon."

Rona nodded. "That sounds fine," she agreed.

Tammy set a bowl of steaming eggs before them and a plate with toast.

Rona hadn't been too enthusiastic about trying the chili and eggs, but the mixture smelled good. She spooned a small portion on her plate. The rich tasting mixture of the spicy chili and the buttery eggs surprised her. Her second helping was much larger.

When Rona and Anna left for work, Anna didn't offer to let her drive. The moderate temperatures of the previous two days had melted the snow and the interstates were opened to traffic. As they rode in silence, Rona began to wonder how much of her and Tammy's conversation Anna had heard. She tried to think of something to say that would get Anna to talk, but nothing seemed right. Before she could come up with anything, they were already pulling into the parking lot.

Rona took the plastic bag holding the lunch Tammy had made her and followed Anna to the third floor. Neither Sharon nor Neal had arrived yet. Rona put her lunch in the refrigerator and started a pot of coffee. Anna walked in while it was brewing.

"Thanks for starting the coffee," she said.

Rona nodded.

Anna started to leave then hesitated. "Listen, I'm sorry about last night. I can get a little overly zealous about my family."

Rona remembered what Tammy had said about the kids. Both of the kids were smiling more, and Karla was slowly beginning to talk more. Maybe Anna wasn't directly responsible for that, but she offered a sense of security that contributed to it. Tammy was right. "No. I shouldn't have said what I did. You and your family have been kind to us. We're indebted to you."

Anna frowned. "I don't want you to be indebted."

"Then what do you want?" Rona's sense of appreciation was fleeing quickly.

"I wanted you to have another chance. You're a good person."

"How do you know that?"

"Because you helped me, even though you knew it would cost you a safe place to spend the night."

"That was Tammy's idea," Rona said as she folded her arms across her chest and stared at the coffeepot.

"It may have been Tammy's suggestion, but I don't think you would have listened to her if it was something you didn't really want to do."

"So you think you have me all figured out, do you?"

"I think you've been hurt by someone you love. Now you keep everyone at arm's length to avoid being hurt again."

Rona snorted. "And maybe you don't know your ass from a hole in the ground."

Anna shrugged. "Well, there are days when I would be the first to agree with you on that." She took two cups from the cupboard and poured their coffee. "Let's work out a compromise for the rest of this week. This is strictly between you and me. This won't affect Tammy or the twins in any way." She turned and handed the cup to Rona before continuing. "Here's the deal. I won't preach about my family anymore, and you don't do anything that might cause either of us any regrets." She held up her cup.

Rona almost dropped the cup. "I don't know what you're talking about."

Anna ignored her as she continued to hold her cup out. "Do we have an agreement or not?" she asked.

Rona nodded.

Anna smiled slightly and clinked her cup against Rona's. "Good. Sharon won't be in until around eight. You can use her computer until then. I've already booted it up for you." She turned and left Rona staring after her. Anna seemed to know her plans. Did she really, or was she guessing? Suddenly it hit her that if Anna were to kick her out now, she could be back on the streets. Her knees began to shake. She held onto the counter for support. It was several minutes before she was able to walk to Sharon's desk and start working. Even then, her concentration kept drifting and she found herself staring blankly at the stack of papers.

She was clearing away her things when a short heavyset woman she assumed was Sharon came in. "Hi. I'm Rona Kirby," she said.

126

Rona was relieved to hear Anna coming down the hallway.

"I leave for a weekend and you replace me," Sharon called out in a low voice tinted with a slight Jamaican accent. She pulled her coat off and draped it over a chair.

"Oh, don't you wish," Anna replied as she gave Sharon a hug. "Rona is going to help you catch up and do the database."

Sharon smiled and extended her hand to Rona. "Then I'm very glad to meet you. I'm Sharon Waddell."

"How was your unexpected long weekend?" Anna asked.

"Girl, we played in the snow like we were children." She laughed. "My husband, Martin, and I have two boys. Ky is seventeen and Benny is fourteen," she explained to Rona. "It's the first time any of us had ever seen snow. Benny took the wheels off his skateboard and started *snow surfing*. Of course, Martin had to try it and almost broke his neck."

"And how did you do?" Anna teased.

Sharon held out her arms as if she were surfing. "I was a natural."

"Sharon broke her arm testing Ky's first skateboard," Anna told Rona.

"Those things aren't easy," Rona replied. "You should try it sometime."

Anna held up her hands. "No, thank you. I like having my feet firmly planted on the ground."

"That's our Anna."

Rona looked up to see a young man standing in the doorway wearing a dark suit and overcoat.

Anna and Sharon called out greetings before Anna introduced her.

"It's nice to meet you," Neal said as he shook Rona's hand. She saw his eyes take her in before he asked about everyone's weekend. As the three co-workers discussed their weekend, Rona picked up the rest of the papers from Sharon's desk and wished she could sneak away to the conference room.

Neal finally left to go to his office when Anna began to explain

127

to Sharon that they needed to rent a computer for Rona to use. Until it arrived, Rona could assist Sharon with whatever she needed help on.

"I'll get her started on putting the packets together," Sharon said. "Come on." She picked up her coat and motioned for Rona to follow her.

The time flew by for Rona. She had a third of the packets stuffed with marketing materials ready by the time Sharon came by to see if she wanted to order lunch.

"We usually order something and I go pick it up. Then we all eat here in the conference room." They looked at the table covered in papers. "Or in the break room," Sharon added.

"I brought a lunch," Rona told her.

"Okay, but you're welcome to join us."

Rona nodded and thanked her.

By the time Anna came by to tell her lunch had arrived, Rona's back was starting to ache from bending over the table so long.

They were already seated when she took her lunch from the refrigerator.

"Anna tells me you worked some kind of magic with the thermostat Saturday," Sharon said.

"I did a little adjusting," Rona said coyly as she sat down.

"Whatever you did, I thank you. I'm always freezing in here and today I'm as warm as toast."

Rona opened the lunch Tammy made for her and found a ham and cheese sandwich and a bag of chips. In a separate baggie were some Oreos.

"I want what she's having," Neal said as he sat down with a small salad.

"I'll share my Oreos," Rona offered.

Neal turned out not to be the stuffed shirt she first thought he was. Between him and Sharon, they laughed throughout most of their lunch hour. They all shared her cookies and Neal teasingly encouraged her to bring more the next day. After leaving the boisterous lunch group, Rona was concerned that the afternoon might drag. She was surprised when Anna came in and told her it was quitting time for Rona.

"I'm sorry, I didn't think about this sooner," Anna said. "I'm so used to working until six or later that I never even thought about how we would work out getting you home."

"I can take the bus," Rona told her.

"I hate to have you do that. It's so far out, I'm sure you'll have to transfer at least once." Anna ran a finger over her lip. "You could take the car and go on home, but then you'd have to come back and pick me up."

Rona thought about it for a moment. "Can I offer another suggestion?"

"Sure."

"I wanted to start looking for a job. If you wouldn't mind, I could work a split shift—like from six-thirty until ten-thirty and then come back at two and work until six. If you have to stay later than six I can just hang around."

Anna nodded. "Sure, that'll be fine. You can use the car then."

Rona shook her head. "I wouldn't feel right taking your car."

Anna waved her off. "You'll be able to cover a lot more territory with it."

"Thanks."

"Good, then that's what we'll do starting tomorrow. But for today you're stuck."

"Actually, I need to run an errand."

"Great. I'll get you the keys."

"No. It's nearby," Rona lied. Anna's car didn't need to be near where she was going. With a quick good-bye to her new co-workers, Rona went to retrieve her meager possessions that she had stored beneath the floorboards of an abandoned building several months ago.

Chapter Eighteen

It was almost six by the time Rona made it back to Anna's office complex. She clutched the battered black bag to her chest as she waited on the elevator. After retrieving the bag, she had taken time to remove it from the protective plastic she had originally wrapped it in. A quick glance inside showed everything was just as she had left it.

"Can I help you?"

She turned to find a security guard dressed in a navy blue uniform and holding a clipboard. She experienced a moment of panic before she realized she had a right to be in the building. "No, thanks."

"I'm sorry, ma'am, but do you have an appointment with someone?" The elevator opened but he motioned for her to move to the other side of the hallway.

"I work for Pagonis Investments on the third floor."

"Pagonis?" he repeated. He studied her for a moment. "Your name, please." He raised the clipboard and began to flip through papers.

"Rona Kirby. This is my first day."

He looked at her again before he waved to her. "Ma'am, would you come with me, please?"

"Why? I told you I work here."

"Your name isn't on my list. With this being your first day and all, I'm sure they just forgot to call us, but I can't let you go up until I verify who you are."

Rona started to argue, but the look on his face stopped her. He wasn't unkind, but he clearly had a job to do. She followed him to the little office down the hall. She stood by the door as he placed a call. "There's no answer," he said, watching her.

"Try again. The receptionist has already left for the day. Do you have a direct number listed to Anna Pagonis?"

He glanced at the clipboard again and dialed. "Yes, this is security. I have a Rona Kirby down here. She says she works for you." He listened for a moment. "You didn't call to advise us you'd hired anyone." He listened and nodded, finally thanking her and hanging up. He picked a pen up from the desk and began to write. "I'm adding your name to the roster. You shouldn't have any more trouble," he told her.

"Has there been some sort of trouble?"

"A couple of bums tried to snatch a woman's purse in the parking lot a few nights ago."

"Wow. Did you catch them?" Rona tried to sound interested enough to keep him talking, but not so much as to sound nosy. She didn't want him to quit talking.

"No. The woman filed a complaint the following morning. Apparently the old security company had a few personnel problems," he said as he tossed the pen back onto the desk.

"You're with a different company?"

"Yeah, the building manager fired the other guys and hired us."

Rona politely said good-bye and left. As she rode up the elevator, she couldn't help but smile. So, Anna wasn't such a pushover after all. For some reason, she was glad.

Anna's office door was still unlocked when Rona reached the third floor. She went in, intending to wait in the conference room, but Anna came out of her office with her coat on and carrying her

131

briefcase. "I'm so sorry about that," she said when she saw Rona. "It's my fault. I should have called them to let them know you started working here today. It completely slipped my mind."

"That happens sometimes with new policies," Rona said.

Anna stopped and looked at her. "What do you mean?"

"I mean the old security company didn't require you to do that, did they? I'm sure they couldn't have cared less who came and went out of the building. In fact, you didn't even have a security guard here during the day."

Anna rolled her eyes. "You probably know more about this place than I do." She flipped off the lights in the break room. "I'm ready to go if you are." She noticed the bag Rona was holding. "What did you find?"

Rona shrugged. "It's just some personal papers I'd left somewhere where they would be safe. I went and got them."

Anna nodded. "I wonder what Tammy's fixing for dinner. I'm starved."

"To be so skinny you sure eat a lot," Rona teased.

"I'm not skinny," Anna protested. "I've been told I'm quite fine." She tossed her hair.

"That you are."

Anna stopped so suddenly that Rona ran into her. She automatically slipped her arms around Anna to catch her. Rona gazed into Anna's dark eyes.

"You're not so bad yourself," Anna replied softly. She pulled away and headed for the door.

Rona was so shocked that she was unable to move for a long moment. When she finally did, she had to run to catch up. As soon as they were in the elevator, Anna began to chatter about the basketball game that was supposed to be on that night.

"I'm not a basketball fan," Rona admitted.

Anna looked at her, clearly appalled. "We're going to have to change that. No one can survive my family without being a Spurs fan. When they won their first championship in '99, we threw a huge party. In fact, there's a game Sunday. Mom is making her specialty, pastitsio."

Before Rona could refuse, the elevator opened and Anna was sailing across the lobby. Anna rambled on about basketball most of the way home. Under normal circumstances, Rona might have been irritated, but she couldn't stop thinking about Anna's comment. When did Anna start looking at her? *When did I start noticing her?* She was still mulling over that question when they pulled into the garage.

The twins met them at the kitchen door. Tammy was washing a bunch of lettuce.

"We went to Auntie Tina today," Katie announced proudly.

"Who's Aunt Tina?" Rona asked, turning to Tammy.

"Athenians," Tammy corrected. "Your mom called this morning and invited us to lunch."

"Really," Anna said. She seemed bemused. "Did you like it?"

"I liked the ba-la-la," Katie replied.

"Yes, I like the baklava too," Anna agreed. "Did you bring me some?"

Karla nodded.

"You did. Where is it?"

"On the table," Karla replied.

"Let's eat some." Anna started toward the table with the twins on her heels.

Tammy cleared her throat and looked at the girls. "None for you two until after dinner."

Anna stopped. "Oops," she said. "I guess I should wait too. What are we having, by the way?"

"I fixed a pork roast. I thought we would eat in about twenty minutes."

"I'm going to go change," Rona said as she left the room. She hid the black bag under the bed and changed into sweats and her sneakers before carefully hanging up her new clothes in the closet. Despite the hassles of all the shopping, she was forced to admit that it felt good to know the clothes she was wearing were hers and that they fit correctly.

When Rona went back downstairs, Tammy was in the kitchen alone.

133

"I'm sorry about last night and this morning," Rona said. "You were right about everything—Anna, the haircut, the clothes, the boots—everything." She looked up to find Tammy smiling at her.

"I'm glad to hear you finally appreciate my keen sense of style," Tammy said as she handed Rona the end of a carrot that she had been grating into a salad bowl.

"You know I can be a butt," Rona admitted as she munched on the carrot. "Do you want me to help with that?"

"No. I'm almost done. How was your first day at work?"

"Good." Rona told her about Sharon and Neal.

"They sound like nice people."

Rona nodded.

"Did something happen on the way home?" Tammy asked.

Puzzled, Rona glanced up. "No. Why?"

"Anna seemed sort of flustered when she came in. I've noticed she talks a lot when she gets nervous."

Rona's face flushed when she recalled how Anna's body felt pressed against her own.

Tammy shook her head as she turned to check the roast. "Like I said, you should never play poker."

"When are we playing poker?" Anna called as she walked in. "I love to play."

Rona turned to stare at her. "I'm seriously considering putting a cowbell around your neck. Do you always walk so softly?"

"I wasn't walking any differently than I always do. You just weren't paying attention," Anna replied as she grabbed a cucumber slice from the salad bowl. She gave Rona a dazzling smile before biting into the cucumber.

"Dinner's ready," Tammy announced.

It took Rona a moment to tear her gaze from Anna's lips. "I'll go get the girls," she mumbled as she rushed out of the kitchen.

134

Chapter Nineteen

The following day, Rona went to the state employment office during her lunch period. It seemed like the logical place for her to start looking for work. She had glanced over the classified ads in the newspaper, but they all seemed to require more skill or education than she had or else they sounded like scams. She wondered if anyone really believed it was possible to earn five thousand dollars a week by stuffing envelopes.

The counselor assigned to her at the employment office scheduled her for a series of tests to see which jobs she would be most qualified for. She took the tests during her lunch on Wednesday and Thursday. As she suspected, she scored higher on tasks that required good hand-eye coordination. When the interviewer asked her about previous jobs, Rona told him about the band. He simply shook his head and informed her that job listings for musicians were rare. He promised he would call if a suitable position opened up. In the meantime, he suggested she consider furthering her education.

Back at the office, she had entered the final address listings into the database Wednesday morning. Sharon helped her print out the labels. By Thursday afternoon, they were affixed to the packets and ready to be mailed out. Anna asked her to come in on Friday to help Sharon with a multitude of small tasks that had been slowly building up.

On the drive in Friday morning, Anna seemed quieter than usual.

"You seem deep in thought," Rona said.

"I was just wondering if you'd heard anything from the employment office."

"No. I don't think they had much hope in finding me anything."

"I was talking to Matt Devers yesterday. He's the lawyer down on the first floor. He happened to mention that he has several file cabinets of material that he needs to log and then send to an archive. When I told him I had hired a temp, he wanted the name of the agency and we sort of worked out a deal, if you're interested."

"Yes, I'm interested. What would I have to do?"

"It sounds like you'd be compiling a log of the files and then making sure the right files were placed in the correct box."

"I can handle that. Should I go see him?"

Anna switched lanes. "Yes. If you like, I'll call him this morning and see when he's available to talk to you."

"Thanks, I'd like that."

Anna glanced at her and smiled.

"What?" Rona asked.

Anna shook her head but kept smiling.

Rona met with Matt Devers at noon. His secretary was at lunch when she arrived and he was watching the front office himself. Devers was a middle-aged man with a severely receding hairline and thick glasses. His wardrobe of an open-necked white shirt, tucked into tan Dockers, and brown loafers seemed more appropriate for a college student than for someone with his own law office. His office space was much smaller than Anna's office. The lack of artwork and plants gave the space a rather sterile feeling. He showed her the file cabinets that were jammed into a small room with tall teetering piles of files stacked on top of them.

"As you can see, I ran out of space a long time back. All of the loose files on top, along with these two cabinets here, need to be sent to an archive." He quickly explained what he needed done with the files. "Did Anna tell you the agreement she and I worked out?" he asked.

"No, just that you mentioned needing these files archived."

"As you can see, I don't have any space to set up a computer for you to work at. Anna agreed to let you stay in her conference room and work there. I'll bring you a box of files and when you complete it, I'll bring another one. If something comes up and Anna needs to use her conference room, it won't take much effort to move my stuff out of the way."

Rona wondered how any of this benefited Anna.

As if anticipating her question he continued. "In return, I'll pay the full cost of the computer rental." He motioned to her. "Let's go back to my office where it's more comfortable." As soon as they sat down, he got right to the point. "I don't know what the financial arrangement was between you and Anna, but I've had my secretary call several temp agencies and she's assured me that I shouldn't pay more than eight dollars an hour."

Rona started to tell him that the wage was more than fair but he stopped her.

"I'm sorry, but the salary is really not open for negotiation. You'll be paid each Friday afternoon, and I don't foresee this project taking more than two weeks." He peered at her through his thick glasses. "What are your thoughts on the matter?"

"I think I'll be ready to start Monday morning."

"Good. Anna explained to me about how you've arranged your time and that's fine with me. I'm usually in the office until at least seven each night. Of course, you realize that you are not allowed to look at the contents of the files or to mention anything you might accidentally see."

"I understand completely."

"And all the files must be brought back to the file room each night before you leave."

Rona nodded her agreement.

He stood so suddenly it startled her. "My secretary will give you all the necessary forms to complete on Monday. Have a good weekend." He held out his hand.

As Rona stepped into the elevator, she saw the security guard and waved.

"Hello, Ms. Kirby, how's the job?"

"Good," she said. "Have you had any more trouble with muggers?"

He smiled. "No, ma'am. You're safe on my watch."

She smiled and waved again as the door closed.

They were sitting at the table playing hearts that night when the phone rang. Anna answered it. "Hi, Mom. Yes, the babies are fine." She looked at Tammy and smiled.

Rona pretended to arrange her cards as she listened to the one-sided conversation.

"No," Anna replied. "I can't go to church Sunday, but I'll definitely be there for dinner. Are you still making pastitsio? . . . Oh, good. I've been craving it. What can I bring?" She made a notation on a pad. "I'll stop by the bakery on West Avenue and buy some of the sourdough bread you and Dad like so much . . . I'll ask them . . . okay . . . Yes, I'll call you back tonight." After hanging up the phone, she turned to Tammy and Rona. "She called to invite you all to Sunday dinner. She's serving pastitsio."

"What is that?" Rona asked.

"It's sort of like lasagna, only it doesn't have quite as much sauce," Anna explained.

"I wouldn't want to intrude," Tammy said.

Anna chuckled. "You wouldn't be intruding. She wants to see the *babies*." She stressed the ending and made them both smile.

Rona and Tammy glanced at each other.

"Come on. There's a Spurs game Sunday afternoon. It'll be fun."

"If you're sure we won't be intruding," Tammy said.

"No, not at all. As you saw, Mom loves to feed people."

"Where does your family go to church?" Tammy asked.

Rona found it odd that she didn't seem the least bit embarrassed to acknowledge that she had been listening to Anna's call.

"We're members of Saint Sophia's Greek Orthodox church. I don't go as often as my parents would like, but Sunday morning is the only free morning I have, and I tend to hoard it. We usually get together after church for Sunday dinner."

They started talking about religion and Rona tuned them out. She'd had enough religion to last her into the next lifetime.

Chapter Twenty

The entire Pagonis clan and their guests gathered in the living room of Anna's parents to watch the early-afternoon basketball game between the San Antonio Spurs and the Memphis Grizzlies. In a rare moment of openness, Tammy admitted that she had once gone to Memphis to visit Graceland and had fallen in love with the city resting on the banks of the mighty Mississippi River. To add a sense of competition to the game, Tammy and Rona opted to cheer for the Memphis team. Rona wasn't much of a basketball fan but understood enough to get caught up in the spirit of the event. The game was close and each basket or missed shot produced a loud roar of cheering or groans.

At halftime, the group broke up to head back to the kitchen or to slip outside for a breath of fresh air. Rona stood and stretched. She and Tammy had spent the previous day lazing around watching television. It had been too wet and cold for them to venture out and Anna had worked until after four. Afterward, when Anna came home, she mentioned she needed to go to Wal-Mart to restock the snack supply for the office. They rode along with her. Rona was finally able to purchase some underwear.

"Go get more food," Mr. Pagonis said as he returned with a plate of cheese and bread. "You're too skinny, like Anna."

"I'm headed that way," Rona assured him as she went in search of an empty bathroom. On her way back, she stopped in her tracks. Her mouth watered as she gazed at the beautiful old upright piano that was the center attraction in a small room that her grand-mother would have called a parlor. The piano's ornate cabinet had been refinished in a brilliant hand-rubbed lacquer finish. Framed photos graced the top. She stepped into the room, telling herself she only wanted to get a better look at the photos. As she grew closer, she could smell the rich aroma of lemon oil. Tucked beneath the instrument was a small piano stool on wheels, with an embroidered seat. She rolled it out and studied the warm hues of the threads used to create the rose design before sitting down at one of the finest pianos ever made, an 1897 Ivers and Pond. She recognized it from the book on antique pianos her piano teacher had kept on the coffee table in the waiting room. Rona had flipped through the book dozens of times while waiting for the student's lesson before hers to end.

Her heart pounded as she opened the lid to reveal the keys that had aged to a light shade of warm honey. She could almost feel the soul of the piano humming beneath her hands as she placed her fingers on the keys. Her right thumb twitched and the rich tone of middle C stirred her blood. She tried to draw her hands away. The piano's magical pull refused to release her. As years of practice took over, she closed her eyes and allowed the music to flow from her heart. A music teacher had instilled in her the love of classical music. She let the music go where it wanted as the thundering hooves of the galloping horse in Schubert's "Erlkönig" gave way to the insistent rhythm of a Chopin polonaise. Her fingers flowed into a wandering, chromatic theme reminiscent of a Liszt sonata and then slithered into his darker "Totentanz." Escaping the darkness, she launched into the almost dance-like work of Brahms's "Ein Kleiner, Hübscher Vogel," where love's pleasures and pains are compared to a bird's life. The sound of the bird's wings spun away into the repetitive melody of Schubert's "Gretchen am Spinnrade."

Rona's body rocked in time to the composer's interpretation of the mournful mood of a woman sitting at a whirring spinning wheel. The music stopped as spontaneously as it had begun. She took a deep breath as if to inhale the last notes. The thunderous sound of applause brought her to her feet. Anna and her family stood crowded together just inside the doorway. She squirmed with embarrassment under the attention.

"You play beautifully," Mrs. Pagonis declared as she rushed forward and grasped Rona's arm.

"Why didn't you tell us you could play so well?" Mr. Pagonis asked as he stepped to her other side.

"Play something else," one of the children yelled. Others instantly took up the cry.

She glanced at the eager faces before her. It had been so long since she'd played for anyone. The actual performance was secondary for her. The thrill was in creating the music. The joy of sitting down and writing a composition, whether it was a work so powerfully raw it threatened to rip the throat from the performer, or the creation of a ballad so poignant it brought tears to the eyes of the listener, or a playful tune that caused even the hardest of hearts to open up.

A tug on her pant leg made her look down. Karla was gazing up at her with those solemn blue eyes. "Please, Rona. One more."

Rona smiled. "Just one and then it's time to go watch the rest of the game," she said.

Karla nodded happily.

Rona sat down before turning back to the child. "What do you want to hear?"

"The one you hum."

"The one I hum?"

Again, Karla nodded.

"When was I humming?" Rona asked.

"You hum all the time," Katie joined in.

Confused, she glanced at Tammy for help.

"I'm not sure if it's the one she's talking about, but there's one song that you often hum," Tammy said. "I've never heard it before."

"Do you remember how it goes?"

Tammy closed her eyes and concentrated for a moment. "It's something like this." She hummed a couple of slow bars.

"That's it," Karla cried.

Shocked by the all-too-familiar tune, Rona could only stare. She didn't realize she hummed aloud and she certainly couldn't remember humming the song Tammy indicated. She looked at the keyboard. She hadn't played the song since before Mary died. Could she get through it?

Someone moved to the side of the piano. She looked up to find Anna watching her. Uncomfortable with the intense scrutiny, she closed her eyes and let her hands seek out the keys that would breathe life back into the composition that she thought she would never play again. She had written this song for Mary and couldn't bring herself to sing the words. As she played the slow undulating melody, snapshots of their happy times came back to her. The first time they met, their first kiss, Mary's laughter, making love, the band, the way the rain sounded against the window of their tiny one-room apartment. She used the piano keys to once more experience and express the joy Mary had brought into her life. When the last note faded, she opened her eyes to find tears on Anna's cheeks. She looked into those dark eyes and felt them drawing her in. A burst of applause momentarily disoriented her. She forced her gaze from Anna and turned to Karla.

"Is that the song?"

"Yeah. I like it."

"Good. Now let's go watch the rest of the basketball game," she urged. There was a flurry of activity as the group made their way out of the room.

Rona carefully closed the lid on the piano and rolled the stool back underneath. When she turned, Anna was still standing in the doorway.

"What's the name of that song?" Anna asked. "I'm not familiar with it."

" 'Lover's Dream,' " she replied as she walked to the door. Anna didn't move.

"It's a beautiful song. I'm surprised I've never heard it before," Anna said.

Rona licked her lips and glanced away.

When she didn't reply, Anna asked. "Do you know who wrote it?" Anna stepped toward her.

"Yeah." She took a deep breath and fought the urge to retreat. She started to answer, and the words died as Anna leaned in and kissed her. The kiss slowly intensified until her arms slid around Anna's waist. A hand cupped the back of her head as another settled on her lower back pulling her closer yet.

The moment was interrupted as shouts of approval erupted in the living room.

"Hurry up, you two," Julian shouted. "The Spurs just scored again."

"Remind me to swat him," Anna said and laughed softly before stealing another quick kiss. "Promise me that this can be continued at a later time."

"I'm looking forward to it," Rona replied, surprised to realize how much she meant it.

Chapter Twenty-one

Rona stared at the television feigning interest in the final moments of the game, when in truth all she could think about was the woman sitting less than five feet behind her. If she were to turn around and reach out her hand, she could touch Anna's warm smooth skin. It had been a long time since she'd been held in someone's arms like that. Almost two years had passed since Mary's death, and even before her death, she had been in so much pain lovemaking wasn't possible. At first, they thought it was nothing more than a cold, but the cough wouldn't go away. Mary waved off Rona's concerns, insisting it was nothing more than allergies caused by the smoke-filled bars they played in. The band was beginning to get some recognition. On average, they played four nights a week. Sometimes, when they were lucky, they were booked six nights a week.

Lenny, the band's lead guitarist and backup vocalist, was the first to mention Mary's loss of lung capacity. She occasionally failed to hold the note for the duration needed. Then it started to become more and more noticeable. By the time Rona was able to convince her to see a doctor, it was too late. The lung cancer was inoperable. That was when the real nightmare began.

From the beginning of the relationship, Mary handled their money and paid the bills. Rona assumed they were doing all right financially. She knew they weren't rich, but they lived a simple lifestyle. On those rare occasions when she did want something like a CD or new clothes, Mary said they could afford them. Rona received a rude awakening when the gigs stopped coming in. That's when she learned they had been living on credit cards and owed over twelve thousand dollars. They had no health insurance and very little cash. When they were no longer able to make even the minimum payment on the debts, the credit card companies began to get nasty. The phone was disconnected for failure to pay and mercifully stopped the endless calls from collection agencies. It was much easier to ignore the collection notices that arrived in the mail, and after the first encounter with a collector who came knocking at their door, they learned to ignore the insistent knocking that seemed to increase with each week. Since they had no health insurance, Mary was at the mercy of free clinics for checkups and a county hospital that insisted on full payment before each treatment. She applied for government assistance, but a mountain of red tape delayed it until a few weeks before she died. The medical card helped some but still didn't cover everything.

After Mary's diagnosis, the band tried to hang on, but without a lead vocal, it quickly fell apart. Lenny left first. He joined the Navy. Zac went home to Lubbock and Eric moved to California. Rona quickly discovered how immersed their lives had been with the band. The only friends she had were those who began showing up after the band began to make a name for itself. They were the first people to disappear when there was no longer a band. She and Mary quickly found themselves alone. Rona got a job as a night watchman, but she quit as soon as she realized that taking care of Mary was a full-time job. With no income, Rona was forced to sell her keyboards and equipment to help pay for the medical treatments and buy food. The only thing from the band they kept was Mary's battered old Martin guitar. On her good days, Mary could find some comfort in strumming the songs she once sang. When the money from the equipment was gone, Rona sold the car, then their meager household furnishings, and when everything else was gone, she turned to her family in desperation.

Her mother hung up the moment she mentioned Mary's name. Then Rona swallowed her pride and called her father. She never made it beyond his secretary. When Rona insisted on speaking to her father, the woman told her in a quiet, embarrassed voice that her mother had already called to warn him Rona would be calling to ask for money. He didn't want to talk to her. She considered calling her brother and sister, but they were merely carbon copies of their parents. When she hung up the phone that day, she swore she would never again make any effort to reach out to her family.

The landlord of the small apartment she and Mary had shared for nearly four years was decent enough. He didn't push too hard for the rent while Mary was living, or immediately after her death when Rona sank into a seemingly bottomless pit of depression. Eventually, though, even his tolerance ran out. When he evicted her, all she had was a small suitcase containing a few clothes, Mary's guitar and ring, and the battered notebook containing her songs.

The guitar and suitcase were stolen the first week she was on the street. She had fallen asleep in an alley with the notebook in her arms. Mary's ring was on a chain around her neck. The suitcase was beside her with the guitar resting on top of it. When she awoke, the suitcase and guitar were gone. She checked all the pawnshops in the area, but the Martin never showed up. With nothing to keep her in Austin, Rona gave up and started walking with no destination in mind. She simply wanted to go someplace new where there wouldn't be a painful memory on every corner.

One night shortly after she arrived in San Antonio, she was sitting beneath a bridge when a homeless guy tried to grab her note-

147

book. She managed to fight him off. It was then that she realized how much the contents meant to her. It took her two days to find the perfect spot, an abandoned building that she could easily and discreetly access through a back fence. After prying up a couple of loose boards from the floor, she removed Mary's ring from around her neck and secured it inside the notebook by slipping it over one of the clamps before closing it. She carefully wrapped the binder in a large piece of plastic she found before tucking it beneath the floor and stomping the boards back into place.

It had felt so wonderful to be able to play a piano again, but her true enjoyment came from creating music and lyrics that made people stop and listen. She would never sing the words to "Lover's Dream," because they were too painful and her own voice was mediocre at best. She had written the song for Mary, who had a beautiful voice with an amazing range. Perhaps she could write again. If she could find a full-time job, she could purchase a small keyboard.

She sensed movement behind her. With a quick glance back, she saw Julian follow Anna out to the kitchen. Would it look odd if she followed them? She wanted to talk to her again. *You want to kiss her again*, a small voice teased. She gave the thought some consideration and decided it was true. She did want to kiss her again and make love to her. The fantasies and masturbating weren't enough. She wanted to touch Anna.

A sudden rush of warmth washed over her. What sort of lover would Anna be? She was a great kisser. Rona didn't have a wealth of experience, but she suspected there was a smoldering fire waiting to burst into flames of passion within the quiet woman.

It wasn't long before Hector and Pietro drifted away toward the kitchen. When Lupie and Polly followed, she gave up thinking about getting Anna alone and turned her attention back to the game. Memphis was losing badly. Tammy didn't seem to care. She and Mrs. Pagonis were sitting on the couch engrossed in a quiet conversation. The twins were in the corner playing with five or six of the younger Pagonis children. Mr. Pagonis was dozing in his recliner and Gina was helping three-year-old Ellen wrap her baby doll up in an old blanket. Rona let the peaceful atmosphere settle around her. This felt right. She would like to have a house filled with running children, but she couldn't envision them being her own. She was thirty-six and for the first time in months, there was a slight glimmer of hope in getting her life back on track.

"You look a million miles away."

She turned to find Gina sitting down beside her. "I was just enjoying the peacefulness."

Gina smiled. "It does get a little loud when we're all here," she admitted.

That wasn't what Rona had been referring to, but she let it go.

"You play the piano beautifully," Gina said.

Rona glanced down. "Thanks. It's been a while since I've played."

"Would you consider giving lessons?"

She looked up, surprised. "You want to learn to play the piano?"

"No. It's not me. Julian and I have been thinking about sending the twins. I think it would be beneficial to them."

"What will you do when they grow up and want to join a band?" she asked, sounding a little harsher than she intended.

Gina tilted her head to one side. "Is that what happened to you?"

She smiled. Gina had turned the question back on her. "Something like that," she admitted. "What did you have in mind as far as lessons?"

"I've made a few calls and it seems like the norm is one lesson per week, and the cost ranges between twenty and twenty-five dollars an hour. We would prefer that they have their lessons individually. We'd also like to start them out with thirty-minute lessons. I'm afraid an hour is too much."

"That sounds good, but I don't have a place to hold lessons."

"If you don't mind, you could come to the house. We haven't actually purchased a piano yet."

"Don't."

Gina looked at her in surprise.

"Pianos are expensive and they're costly to maintain properly," Rona said. "If you want the kids to take lessons, buy an electronic keyboard. You can get a good one for much less than a piano will cost. That way, if the kids don't want to continue, you won't be stuck with an expensive mistake."

"That's a good idea. When can you start?"

"If you're serious, I can start anytime. I work until six."

"Great," Gina said. "Let me go find Julian and we can work out the details."

As Gina rushed off, Rona leaned back. If she charged ten dollars per lesson that would bring in an extra twenty dollars a week. That wasn't much, but eventually she'd be able to purchase a used keyboard of her own. Maybe she could even find a band that needed a songwriter. She stopped. She didn't want to think that far in advance. It was tempting fate to want something too badly.

Chapter Twenty-two

It was after seven when they finally pulled into Anna's driveway. The twins were in the backseat with Tammy, telling her about an animated creature that was a sponge or something. Rona tried listening to them, but Anna's quiet presence beside her was distracting. They hadn't had an opportunity to be alone since the kiss. Just thinking about it made her pulse quicken. As the car pulled into the driveway and they waited for the garage door to rise, Rona wondered how late Tammy and the kids would stay up. Would she and Anna make love?

When Anna pulled the car into the garage and pushed the remote to close the door, Rona practically jumped out of the car.

"Come on," Tammy urged the girls as she helped them out of the seatbelts. Rona opened the back door to help Karla out of the car.

Once inside, Rona struggled to maintain a semblance of normal behavior as they all made their way to the den. Twice she looked up to find Anna watching her. When their gazes met, Anna gave her a small suggestive smile that made a thin sheen of sweat break out along her hairline. Rona fanned herself with a magazine from the table beside the couch.

"Is the heat too high?" Tammy asked.

"No, why?" Rona stammered.

Tammy started to say something but stopped and looked from Rona to Anna. She grinned slightly. "Girls, it's time for bed." They began their normal complaint, but tonight she scurried them off. "I'm exhausted too. Good night." Without waiting for a response, Tammy left.

"Were we that obvious?" Rona asked, staring at Anna.

"Hey, it wasn't me fanning myself."

"It was your fault."

Anna tried to look innocent. "What did I do? I was just sitting here minding my own business."

"Yeah, right."

Anna moved to the couch and turned to face her. "It was those looks you kept sending me," she said as she brushed her thumb over Rona's cheek. "You have beautiful skin."

Rona turned her head slightly and kissed Anna's hand. "Would you mind if we saved the talking for later? I've been wanting this all afternoon." She leaned forward and kissed Anna. As the kiss deepened, she began to push her back onto the couch.

"No," Anna whispered. "One of the kids might come down." She stood up and took Rona's hand. "Come with me. I don't want to have to worry about anything except pleasing you."

Rona moaned softly. "Let's go."

They rushed to Anna's room. With the door closed, Rona pulled Anna into her arms. After several deep kisses, she stepped back and eased Anna's sweater off. As she began kissing her again, she let her hand drift up Anna's side until her fingers encountered the satiny material of her bra. Without removing it, she held Anna's ample breast in her hand and let her thumb caress the lacy barrier until she felt the swollen nipple. She released the bra clasp as she kissed her way down Anna's chest and with slow deliberation pulled the nipple into her mouth.

Her own need grew as Anna began to make soft sounds of pleasure and pulled her toward the bed. Rona eased her onto the bed and straddled her thighs. She kissed her deeply as she unbuttoned Anna's jeans and took her time in lowering the zipper. With slow deliberation, she ran her tongue around each nipple. As the small buds grew firm, she sucked them into her mouth, causing Anna to arch her back and gasp.

"Yes," Anna whispered as Rona trailed her hand steadily downward until the jeans made it difficult for her hand to move. She sat up, eased the jeans off and dropped them onto a trunk at the foot of the bed. Never taking her gaze off the beautiful woman before her, she stretched out beside her and trailed her fingers along the inside of Anna's bare thighs. When Anna began to squirm, she kissed her and worked her hand into the top of the panties. She slid her fingers into the creamy wetness and began to leisurely stroke the heated flesh. When Anna's hips began to match the rhythm of her fingers, Rona's kisses deepened. When her own desire became so intense she found it difficult to concentrate, she finally relented and offered the release that was so desperately being sought. Anna's body arched sharply and seemed to hang in space for a moment before she released a long shuddering gasp. Rona held her until the tiny aftershocks of pleasure faded.

"I knew you would be fantastic," Anna said, her voice still husky with desire.

"That was just a quickie to take the edge off."

"It felt like the top of my head was about to come off."

Rona kissed her cheek. "You'd better be careful. I have a long night planned for you."

"Talk, talk, talk. Is that all you can do?"

"Perhaps we should see." Rona eased her hand from between Anna's legs and sat up. In one smooth move, she stood up and turned Anna sideways across the bed. She knelt by the bed and helped Anna scrunch forward until her hips were on the edge of

153

the mattress. With her hands, she pushed the long legs open, then used her thumbs to spread the swollen lips. She used the tip of her tongue and her warm breath to tease until Anna was begging for relief. Instead of offering the release Anna wanted, she ran two fingers through the wetness before slipping them slowly inside and then easing out. With each insertion, she went a little deeper until her fingers were fully engulfed.

"More," Anna gasped.

Rona added a third finger and began the acclimation process all over. As Anna's arousal escalated, so did her need. Rona squeezed her fingers into a tightly pointed cluster and began a slow rhythmic action. She felt the first faint trembling and reminded herself not to hurry. The trembling intensified. She increased the tempo of her penetrating movements.

"Faster," Anna pleaded as she pushed herself deeper still onto Rona's hand.

Suddenly the bed began to creak furiously as Anna cried out her pleasure. Rona waited until the cries were melting into whimpers before she removed her hand and buried her face between the trembling legs.

"I . . . I can't," Anna breathed.

Rona ignored her and continued her feasting. It wasn't long before Anna's body began to rock once more. Her hands clamped around Rona's head pulling her ever closer until she came in an explosive orgasm.

Rona felt Anna slowly release her death-grip on the comforter. Half of her body was dangling over the edge of the bed.

"I don't have the strength to scoot back or to pull you up from the floor," Anna mumbled. "You're going to have to make it back up here on your own. My muscles have been replaced by dishrags."

Rona smiled as she stretched out beside her. "You would probably be more comfortable if you were to get back on the bed."

"Yes. I'm sure I would, but I told you I can't move."

"I know. Come on, my little dishrag. I'll help you." Together they managed to work their way to the center of the bed. "You're cold. Let me get you under the covers."

Anna sat up slowly and helped pull the comforter and sheet back. After they were in bed, she reached over and switched on a bedside lamp. "This is really embarrassing," she said. "You're still in your clothes."

"I can help with that also." Rona got out of bed and peeled off her clothes before hopping into bed naked. "Now do you feel better?" She pulled Anna into her arms and kissed her. "I can't seem to get enough of you." She rested her hand on Anna's stomach. It had been too long since she'd touched a woman. She took her time exploring every curve and indentation. The small indentation behind Anna's ear became particularly fascinating. She noticed how Anna would make a delicious little shiver each time her kisses worked their way to that area. After several sweet minutes, she pulled Anna on top of her and buried her face between her breasts. Their weight caressed her face as she took first one and then the other into her mouth. She squirmed with pleasure as the nipples enlarged and hardened beneath her tongue. Anna's breath quickened as Rona slipped her hand between their bodies and began gently raking her fingertips through Anna's thick pubic hair.

"I want to touch you," Anna whispered.

Before Rona could protest, Anna slid a knee between Rona's legs and pushed them apart. As her mouth claimed Rona's lips, her fingers began a subtle movement below that gradually increased in pressure. Rona felt the first tiny spark of release and held her breath until her body began to tremble. Just when she thought she couldn't tolerate another moment, Anna gave her the release she so desperately needed. The bed creaked loudly, but she couldn't stop the mad thrashing that Anna's hand was causing.

Slowly her body began to relax.

Anna stretched out alongside her. "That was nice."

"It was a pretty good start."

"It's been a while since I've been with anyone," Anna admitted. "I was a little nervous."

"Me too."

Anna sat up and leaned on her elbow. "You were nervous?"

"Yeah. I was afraid you were going to wake up the neighborhood with all that shrieking."

Anna gently swatted her shoulder. "You weren't exactly quiet as a mouse. Tammy and the neighbors must have thought we had a revival going on over here."

"A revival?" Rona asked, confused.

Anna fell back on the bed and began to thrash wildly. "Oh, God. Oh, God," she moaned in exaggerated ecstasy.

"I didn't do that!"

Anna began to laugh.

"You are so going to get it," Rona said as she pounced on Anna and began to tickle her.

"No," Anna squealed. "I can't stand being tickled."

"Take it back," Rona said, her fingers poised for a new round.

"Yes. Yes. Yes. I take it back."

She looked so sexy with her dark hair mussed and her eyes sparkling with mischief. "You're so beautiful," Rona whispered as she leaned down to kiss her. The kiss became more intense and they made love again.

Afterward, as they cuddled beneath the blanket talking, Rona told her about Gina's offer.

"How do you feel about giving lessons?" Anna asked.

"I've never tried it, but I told her I'd like to give it a shot. I can still remember my first few lessons, so I think I can help the kids. I'm going over tomorrow night, after work. We've agreed to try the lessons for a month. After that, if Gina and Julian are satisfied with how things are progressing, and the kids are enjoying the lessons, then we'll work out a plan."

"I'm embarrassed to admit how hot I got today watching you play," Anna said. "I've never seen anyone so . . . so . . ." She struggled for the word. "I can't explain it. You were so intense and the music seemed to be pouring out of you. It was as if you were making love to the piano." She stopped suddenly and looked away. "You must think I'm some kind of nut."

Rona smiled and hugged her closer. "You're in bed with me, so you obviously are," she said.

Anna wrapped an arm around her waist. "You know, if you like giving lessons, you could probably find other students. There are several kids in the surrounding neighborhoods."

"Whoa," Rona cautioned. "Let's wait and see if I survive my first day."

"Sorry. I can get carried away. If someone asks me for a piece of gum, I try to give them the entire pack."

She smiled. "Anna, you're a good person."

"I'm a pushover."

"It sounds like there's a story behind that."

Anna grimaced. "You don't want to hear that story."

"I want to know everything about you."

Anna took a deep breath and slowly released it. "Her name was Patricia Braden—Patti. We met at a fund-raiser hosted by the local gay and lesbian political caucus. Patti introduced herself to me while we were standing in the buffet line. I was flattered that this strikingly beautiful woman with the long chestnut hair seemed to be seeking me out from the hundreds of other women in the crowd. As the night progressed, I found out that she had recently moved to San Antonio from New York. She was an artist who, according to her, had become tired of the unending madhouse of the city that never slept. She originally came to San Antonio to attend the gala opening of a friend's gallery and fell in love with the city's relaxed, easy pace. She invited me to meet her at the McNay Art Museum the following day."

Rona suspected she was about to discover the story behind the box marked *bitch*.

"I had never visited the McNay and Patti was like a gigantic fountain of knowledge. She told me the history the museum. She talked about O'Keeffe, Van Gogh, Cézanne and Gauguin." Anna looked away before continuing. "For the next two weeks, every free moment of my time was consumed with Patti. When she mentioned she might have to return to New York because her prospects of finding work in San Antonio's limited art world were almost nonexistent, I panicked. Like a complete fool, I begged her to move in with me so she could dedicate her time to her own paintings." She glanced at Rona. "Pretty stupid, huh?"

"No, you loved her and trusted her. What happened?"

"I went beyond stupid and added her name to my personal credit card and bank account. A few days later, I came home from work and she was gone and so was my bank account. The only thing she left behind was a six-thousand-dollar credit-card bill."

When she had finished, Rona kissed her forehead. "I promise I won't ever use you." As she made the promise, she realized she meant every word.

"Tell me something about yourself," Anna prompted.

Rona took a deep breath. She hadn't talked about Mary to anyone. "What do you want to know?"

"Everything eventually, but for now whatever you feel like talking about."

She started her story with the band. Gradually she spoke of Mary, the cancer and the funeral. When she cried, Anna kissed away the tears.

"Do you mind if I ask how you ended up on the streets?" she asked after Rona composed herself.

"I couldn't work when Mary was so ill. Afterward, I didn't care if I lived or not. By the time, I started to care again it was too late. I was already on the street."

"Don't you have family? What about Mary's family?"

"I have two very religious parents, a brother and sister. Do they consider me family? No." She took a deep breath. "When the band fell apart, I called my parents asking for help. Neither one of them would even talk to me. Mary grew up in Florida. Her mother was a crack addict and died soon after she was born. Mary grew up in foster homes."

"What about friends? Couldn't someone have helped you?"

"We didn't really have friends outside the band. There were a few groupies, but when the band's bookings disappeared, so did they."

Anna held her close and kissed the top of her head. "Those days are over now. Let's talk about happier times." They whispered like schoolgirls until, sometime in the early hours of morning, they finally fell asleep.

Chapter Twenty-three

Rona opened her eyes slowly and smiled. Anna was sleeping on her side with her back pressed up against her. It had been a long time since she had spent the night with anyone. She had almost forgotten how nice it felt to wake up with a warm body next to her. She rolled over onto her back. Anna turned over and wrapped her arms around her.

"Is it time to get up?" Anna asked in a sleepy voice.

"We still have a few minutes."

"Good. Someone kept me up last night. I didn't get much sleep."

"I know the feeling," Rona whispered as she kissed Anna's shoulder.

"Someone kept you up, too?"

"Yes. There was a little nymphomaniac who wouldn't let me sleep."

"You lucky devil you," Anna muttered. "Did you get her name and number?"

Rona hugged her. "You're not going to believe this, but I'm starving."

Anna sat up quickly. "Me too. Let's scramble some eggs."

"Do you think we should shower and dress first?"

"Why?"

"It would be awkward if Tammy came down and we weren't dressed."

"Good point." Anna gave her a quick kiss. "I'll meet you in the kitchen in twenty minutes."

Anna turned the bedside lamp on and smiled as Rona jumped out of bed and began to yank her clothes on.

"First one done starts the coffee," Anna said.

Rona leaned over and gave her another kiss. "I'll put it on before I go up to my room."

"You're so sweet."

"No, I'm not. I just don't like your coffee."

"Ouch. Too much honesty isn't a good thing," Anna said.

"Don't worry about it. You have other qualities that are much more important than coffee."

Anna's eyes sparkled. "Like what?"

"I'll have to postpone that demonstration until tonight."

"How am I supposed to spend the day trying to concentrate on investment returns when all I'll be thinking about is tonight?"

Rona slipped her hand beneath the cover and caressed Anna's breast. "You've got a point. Maybe we should—" The alarm clock clicked on and the sound of Boy George howling about a chameleon filled the room. Rona looked at the radio and grimaced. "I've never been able to figure out what the heck he's singing about."

"Go shower," Anna said and laughed. "We'll talk about it over breakfast."

Rona tiptoed up the stairs. She felt like singing and dancing a silly jig. No noise came from Tammy's room as Rona slipped into her room. She managed to control her jubilation until she was in the shower. She sang and whistled until her jaws ached.

It was closer to twenty-five minutes before she walked into the

161

kitchen and was greeted by the smell of freshly brewed coffee and frying bacon. "Sit down and enjoy your coffee," Anna said as she popped two slices of bread into the toaster. "I'll have the eggs scrambled in a jiffy."

"Such service. I could get spoiled by this."

"Good. Everyone deserves to be spoiled occasionally," Anna said as she broke eggs in a bowl and began to whip them.

Rona found herself smiling as she watched Anna work. "Does that mean I'm supposed to spoil you in return?"

Anna winked at her. "You already have."

"How?"

"I could tell you in great detail, but then we'd probably be late for work." Anna poured the eggs from the bowl into a preheated skillet. "Maybe we should limit our conversation to something less stimulating."

The toaster spat out the bread. Anna grabbed it and divided the eggs onto the plates already containing strips of crispy bacon. After setting the plates on the table, she topped off their coffee and gave Rona a quick kiss. They both ate with gusto.

"Somebody was hungry this morning," Tammy called from the kitchen doorway.

Rona glanced up and smiled. "We left you some coffee."

"I'm the chief cook this morning," Anna said cheerfully. "What'll you have?"

"Coffee is fine for now. Something sure put you two in a cheerful mood."

Rona felt a blush race up her neck and for once even Anna seemed at a loss for something to say. She could feel Tammy's gaze moving back and forth between them.

When neither of them spoke, Tammy said, "I have a job." That got everyone's attention.

"Congratulations," they both replied at once.

"Where are you working?" Rona rushed on.

"Mrs. Pagonis offered me a job working at the restaurant. One of their waitresses on the lunch schedule had to leave. Her husband is in the military and he was transferred to Kentucky. I'm starting today."

"What about the kids?" Rona asked.

"The church Anna's parents attend has a pre-kindergarten program. Mrs. Pagonis thinks I'll be able to get the girls enrolled, and there's a room at the restaurant where they can stay until then."

Anna leaned back with her coffee. "We practically grew up at the restaurant," she said. "My parents couldn't afford to hire a babysitter when they first started out. Dad converted a small room off the kitchen for us to stay in. We had a television, books and games. He even put a couple of bunk beds in so we could rest if we were sick or tired. Over the years, they've let employees with small kids use the space. It's sort of a mini-daycare."

"Wow. That's nice," Rona said as she came back to the table with Tammy's coffee.

"I think it's time I started contributing to the household expenses," Tammy said. "With both jobs, I can afford to help out some."

Rona nodded. "I could too."

Anna started to protest but was quickly overruled. It took them a few minutes to all agree on what was a fair percentage. They finally agreed that Anna would pay fifty percent of the household expenses and Tammy and Rona would contribute twenty-five percent each.

"Aren't you worried about your husband finding you? I mean, my parents will insist you file the necessary employment records."

Tammy stared into her coffee for a moment before meeting Anna's gaze. "I'm tired of running and hiding. I'm tired of my kids having to suffer for my cowardice. If Wayne finds me, then I'll have to face whatever happens. I can't keep running."

"I appreciate your courage," Anna began, "but I don't want my parents caught between you two."

Rona's gaze shifted between the two women as a whisper of tension eased into the room.

Tammy took a deep breath. "I wouldn't do anything to put your parents or you in any kind of danger. If you're not comfortable with me working at the restaurant, I'll look elsewhere."

Anna stared into her coffee. "Take the job. I know they'll treat you right, and you'll be able to keep the girls nearby. You understand I'll have to talk to my parents and warn them about the possibility of Wayne Daniels showing up."

"I've already told your mother," Tammy admitted.

Rona noticed a look of respect in Anna's eyes as she nodded at Tammy.

The evening Rona stood on a slightly elevated section of the street a few doors down from Julian and Gina's and gazed at the distant glow of the city. Julian had offered to drive her home after the kids' piano lessons but she declined. She wanted to walk. The weather was cool and the air crisp. A sharp fragrant scent teased her nostrils. It took her a moment to recognize it as wood smoke. She glanced at the surrounding rooftops until she located the telltale signs of a wood fireplace.

As she walked on through the sedate neighborhood, she thought about the thousands of homeless people scattered across the city. Her hands closed around the twenty dollars she earned from the piano lessons. A strong gust of cold wind blew a scattering of dry leaves past her and worked its way through her clothing. Hunching her shoulders against it, she made up her mind that tomorrow she would start searching for Malcolm. Maybe there was some way she could help him. She stopped when she started up Anna's driveway and saw the warm glow of light from the kitchen window. It felt good to know someone was waiting for her inside. She didn't have a key and had to ring the doorbell. Anna answered it so quickly, Rona wondered if she had been watching for her.

"Hi," Anna said as she closed the door behind them. "Welcome home." She leaned forward and kissed her.

Rona returned the kiss quickly before asking, "Where are Tammy and the kids?"

164

"Upstairs. Tammy was exhausted after working today. She said she was going to take a long hot bath and crawl into bed."

"I think she's figured us out," Rona said as she removed her jacket and draped it over a chair.

"Before I forget it, I have something for you." Anna pulled out a small box of candy. "It's Valentine's Day. Since we just . . . well, with last night being the first time . . ." She finally gave up and removed a key from her pants pocket. "I had a key made for you." She handed it to her.

"Thank you." Rona didn't know what to say. It hadn't occurred to her to buy Anna anything for Valentine's Day. "I didn't buy you anything."

"Don't worry about that. I shouldn't have either. It was a spontaneous gesture. Please, don't think of it as anything other than a box of candy."

"Maybe I should go outside and come back in. Then we can start all over."

"I don't want you to leave." Anna hugged her. "I missed you at dinner."

Rona ran her hands down Anna's back. "I'm here now," she said and kissed her.

"Aren't you hungry?" Anna asked as Rona slipped her hands beneath her shirt.

"Yes, I am." The clasp on Anna's bra sprang free beneath Rona's hands. "Do you have work to do this evening?" Rona's lips were moving slowly along Anna's neck.

"No."

"Good, because I have a lot of things I need to get taken care of."

Anna's voice betrayed her disappointment. "Like what?"

"This." Rona's mouth claimed Anna's nipple.

Anna pulled her closer. "We can't do this here."

They slowly made their way to Anna's bedroom.

Chapter Twenty-four

Rona began searching for Malcolm during her lunch breaks. She was glad Matt Devers had agreed to her unorthodox schedule. On Tuesday, she started by looking in their usual haunts. No one had seen him. On her way back to work, she stopped by the Taco Haven, a small hole-in-the-wall taco joint that allowed the rougher-looking elements among the homeless to come inside to buy and eat their food. Most other places wouldn't permit them inside. Anytime she and Malcolm acquired a couple of dollars, they would head to the Taco Haven, where a dollar bought a taco and a small cup of coffee.

When she arrived, Domingo, the owner, was sitting in his usual spot behind the counter reading *La Prensa*, San Antonio's bilingual newspaper. Only two of the booths were occupied with other customers.

"*Hola*, Domingo," Rona said as she sat at the counter near him.

"*Buenas tardes, senorita*. I was beginning to wonder if you were okay," he replied, without lowering his paper.

"I found a job."

He folded the paper slowly and placed it under the counter before turning to look at her.

She found herself wondering how old he was. His back was stooped, but his hair was still glossy black. The extensive network of wrinkles on his face seemed to indicate that he was well advanced in years, but when he moved there was a quickness and sureness that indicated a much younger man.

"That's good," he said. "People should work. Are you hungry?"

"Yeah." She ordered two tacos and a cup of coffee. "Have you seen Malcolm recently?"

He shook his head as he poured her coffee. "Last time was when he was here with you," he said as he disappeared into the kitchen to get her food.

She was trying to think of other places she could look tomorrow when he returned with the two steaming *carne guisada* tacos. He returned to his newspaper while she ate. As soon as she finished she stood. He again folded his paper and made his way to the cash register.

"If you see Malcolm, will you tell him I'm looking for him? Tell him . . ." She hesitated. How could he contact her? "If he could just tell you where he's hanging out, I'll find him."

He nodded and returned her change, then returned to his paper. Rona put down a tip larger than the amount of her bill and left.

On Wednesday, she called the Taco Haven just before leaving the office. Domingo still hadn't seen Malcolm. She expanded her search to areas where she thought he might have moved to. She passed on a message to everyone she spoke with asking Malcolm to contact Domingo.

That night, long after Anna had drifted off to sleep, Rona lay staring at the bedroom ceiling. She felt guilty for not trying to contact Malcolm sooner. They had watched out for each other. "Why aren't you sleeping?"

Anna's voice startled her. "I'm sorry. Did I wake you?" Rona asked.

"No." Anna turned to face her. "What's wrong?"

In the dim glow from the back neighbor's security light, Rona could see Anna gazing at her.

"I'm a little concerned about Malcolm. He's a friend of mine and we sort of looked out for each other when things got bad. I've been trying to find him, but no one's seen him for several days."

"Could he be at one of the shelters?"

"I don't think so. He hates them, too. I checked all his usual hangouts, so either he's left or the police picked him up."

"For what?"

"It could have been vagrancy or panhandling." Malcolm wasn't above panhandling or picking an occasional pocket, but to her knowledge, he didn't resort to violent crime.

Anna was still for several seconds. "Is there anything I can do to help find him?"

Rona hugged her. "No. I'll go back tomorrow at lunch and start asking around again."

Anna hesitated. "You understand that I wouldn't feel safe having a strange man in the house."

She kissed Anna's forehead. "I wasn't expecting you to take him in. I just need to know he's okay. Go on back to sleep."

"What about you?"

"Don't worry about me."

Anna leaned over and kissed her. The kiss grew steadily more urgent. Rona closed her eyes and let the kiss burn away all her worries and fears. When Anna's hand eased down her stomach and slipped between her legs, Rona rolled over onto her back and pulled Anna on top of her. She opened her legs to give Anna's insistent hand more space. As the fingers brought her closer and closer to orgasm, she wrapped her arms tightly around Anna's body and arched her body upward. When release finally came, she burrowed her face in the warm shoulder above her and cried out her pleasure. After making love, they slept.

᪐

The following day, Rona again called Domingo. There was still no word of Malcolm. She had already covered the relatively small amount of distance she could reach on foot during lunch. All she could do now was wait until Saturday when she could hitch a ride in with Anna and spend most of the day searching for him. She decided to use her lunch break to shop for a couple of basic beginning piano music books for her students. Gina had agreed to reimburse her for the cost. Using some of her carefully hoarded money, she walked to a nearby music store to search through their selections.

After making her purchases, she glanced over the ads on the bulletin board. There was a flyer announcing that the store needed a full-time sales clerk. The position started at four hundred dollars a week. She reached for the flyer but stopped when she saw a bold line across the bottom stating that at least a year of sales experience was required. She had none. Looking over the rest of the board, she found no ads from anyone looking for a keyboard player, but there were a couple of business cards offering piano lessons. On a whim, she borrowed a three-by-five card from the guy at the counter and wrote out her own ad offering piano lessons. She used the phone number of Anna's office as a contact source. She felt a tad guilty as she pinned the card onto the board. She should probably have asked Anna before she started using her phone number. Before leaving, she strolled through the area where the pianos and organs were displayed. A short, thin woman was showing an electric keyboard to a man with a girl who Rona guessed to be fourteen or fifteen. The girl was in the process of trying to bang out some tune that sounded vaguely familiar to her.

"This one isn't any good," she whined to her dad.

"This is the latest model. You've tried everything else we have," the saleswoman said as her hand went to her temple.

Rona had seen dozens of kids like this girl. They were spoiled rich kids who came to River Center Mall and pushed their way through the crowds as if they owned the place.

"They've been in here for an hour."

Rona flinched. She was so engrossed with eavesdropping that

169

she failed to notice the sales clerk who had given her the card walk up behind her.

"What's the problem?" she whispered back.

"The kid's a brat who thinks she has more talent than she does. She keeps trying to play that Norah Jones song 'Come Away With Me,' and she can't. So she blames it on the keyboard." He rushed on. "My guess is the guy's a weekend dad who's willing to buy whatever the kid wants."

"So, why don't they buy one?"

The clerk chuckled. "That's going to be pretty tough. The kid wants the one that sounds like Norah Jones's piano. When she screws it up, she blames the keyboard. Verna's wasting her time with them. They'll end up going somewhere else."

Rona nodded. "I noticed you were looking for a sales clerk. If I sell this guy a keyboard, can I have the job?"

He glanced at her and shrugged. "You'd have to ask Verna. She's the owner."

"Then let's get her over here."

The clerk hesitated, and they stood watching the man and his daughter for a while longer.

"He's going to leave," Rona pushed. "I know I can sell him a keyboard."

"Wait here," he instructed.

Rona watched as he went over and pulled Verna aside. Rona nodded slightly as the woman excused herself and came over to her.

"What makes you think you can sell him a keyboard?" she asked. "How much sales experience do you have?"

"None, but I know people and I know music. You're about to lose a sale."

"Which one do you think is most suitable for her?"

"With her talent, the cheapest one Wal-Mart carries, but to show you I can do it, I'm going to sell him that Yamaha." It was a PF-1000, top of the line.

The woman scoffed and shook her head. "That particular model carries a forty-one-hundred-dollar price tag."

Without waiting for her agree, Rona handed the sales clerk her bag and sat down at the Yamaha. She did a few quick scales to limber up prior to launching into the song. Before she was halfway through the first verse, the kid was racing toward them.

"That's the one I want," she yelled and pointed toward the digital piano.

Rona continued playing.

"I want that one," the girl insisted again.

"This is a professional quality instrument," Rona said. "I would recommend something much cheaper for someone at your level." She played a few more measures before she stopped and stared directly at the girl. "There are some very nice keyboards at Wal-Mart that sell for a fraction—"

"I can play just fine," the girl huffed, glaring at Verna. "You did something to the buttons to make this one sound better." A radical transformation overcame the girl as she turned to her father. "Daddy, you said you wanted me to learn to play the piano. How can I possibly learn anything on those horrible things she was trying to sell you?" Without turning from her father, she pointed toward Verna.

"Alexis, this appears to be a complicated piece of equipment. Perhaps you should start with something simpler."

Rona stared in amazement as a large tear formed and spilled gracefully from the girl's eye. It rolled down her cheek as if a director had cued it into the script. "You don't think I'm smart enough to learn to play. Maybe you should take me back to Mom's."

The man glanced nervously at Rona and cleared his throat. He tried to pull the girl away from her captive audience, but she held her ground.

Rona turned back to the keyboard and softly played another Norah Jones tune.

Alexis stared daggers at her before burying her face in her

171

father's chest. The shrieking rage exhibited earlier was replaced with silent shoulder-shaking sobs.

The man's shoulders drooped as he awkwardly patted her arm. "Don't cry. You know I can't stand it when Daddy's little angel cries."

Rona would have sworn she heard either Verna or the clerk snicker.

The guy turned to Verna. "We'll take this one."

A suddenly dry-eyed Alexis squealed and hugged her father. "You'll see," she promised him. "I'll sound wonderful on this one. Oh, Daddy, you are so awesome."

Rona headed to the other side of the store and waited until Verna completed the transaction and the customers left.

Verna walked over to join her. "I'm Verna Holland, the owner."

Rona introduced herself.

"I really shouldn't have allowed that to happen," she said as she sat on a piano bench near Rona. "It wasn't very honest. You know she didn't have the talent to play this instrument. It's entirely too complicated for her."

"Yes, but she's happy because she got what she wanted. Daddy's happy because he bought what she wanted. You're happy because that was a big sale. Now the question is—am I going to be happy about getting a job?"

Verna looked at her. "Let's try it on a trial basis for three weeks. For future reference, we really do try to match the instrument to the customer, so no more stunts like today."

Rona felt like jumping up and down and doing her own shrieking, but instead she merely thanked her.

"When can you start?" Verna asked.

"Is a week from Monday okay?" Rona asked, sounding much calmer than she felt. "I'm working at a temp position now, but it's about to end."

"That's fine. Jerry wants to start working nights and weekends in two weeks, so he'll have a week to show you the ropes." She stood and motioned for Rona to follow her. They entered a small office with catalogs and music journals piled everywhere. Verna opened a file drawer and pulled out several papers. "These are standard employment forms. Fill them out and bring them back when you come in. The store opens at nine, but you'll need to be here at eight-thirty." She gave the forms to Rona and shook her hand. "Welcome to Holland's Music Center."

"I'll see you a week from Monday," Rona said as she turned to leave.

"And don't be recommending customers shop at Wal-Mart anymore, either," Verna called after her.

Rona couldn't wait to tell Anna the news. As she started back to the office, her bag of sheet music in hand, she stopped and turned her face to the warm sun. The cold fronts were temporarily forgotten as the temperature hovered around sixty degrees. As she stood there, she saw a homeless man slip into an alley across the street. He brought back her concerns about Malcolm. Since she still had time to spare, she decided to run by the police station to see if maybe he was being held there.

"I thought I heard someone," Anna said as she walked out of her office. "You're back early."

"Where is everyone?" Rona asked, following Anna back down the hallway.

"Neal had a lunch date and Sharon needed to run some errands." Anna leaned against the front of her desk and studied her. "What's that sly little smile all about?"

"I found a job."

"Congratulations," Anna said and gave her a hug. "Tell me all about it."

Rona quickly told her how the job offer came about.

"Why were you so sure he would buy such an expensive model?"

"The kid was a brat. She was used to getting everything she wanted. Besides, what did I have to lose?"

Anna pulled her into her arms. "We're going to have to celebrate," she said as she nuzzled her face into Rona's hair.

Rona pulled her closer as a delicious tingle began to warm her body. "This is not the place to start something you may not have time to finish."

Anna glanced at her watch and sighed. "You're right. Sharon could be back anytime now." She gave her a quick kiss before releasing her. "All right, I'll be good. Have you heard anything about Malcolm?"

"No. No one seems to know where he is. I've looked everywhere I can think of. I even went to the police station."

Anna hugged her. "I'm sorry. Is there anything I can do to help you locate him?"

"No," Rona replied as she rested her head on Anna's shoulder. "I don't know where else to look. Maybe he left." Or maybe he didn't survive the freezing weather, she thought. They heard the door to the front office open. Rona stepped away and gave Anna a teasing smile. "Can you imagine what we would have been doing if I hadn't shown extraordinary willpower?"

"I know exactly what I would have been doing. That's why it's going to be a really long afternoon," she replied as she brushed past Rona and ran her fingertips up her leg.

Chapter Twenty-five

That evening, Rona and Tammy sat at the kitchen table discussing Rona's new job, while the twins were upstairs playing. Anna was still at work.

"Do you ever get scared?" Tammy asked.

"About what?"

"You know. Everything seems to be working out for us, but sometimes I wake up at night scared that it's all a dream. That some morning I'll wake up back on the streets and this will have all been a dream."

Rona squeezed her arm. "It's not a dream and we won't ever be back on the streets."

"How can you be so sure? It happened before. Why couldn't it happen again?"

"It won't happen again because we're both smarter now than we were. More important, we're not alone anymore. Even if Anna and her family were to disappear from our lives, we'd still have each other."

Tammy nodded. "Speaking of which, you seem to be staying up awfully late," she said as she gave Rona a knowing smile.

"I didn't realize you'd been waiting up for me."

"How could anyone sleep with you bounding around like a colt in springtime?"

"Sorry, I thought I was being quiet. I'll tiptoe up the stairs."

Tammy laughed. "Oh, you make it up the stairs just fine," she said. "It's once you get in the shower that you start singing at the top of your lungs."

Rona felt herself blush. "I didn't think anyone could hear me over the sound of the running water and with the bathroom being so far away from you."

"I'm just grateful you can carry a tune." With her fingertip, Tammy traced the pattern on the tablecloth. "Things seem to be going well with you."

"You are so nosy," Rona said and smiled to take the sting out of the words.

"I'm not nosy. I simply have an insatiable curiosity." She waited for Rona to respond. When she didn't, Tammy gave a loud huff. "Well, aren't you going to tell me anything?"

"Like what?" Rona asked.

"Like, is this serious? Since you aren't making it to your room until five or later, I think it's safe to assume you two aren't sitting around playing dominoes."

"No. We aren't playing dominoes," Rona said and chuckled. "It's still too early to know how serious it is, but . . ." She hesitated. "I think with time it could be."

Tammy stood and hugged her. "I'm glad. You deserve to be happy."

The sudden demonstration of affection embarrassed Rona. She tried to cover it. "Does that mean you're no longer worried I'm going to rip her off?"

"You're not the type to hurt someone you care for," Tammy replied. She walked to the kitchen window and stared out. "Look at those kids. Don't you wish you had that much energy?"

Rona joined her at the window to watch a group of kids playing football at the house across the street. The earlier warmth of the day was slipping away, but they didn't seem to notice.

"I've been sitting so much these last couple of weeks," Rona began, "that I feel like my backbone is starting to compress."

Tammy stifled a yawn. "Being on my feet doesn't bother me so much. It's the constant hurrying."

"Is the restaurant that busy?"

"Yes. Today we were so busy that at one point there was a twenty-five-minute waiting time to be seated for lunch. I can't imagine how busy they must get for dinner. It's so hectic we're almost running sometimes." She yawned. "I'm so tired."

"That's why I ordered pizza for dinner tonight," Anna said as she strode into the kitchen.

Rona and Tammy both jerked in surprise.

"Anna, I swear I'm going to put a bell around your neck," Rona replied.

"Why?"

Tammy turned to face her. "You have a way of sneaking up on people, and you move so fast."

"It's the carpet in the hallway," Anna said as she raised her hands palms up. "And I can't help it if I have all this energy."

"Maybe you could find a more productive way of releasing that energy," Tammy offered as she left the room. She stopped at the doorway and looked back. "I'm going to get the girls washed up for dinner. I'll make sure we make plenty of noise before we walk in. I wouldn't want to surprise you trying to burn off any of that energy."

Rona laughed at the look of surprise on Anna's face.

"What are you laughing at?" Anna asked as Tammy disappeared. "Did you tell her about us?"

"No. She figured it out all by herself." She walked over and kissed Anna's cheek. "I told you half the neighborhood could hear you."

Anna's face turned red. "She told you she heard us?"

177

"When is the pizza due to arrive?" Rona asked, ignoring Anna's question.

"Not for thirty minutes or so, but if you're hungry I can start a salad."

Rona took her by the hand.

"Where are we going?" Anna asked.

"You've kept me waiting all afternoon and I'm suddenly feeling very energetic." She kissed Anna softly before they left the kitchen.

As they were walking down the hall, the phone rang.

"No," Rona moaned.

Anna stepped into the den. "I have to answer," she apologized as she read the caller identification. "It's Sharon."

Rona walked on to the bedroom, hoping the call would be short. She sat in the chair at Anna's dresser. As time slipped by, she began to pick up the various bottles and tubes sitting on the dresser to read the labels. A few she opened to sniff. When she had gone through the small inventory of products, she opened the wooden jewelry box. Inside she found a white jeweler's box containing a string of pearls and matching earrings. Several rings and gold bracelets were neatly laid out within the larger container. She was about to close the lid when she noticed a beautiful gold and enamel pendant watch on a gold chain. As she picked it up, she saw a business card beneath it. The decorative engraving on the oval case with scalloped edges was highlighted with black enamel. She turned it over. On the back was an enamel painting of an angel playing a flute and surrounded by a garland of flowers.

"Isn't it beautiful?"

Rona almost dropped the watch.

"I'm sorry," Anna said quickly before Rona had time to scold her. "I don't do it on purpose."

"It was my fault this time," Rona said as she placed the watch back into the box. "I was snooping and got caught."

Anna reached over and took the watch out. "You're welcome to look at anything I have," she teased as she bumped Rona's shoulder with her hip. "This watch belonged to my Yia Yia. It belonged to her mother."

Rona glanced at her.

"Yia Yia was my maternal grandmother. I can't remember ever seeing her without it. When I was small, I used to love to sit on her lap and play with it." She pushed a small button on top and the case popped opened. She held it out for Rona to see. "That's a photo of my great-grandparents."

"It's beautiful."

"It needs to be cleaned and adjusted," Anna said as she gently closed the case. "A friend told me about a shop in Balcones Heights that specializes in antique watches and clocks. I stopped by and talked to the man. He said he could work on it. I just never seem to get around to taking it over to him."

"Is this the guy?" Rona picked up the business card from the box.

"Yes. I'll get it over there someday," Anna replied. As she was putting the watch back into the jewelry box, the doorbell rang. "That must be the pizza."

"So much for all that energy I had," Rona said as she followed Anna down the hallway.

Chapter Twenty-six

Rona stepped off the elevator with the last of the boxes from the archiving project for Matt Devers. The past few days had flown by and she couldn't believe she would be starting the full-time position at the music store the following Monday.

Devers' secretary was on the phone when Rona walked in. Rona nodded to her before going on to the storeroom where all the other boxes were waiting for pickup. As she set the box down, she looked around the room and smiled. Two weeks ago, it had been an overflowing mass of papers. Now, thanks in part to her work, the room was once again neat.

"Looks good, doesn't it?"

She turned to find Devers standing in the doorway. She said, "It's a lot better than it was two weeks ago. As soon as these boxes are picked up for storage you'll have even more room."

He pulled a check from his coat pocket and handed it to her.

With a glance, she saw he had paid her for the full eighty hours. "I finished at two," she told him.

He waved it off. "Close enough. You did a good job." He held out his hand to her. "Thanks for all your help."

Rona thanked him and left. In the privacy of the elevator, she looked at the check again. After deductions, she had earned almost six hundred dollars for the past two weeks. With the money from the piano lessons and the remainder of what Anna had paid her, the little nest egg was growing rapidly. Another trip to the thrift store for more clothes had eaten up part of it, but she still had a little over seven hundred dollars. She folded the check and put it in her pocket. It was time to open a checking account. She would ask Anna where she did her banking.

When she walked into the outer office, Anna was standing in front of Sharon's desk, laughing. "It must be Friday," Rona teased.

"And not a minute too soon," Sharon said.

"I've finished the archiving for Devers and e-mailed him the file, so you can return the computer whenever you want," Rona informed Anna.

"You're finished?" Anna asked.

"That's right."

"Well, it's one of those rare Friday afternoons where I have no appointments until Monday morning. I'm ready to get out of here."

"You're leaving me here alone?" Sharon asked with a sad face.

"No," Anna called as she went back for her briefcase and purse. "I'm leaving you with Neal."

Rona rushed to get her jacket.

"We're being abandoned, Sharon," Neal said as he stepped from his office.

Anna came back down the hall with him right behind her. "Now you know how I feel on all those lonely nights when you two leave at five and I'm still here until the wee hours. Have a nice weekend." She sailed out the door with Rona on her heels.

"Oh, spare us the sad story," Sharon called out as door closed.

Anna continued to babble nonstop all the way to the car.

"How much coffee did you have this afternoon?" Rona asked when Anna finally had to stop to breathe.

181

"None. Why?"

"You seem a little hyper."

The afternoon sun was warm coming through the car windows. "I spoke with my friend Tee this afternoon. She and her partner, Yolie, have a small cabin on Lake Medina. While we were talking, I happened to mention that it would be nice to get out of town this weekend and she offered us the use of the cabin." She looked at Rona expectantly. "I wasn't sure how you would feel about it."

"Where is it? I mean, how far away?" Rona didn't really care. She simply wanted time to think.

"It's less than an hour's drive. Do you want to go?"

Rona considered telling her the truth, that spending the weekend in a cold drafty cabin wasn't high on her list of things to do, but the animation in Anna's face stopped her. "I think I could handle just about anything, if it meant I'd have a weekend alone with you."

Anna smiled brightly. "Great, then let's get home and pack. This is too good to be true. I want to get out of here before someone catches us or I wake up and discover it's all a dream. I've already called Tammy and told her we'd probably be gone this weekend."

"You're really excited about this, aren't you?"

"It's so rare I have an entire weekend free, and the cabin is like frosting on the cake," Anna said as she reached over and squeezed Rona's hand.

"If we have time before we leave, I need to open a checking account," Rona said.

Anna looked at her and smiled. "For that, we can take time."

Anna pulled the car into the parking lot of a small general store. "This is the last store before we reach the cabin. I need to buy milk." She handed Rona the keys. "But first I have to find a restroom."

"You go find the restroom and I'll get the milk," Rona said as she stepped out of the car. The store was small but looked clean, and the road out front was paved and in good condition. Maybe the cabin wasn't going to be out in the middle of the boonies after all. She began to relax as she looked around. There were scattered patches of woods around, but they didn't look dark or foreboding. This might be fun, she thought. After all, she loved the water. Feeling better about the trip, she walked into the store. An elderly man and woman sat behind the counter. Both spoke to her as she entered. As she browsed the well-stocked aisles, she tried to remember if there was anything other than milk they might need. They had packed enough food for a small army. Nothing caught her attention, so she grabbed the milk and returned to the cash register.

The man came over to ring up her purchase. "You new around these parts?" he asked.

"Not really. I'm just here for the weekend."

"You got a place nearby?" he asked as he gave her the total of the purchase.

"I'm staying at a friend's cabin up on the lake," Rona replied. She took some money from her pocket.

He pulled his lower lip in and nodded. "Reckon you know to be careful with the bears."

Rona's head snapped up. "Bears?"

"Yep. It's 'cause of all them deer hangin' around up there. Bears just can't resist the taste of venison."

"John," the woman scolded.

"Now, Eleanor, if these girls are goin' to be stayin' up there on the lake all alone, they need to know about them bears."

The woman looked at him and shook her finger.

"Okay." He shook his head and handed over her change. "Don't ever get married." He sighed. "After you do, all the fun is just plain gone."

"Lordy, here he goes again," the woman said as she stood. "I'm going to check on dinner. You be good, old man."

Anna poked her head into the doorway. "Ready?"

Rona looked from the man to his wife and back.

He leaned forward and whispered, "You keep a close lookout for them bears. You most likely won't see any durin' the day, but they'll be comin' out after dark." He winked.

"John," the woman's voice came from the back.

He rolled his eyes. "Don't ever get married." He sighed again and shuffled off.

"What was all that about?" Anna asked when they were back in the car.

"Nothing, he was just having fun with me," Rona said as she stared out the window. She spent the rest of the trip probing the darker shadows of the woods.

The stone cabin, with a balcony that extended over the lake, wasn't the crude little one-room structure Rona had envisioned, although it was remote. The last house they'd passed was a good two miles down the road. "Where's the key?" she asked as they stepped out of the car and gazed at the spectacular view of the lake behind the cabin. There was one rather large area of woods across the road from the cabin, but Rona chose to ignore it.

"The back door is locked with one of those keyless entry thingies that real estate agencies use. Tee gave me the combination." Anna pointed to the side of the cabin. "There's a stairway on the side that leads to the back door. I'll go around and unlock it, if you'll start unloading the car."

"You seem to be in a hurry," Rona said and smiled.

Anna stopped and took a deep breath. "You're right. I've been so afraid something would happen to prevent us from coming up here, but I've told Sharon that nothing short of a family emergency was dragging me back into the office before Monday morning." She reached out and took Rona's hand. "I guess I'm a little nervous."

"Why are you so nervous?" Rona asked, ignoring the butterflies dancing in her own stomach.

Anna shrugged. "I don't know. I guess I see us going away for a

184

weekend as another step closer to"—she looked away for a moment—"whatever we're heading toward."

She realized that their nervousness stemmed from two separate issues. With some effort, she pushed away the old man's warning. He was probably trying to scare her, anyway. She needed to prove she wasn't afraid of her own shadow. "I think we should stop worrying about where the relationship is headed and concentrate instead on where that pathway over there leads." Rona pointed to a well-worn path that disappeared around the side of the cabin. The path was in the opposite direction of the larger area of woods. The area immediately around the cabin was open. No large trees or sinister-looking dilapidated shacks were present for undesirable things to hide behind.

"Was that an admission that you've been worrying too?" Anna asked, interrupting her covert surveillance.

"I'm not sure I would say I was worried, but I'll admit to being nervous," Rona said, deliberately leaving her meaning vague. "Let's walk down to the lake before it gets dark. We can unload the car later."

Hand-in-hand they strolled toward the lake. "Why were you nervous?" Anna persisted.

Rona was embarrassed to admit that she had considered the old man's warnings. She decided to play along with Anna's worries. "I don't know. We're already spending most of our nights together, so it's not like I don't already know you snore."

Anna gasped. "I do not snore."

Rona rolled her eyes. "Who told you those lies?"

"You're being horrible." They came around to the side of the cabin and Anna stopped suddenly. "Look," she whispered and pointed to four deer standing near the water's edge in a small grove of trees.

As they stood watching, a large buck came out of the trees and eyed them. Rona instinctively clutched Anna's arm. She was certain that she'd read an article about a buck attacking someone. "Are there a lot of deer around here?"

"Scads," Anna whispered.

Oh hell, was the old codger telling the truth about the bears? A fine bead of sweat broke out along Rona's hairline as she stared at the deer. She considered asking Anna about bears, but if he had been pulling her leg then Anna would think she was silly.

Anna apparently mistook Rona's clinging to be a sign of excitement, because she continued to stare, starry-eyed, at the animals. "I think the doe closest to the water is pregnant," Anna said softly.

Even more reason for the papa to be protective, Rona decided as she eyed the sharp points of the buck's rack. "It's getting dark. Maybe we should go back and unload the car now," Rona said. "We wouldn't want to scare them away." As they walked back to the car Rona kept glancing behind them. She wasn't going to tell Anna, but she was a city girl through and through. As far as she was concerned, wildlife observation was best done from inside the house.

While Anna went to unlock the door, Rona quickly grabbed their suitcases from the car. After she was sure Anna wouldn't be able to see her, she raced back to the side of the cabin and peeked around it to make sure the deer were still occupied with dinner and not in the process of sneaking up on her. Satisfied that they didn't appear to be planning any covert attacks on her, she ran back and wrestled out the enormous ice chest filled with food.

By the time Anna opened the front door, most of their things were waiting for her on the front porch. "Why didn't you wait and I could have helped you with that?" she asked.

Rona grabbed an armload of things. "I'm anxious to get the weekend started," she replied as she made one more sweep of the perimeter.

The cabin had two bedrooms, one on either side of the cabin. They both provided clear views of the lake. Rona took their bags to the guest room.

She opened a set of French doors and stepped out onto a large balcony that ran across the entire back of the cabin and protruded over the lake. "Wow. Now this is a view." She could appreciate the beauty of the place much more now that she was out of the reach of all marauding wildlife.

Anna came up behind her and wrapped her arms around her waist. "I've always loved it up here."

Rona felt a stab a jealousy. "You've been here before?"

"Yes. I come up once or twice a year."

"Oh."

Anna chuckled. "You're jealous."

"No, I'm not." Rona cringed at the petulance in her statement.

Anna hugged her tighter. "Tee and Yolie occasionally invite me up to spend a weekend with them. I've never brought anyone else here."

Rona knew her reaction was childish, but she still felt an overwhelming sense of relief.

"Let's get the rest of the stuff," Anna said as she kissed the back of Rona's neck.

When everything was inside, Anna turned to Rona. "While I unload the ice chest, would you mind bringing in some wood and building a fire?" She nodded toward the see-through fireplace that separated the living room and kitchen as she began to remove items from the ice chest.

Rona glanced out the window. It was dark. "You want me to walk around in the woods looking for firewood?"

Anna stood up with a carton of milk in her hands and gazed at her.

Rona could see she was struggling not to laugh.

"There's a small room just outside." She pointed to the back door. "You'll find wood stacked inside there."

Rona nodded, but continued to stare at the darkened panes of the window.

"You know what," Anna said as she handed the milk to Rona. "I know where everything is. You might have trouble finding it in the dark. I'll get the wood."

Rona practically snatched the carton from Anna's hand. "Great, I'll unload the ice chest." She put the milk in the refrigerator before going back and grabbing packages of cold cuts. As soon as Anna disappeared out the door, she stopped and breathed a sigh of relief. All kinds of things could be hiding out there in the dark. She removed a bowl containing carefully wrapped eggs from the ice chest and stopped. Anna was out there with those unknown things. The old man could have been telling the truth. Maybe the woman had told him to hush because she didn't want him scaring away the customers. Rona stepped closer to the door to see if she could hear Anna moving around. There was nothing. She eased the door open. Still nothing. "Anna," she whispered. She shivered when there was no reply.

This cabin was exactly the kind of remote place that appeared in those horrible murder thrillers her brother had loved to watch. Clutching the bowl of eggs, she took a tentative step onto the balcony. She tilted her head from side to side, trying to hear beyond the sound of the water lapping against the balcony supports. As she turned to her right, she noticed a thin trickle of light that appeared to be seeping from beneath a door.

Relief washed over her. Anna couldn't hear her calling out because the door to the wood storage area was closed. Rona turned to go back inside, and as she did, something enormous rose up in front of her.

"Bear," she screamed as she dashed back into the kitchen and slammed the door behind her. There was a loud crash just beyond door. The bear was trying to get in. Rona threw her body against the door and locked it. Then she remembered. Anna was still out there getting wood. Had she heard her scream? If so, would Anna lock herself in or would she run to help her? If Anna hadn't heard her scream, she would walk out totally unaware.

Rona searched about wildly for a weapon; the only thing she could find quickly was a broom. It would have to do. If she made enough noise, perhaps she could scare the bear away. At the very least, she could distract it long enough to get Anna safely into the house. Rona threw the door open and charged out screaming at the top of her lungs. She turned in the direction where she had first seen the bear, and seeing nothing, spun in the other direction. It was then she heard the strangled sound. The blood pounding in her ears made it difficult for her to hear. It took her a moment to realize the sound was laughter. She finally located Anna sitting on the floor laughing hysterically. The broom slipped from Rona's hand and clattered to the floor.

"I don't see what's so damn funny," she said in a shaky voice.

Anna tried to stand but slipped back down as a new wave of laughter overtook her.

"I thought you were about to be some bear's dinner."

Anna wiped her eyes and stood. "And you came to rescue me. Oh, how sweet." She wrapped her arms around Rona. "That's the sweetest thing anyone's ever done for me."

Rona saw no humor in the situation, and the continued spasms of shakes overtaking Anna's body told her that she was still being laughed at. "It's not funny," she replied. "I really did see a bear."

"You're absolutely right," Anna said and sniffled. "There's nothing funny about you thinking you saw a bear."

"I did," Rona protested.

"It was me. I had an armload of wood. I had just turned the light off and stepped out of the storeroom when you first walked out. I spoke to you, but I guess you didn't hear me."

"Well, you should have said something else," Rona sputtered.

"I would have, but when you screamed 'bear!' and threw the eggs at me, you scared me so badly I dropped the wood." Anna could barely speak over her laughter.

"Oh, crap. I threw the eggs." She started to pull away to look for the bowl.

Anna held onto her. "Forget about the eggs and look at me."

"Why?" Rona asked. "So you can laugh at me some more."

"No. Look at me, because I need to tell you something."

"What?"

"You running out with nothing but a broom to save me from a bear is the sweetest, bravest thing I've ever seen. I love you, Rona."

Chapter Twenty-seven

The statement hung between them. These weren't words Rona had expected to hear anytime soon, if ever. She wanted to say something, but Anna's declaration caught her completely off guard. She wasn't sure how to respond.

Anna stepped away. "Too soon, huh? I'm sorry."

Rona tried to speak, but still nothing came. She had seen the look of hurt on Anna's face as she turned from her.

"Why don't you finish with the ice chest and I'll clean up out here?" Anna turned away without waiting for her to agree.

Rona went back into the kitchen and stood staring into space. Anna had opened the door to the next step in their relationship, but she hadn't been able to step in. Why couldn't she say the words? She felt strongly for Anna and wanted their relationship to mature. Was she not ready to make that commitment? She tried to form the words in her head and visualize saying them to Anna, but they scampered around like leaves caught in a whirlwind.

"We did a decent job packing the eggs," Anna said as she walked in holding the bowl. "It looks like two or three are cracked, but they're salvageable." She set the bowl on the counter without looking at Rona. "I'm going to bring in the wood and start a fire. It'll get chilly now that the sun has gone down."

Rona watched her walk away. There was already a chill in the air and it had nothing to do with the weather. Not knowing what else to do, she finished putting away the items in the ice chest.

For the next hour, they both kept their distance. When Anna came in with the wood and started building a fire, Rona went to unpack her bag. She left to put away the ice chest when Anna came in to unpack. She was boiling water for spaghetti when Anna came out a few minutes later.

"Are we going to spend the entire weekend avoiding each other?" Anna asked.

Rona shook her head.

"I'm sorry about what I'm said."

An odd queasiness hit Rona's stomach. She turned off the boiling water. "I didn't know what to say," she admitted. Anna turned away before Rona could see her face. "I wasn't expecting you to say . . . that."

"It was just one of those spur-of-moment things," Anna said as she knelt down and began stoking the fire. "It's not like I was about to ask you to marry me or anything."

"Right," Rona said with a chuckle that stuck in her throat and made her cough. She saw Anna's hand brush against her cheek as she pretended to push her hair back from her face.

"We're going to need more wood," Anna said as she rushed out of the cabin.

Rona leaned her head against the refrigerator door. Why couldn't she just say the damn words? She cared deeply for Anna. Mary was the only other person she'd ever felt this way about. I f she loved Mary, then the feelings she was having for Anna must be . . . the same thing. Frustrated, she gave her head a sharp rap on the refrigerator door. She couldn't even think the words. Needing something to do, she turned the water back on before dumping the ice out of the ice chest. When the water was again boiling, she added the pasta and poured the leftover spaghetti sauce into a saucepan to heat. Anna still had not returned when Rona started putting together a small salad. The sauce was simmering and the pasta was draining when Anna finally came back.

"I'm sorry," Rona said as soon as Anna put the wood down.

Anna shook her head. "You didn't do anything. I shouldn't have . . ."

"I care for you deeply, but I'm not ready—"

Anna held up her hand. "Can we please just forget it happened?"

Rona nodded. "If you can forget I thought you were a bear?"

Anna smiled, and the tension between them began to melt. "What possessed you to think I was a bear?"

Embarrassed but relieved that they were speaking again, Rona told her what the man from the store had told her.

"That old fart told me the same thing the first time I stopped in there. Luckily, I knew he was full of stuffing."

"So, there really aren't any bears around here?"

Anna shook her head. "I think you'd have to go all the way to West Texas to find a bear."

"You must have thought I was some kind of idiot." She quickly turned away, but not before she saw Anna's face soften.

"We'll blame your nervousness on low blood sugar," she said as she started removing dishes from the cabinet. "The spaghetti smells wonderful. I packed a couple of bottles of wine. They're in that box over in the corner, if you'd like to open one."

Their conversation remained forced all through dinner. It wasn't until after they moved to the living room and curled up on the sofa together that things began to return to normal. They shared the routine everyday stories of their lives that no one other than a lover wants to hear. It was well after midnight when Rona pulled Anna into her arms and kissed her. In the warm glow of the firelight, she spread a blanket out on the floor. She slowly removed

Anna's clothes before taking off her own and stretching out alongside her. At first, their touches were guarded, but as passion took over, they became more insistent. When Rona slipped her fingers deep into Anna, Anna surprised her by rolling over onto her and sitting up. She drove Rona's fingers deeper inside her as she began a slow rhythmic rocking motion.

With her hand imprisoned, Rona used the thumb of her other hand to help stroke her lover to orgasm. She watched as Anna came with her head thrown back and her body arched and practically vibrating as waves of pleasure shook her, leaving in their wake that special soft afterglow of dreamy eyes and a faint smile. Rona wrapped her arms around her and held her tight. With eyes squeezed shut to stop the tears that threatened, she finally allowed herself to admit how much she did love this woman. She tried to say the words aloud, to tell Anna how she wanted to spend a lifetime with her, but to do so might tempt fate. Instead, she held her. When Anna tried to move to make love to her, Rona whispered, "Just let me hold you."

The fire slowly burned down. When the night air took on a chill, Rona pulled the edges of the blanket around them and continued to hold her. The eastern sky was already beginning to grow light before Rona finally drifted off to sleep.

The smell of freshly brewed coffee dragged her eyes open to reveal Anna sitting on the floor beside her holding out a cup.

"I knew this was the only thing that would wake you," Anna said and smiled.

It took Rona a second to realize that the light was coming from the kitchen and not the sun. "What time is it?" she asked.

"A little after six."

"Why are you up so early?"

"Because there's something I want to show you and we have to rush or we'll miss it. So hurry and get dressed," Anna said as she stood.

"Wait a minute," Rona protested. "Where are you going with my coffee?"

"I'm going to put it in a travel mug. Get dressed. We really do have to hurry."

Rona tried to shake the cobwebs of sleep from her head and concentrate on tying her sneakers. She was buttoning her shirt when Anna returned.

"I brought you a pullover and your jacket. You'll need to wear them both. It's cool out."

Rona picked up the blanket and started to fold it.

"We'll do that later," Anna insisted. "Please, hurry."

Rona grabbed the pullover and yanked it over her head before getting her jacket and heading for the door. "Well, what are you waiting for?" she called back to Anna. "We have to hurry." She started out the front door.

"No, this way," Anna called as she headed out onto the balcony.

Rona followed her down the steps of the balcony. "Where are we going?" she asked as she rushed to catch up.

"Over there." Anna pointed to the far side of the lake. "You're about to see one of the most fantastic sunrises of your life. It looks like the entire lake catches fire."

Rona stopped sharply. "How are we going to get there?"

"In that."

In the dim light, it took Rona a minute before she noticed the small rowboat. She swallowed her groan. "The next thing I know, she'll be wanting to fish," she grumbled as she started running to catch up. She needed that coffee.

When they reached the boat, Anna finally handed over Rona's cup. "Hop in and I'll push off."

Rona climbed in and held on while Anna scrambled into the boat. She took time to grab a quick swallow of coffee, then picked up the oars and started rowing across the lake.

"Hey, you seem to know what you're doing," Anna said as Rona's long smooth stroke sent them skimming across the lake. "I guess you've rowed a boat before."

194

"Please." Rona pretended to be offended. "I am from Michigan. You know, where there are real lakes, not just these little man-made things you Texans have."

"Excuse my ignorance. You're absolutely right." Just when Rona was about to feel smug, Anna added, "Are there any bears in Michigan?"

Rona rolled her eyes and sighed as Anna's laughter danced across the lake.

Chapter Twenty-eight

On Monday morning, Rona stepped off the bus and walked toward the music store. She couldn't remember the last time she felt this relaxed and happy. She and Anna spent the entire weekend hiking around the lake or exploring it in the rowboat. The sunrise was as beautiful as Anna promised, as were the sunsets. Each night they talked until a playful touch or kiss led them to the bedroom. The weekend was so fantastic she hadn't even spent time worrying about coming back and starting a new job today. Her only regret was that because of the difference in their hours, she would no longer be riding with Anna. Riding the bus worked well for her. Even though the trip took almost an hour, she only had to make one transfer and the store was less than two blocks from the bus stop.

A closed sign still hung in the window, but Rona could see Verna inside dusting. She tapped on the window and smiled when Verna looked surprised. "You didn't think I was coming back, did you?" Rona asked when she went in. The store smelled of fine furniture polish.

"It was a toss-up," the older woman admitted.

Rona handed her the employment forms Verna had given her the day she hired her.

"Let me give you the grand tour. If your lunch needs to be refrigerated," she said, gesturing to the small bag Rona was toting, "we have a small fridge in the back storeroom." The showroom consisted of one enormous area, with the various types of instruments claiming their own spaces. Large tables holding wooden boxes filled with sheet music made up the back of the room. Display cases exhibiting small musical accessories sat near the appropriate instruments. The walls held framed posters of famous musicians and ad posters hawking everything from harmonicas to baby grand pianos. As Verna gave her a tour of the sales floor, she also recited the history of the store. Rona's interest didn't pique until she mentioned that the store catered to professional musicians.

"I didn't realize San Antonio had that many professionals," Rona said, knowing that Austin was better known for its music scene.

"You'd be surprised," Verna replied as she led the way back to the front. "Most of them aren't household names like the headliners they perform with." She turned and sniffed. "Not every musician in Texas lives in Austin, you know." She began to arrange a display case filled with harmonicas. "Before my husband, Sam, died, the courtyard would be packed every Saturday night. Attendance was by invitation only. Let me tell you, an invitation from Sam Holland was a guarantee that you were about to be noticed by some of the top music people around. We had music people from Nashville, Los Angeles and Seattle calling us."

"Where's the Courtyard?" Rona asked, thinking she was talking about a club.

"Out behind the store." She nodded toward the back.

"There's a club behind here?"

197

Verna looked at her as though she was daft. "No, there's a courtyard."

"Oh," Rona said, even though she still wasn't certain she understood.

"We'd also have an open mike night once a month." She covered her ears and cringed. "Some of those people were horrible, but every once in a while a jewel would come along."

A tapping on the front glass interrupted them. "That's Jerry. That boy is always late. Would you mind letting him in? The keys are in the door."

Rona trotted to the door and opened it. She wanted to hear more about the courtyard. Before she could bring the conversation back around to it, customers started trickling in. Business wasn't booming, but it was steady. Whenever they had free time, Jerry showed her how to ring up sales and helped her become acquainted with the stock. At first, she wasn't sure how she was going to get along with the boisterous and gossipy twenty-year-old. As she spent more time with him, she began to realize that most of his posturing was an attempt to cover his deep insecurities of an already receding hairline and the ravages of a severe case of childhood acne.

The morning flew by and before she knew it, Verna was sending her off for lunch. There was a phone in the office that Verna said she could use for local personal calls. Rona used it to call Domingo at the Taco Haven. She was disappointed to learn there was still no news of Malcolm. She gave Domingo the store's phone number and asked him to call if he heard anything. Verna was sorting a new shipment of sheet music when she went back to get her lunch.

"Do you still use the courtyard?" she asked.

"No. That was Sam's baby. He would tell me who to invite and I'd make the calls."

"It must have been a real blow to the musicians when he died. There aren't many places for new artists to get noticed."

Verna stopped sorting and looked up. "You know, that never

occurred to me. I was so devastated when Sam died, I didn't think about how anyone else would feel."

"When did he die?"

"It will be three years in May. He was sitting on the back porch and—" Her voice caught. "Our son, Junior, came over to drop off some tool he had borrowed and found him. He'd had a massive heart attack. The doctor said there wasn't anything anyone could have done, but sometimes I feel guilty. If I hadn't chosen that day to have my hair done, maybe I could have done something. There were so many things I never got to tell him." She looked up at Rona. "Do you have someone special in your life?"

Rona nodded. "As a matter of fact I do."

"Well, don't waste time. Make every minute count, because they go by so quickly. Tell him how much you love him every day."

"She," Rona said as a streak of guilt shot through her. She should have told Anna she loved her while they were at the cabin. She had tried to a couple of times, but the words just would not come out.

Verna's hand flew to her chest. "I'm sorry. Sam was always getting after me about making assumptions about things."

"I suppose some people would think you made a normal assumption," Rona replied lightly.

Verna made a short hissing sound. "Normal. What is normal anyway?" She went back to her sorting. "What's her name?"

"Anna."

Verna nodded. "That's a pretty name." She noticed the bag Rona was holding. "You can eat your lunch over there at that table, if you'd like."

"Thanks, but if you don't mind, I'd like to see the courtyard."

Verna looked up and smiled. "Would you really? Let me get the key and I'll show you."

A few minutes later, Rona stepped out into a large rectangular-shaped area created from the backs of buildings. Murals of Texas musicians covered the walls. She began calling off the names of the people she recognized. "There's Buddy Holly, Bob Wills, Selena,

George Jones, Willie Nelson, Stevie Ray Vaughan and his brother Jimmie, Roy Orbison, ZZ Top, Janis Joplin, Freddy Fender, Woody Guthrie, T-Bone Walker, Tish Hinojosa, Lyle Lovett, George Strait, Natalie Maines of the Dixie Chicks." She stopped and shook her head as the paintings continued on around the rectangle. There were many she didn't know, but a couple in particular caught her attention. "I don't recognize those two men," Rona said as she pointed them out.

"The one on the left is jazz trumpeter Nat Adderley. The other is slide guitarist Blind Willie Johnson."

Rona recalled Mary talking about him. "Is he the guy who used his pocket knife as a slide?"

Verna looked at her and nodded with approval. "Yes. He's probably the greatest slide guitarist ever."

Rona noticed for the first time that the music store wasn't a single-floor building. "What's up there?"

Verna squinted at the upper floor. "Jerry rents the upper floor from me. He lives up there."

"You mean Jerry, the guy who's training me?"

"Yes, that's the one. You'd think he'd be able to get to work on time." Verna waved away her remark. "I don't complain because he's around to keep an eye on the store at night and he's always around to help customers when they have an emergency."

Rona continued her study of the courtyard. Weeds had clawed their way through cracks in the cobblestone, and the wooden benches scattered around were in dire need of paint. Only on closer examination did she notice the small alley that ran along the far side. She walked over and took a look. A narrow wooden fence blocked one end and a wrought iron gate blocked the other side. As she stood gazing up at the murals, she could only imagine the great music these walls had absorbed. With its laid-back atmosphere and wonderful acoustics, the courtyard would be the perfect spot for an impromptu jam session. Time stopped as they both became lost—Verna in her memories and Rona in her fantasies of sitting down and playing with some of these dynamite musicians.

After lunch, Rona spent the remainder of her shift learning the ins and outs of the sales counter. By the time she left that afternoon, she felt confident in being able to handle any regular sales transaction.

According to the bus schedule she had picked up, her bus was scheduled to arrive fifteen minutes after her quitting time. If she missed it, she would have to wait an hour for the next one. The ride home wasn't as pleasant as her morning commute. There were several rowdy teenagers on the bus. It was a relief when they got off at the mall. She watched the stops carefully. She didn't want to miss hers. It would take her a few days to get used to the route. After the first stop, she would have a twelve-minute wait for her transfer, and then a thirty-five-minute ride to the bus stop near Anna's house. Since it was Monday, she would go straight to Gina and Julian's for the twins' piano lessons. She was tired, but she was too happy to complain.

Rona could hear the television when she stepped into Anna's living room. Tammy came out of the den. "You look beat," Tammy said.

Rona shook her head and smiled. "The last hour—" She stopped. "Where's Anna?" She followed Tammy into the kitchen.

"She had a late meeting with a client but thought she would be home soon," Tammy said as she pulled a plate from the oven. "I made breaded chops with broccoli."

Rona took the plate. She was starved.

"How are the piano lessons going?"

"They learn the drills I give them, but it's impossible to keep them separated during their individual lessons," Rona said between bites. "When they're together, they want to play the drills together. I'm not sure how I'm going to handle this."

"My girls don't like to be separated either, but I think they'll grow out of it as they get older."

Rona nibbled on the broccoli. "How are things going at the restaurant?"

"Good. I'm adjusting to the pace and the girls don't seem to mind having to stay in the playroom." She sat down at the end of the table. "Did you know Anna's birthday is coming up?"

"No. When?"

"Her actual birthday is March fourteenth, but Mrs. Pagonis wants to throw her a surprise party the Saturday before."

"That's only three weeks away," Rona said as she put her fork down.

"Well, make sure you don't say anything to Anna about it. They want to surprise her."

Rona nodded, already trying to think of something special she could give Anna. It couldn't be any old gift. It had to be something special.

Tammy returned to the den, leaving Rona to eat and think. It wasn't until she was rinsing her plate and putting it in the dishwasher that she knew what she was going to give Anna. It would be the perfect gift. She dried her hands before going to Anna's bedroom and taking the pendant watch and business card from the jewelry box. She would drop it off tomorrow after work to have it repaired. That would be her gift to Anna.

Chapter Twenty-nine

Business was so heavy the following day that Rona ended up working late. She wasn't able to drop the watch off until Wednesday. The trip to the watch repair shop proved much harder than she had anticipated. After changing buses twice, she realized they were making a long meandering loop around the area she needed to be. She ended up having to walk several blocks to reach the shop. In trying to get home, she got on the wrong bus and had to wait forty-five minutes for the bus that would get her to the correct stop. Each time something went wrong, she would remind herself how happy Anna would be when she discovered the watch was working again. Rona was exhausted by the time she finally got home.

Anna and the twins met her at the door. "I was starting to get worried," she said as she lightly touched Rona's arm.

"I needed to run an errand and I ended up on the wrong bus," Rona admitted.

"Maybe we should start looking for a car for you."

Rona shook her head. "I can't afford a car. It won't take me long to learn the different routes." She could tell Anna wanted to say more, but she let it go and nodded.

"Mama saved you some food," Katie announced. "We had Chinese."

"It was a long day for all of us," Anna explained. "I stopped and picked up takeout."

Rona sat at the table while Anna told her about a new client. She tried to listen, but her feet and back ached from all the walking. As soon as she finished eating, they all went to the den to watch television. The next thing Rona remembered was Anna shaking her and telling her it was time for bed.

The following morning, Rona sat on the end of the bed and watched Anna get dressed. "Tee and Yolie want to get together with us for dinner soon," Anna said as she walked to her dresser. Rona held her breath as Anna picked up her wristwatch and put it on. If she opened her jewelry box, she was sure to notice the pendant watch was missing.

She was so busy watching she failed to answer.

"If you're not comfortable meeting them yet, I can beg off."

"No. That's fine."

"Are you sure?" She came to stand by the bed. "What's wrong? You seem jittery."

"I'm just a little nervous about work, I guess. I'd love to meet your friends." She stood and kissed Anna on the forehead. "I fell asleep so fast last night, I didn't have a chance to ask you how your day went," she said, trying to change the subject.

"I received a couple of promising leads for new clients. I have a meeting with one of them today." Anna headed into the bathroom.

"That's great."

"Oh, by the way," Anna called. "I spoke to Julian yesterday. He and Gina are thrilled with the twins' progress."

"I'm starting to feel bad about charging them for two lessons, when both of the kids end up attending each other's session. I should probably just combine them and only charge them for one lesson."

"You shouldn't feel bad. You're still giving them a full hour."

"I guess."

Anna came out of the bathroom ready to go. She opened her arms to Rona. "I don't want to go to work. I'd rather be home with you."

"I'll be leaving in a little while," Rona reminded her. "Do you have any appointments for tonight?"

"No. I don't have anything scheduled, as of now."

"Then why don't we both plan on getting home at a decent hour and getting to bed early." She ran her hand down Anna's side and back up her thigh.

Anna stepped away. "Don't tease me like that when you know I have to leave."

"I didn't do anything," Rona said innocently.

"Yeah, right." Grinning, Anna held out her hand. "Walk me to my car?"

Rona stood in the kitchen doorway and waved as Anna backed her car out of the garage. Afterward, she made her way upstairs. Although she and Anna spent their nights together, she still went to her room each morning after Anna left for work, to shower and get dressed for the day. She met Tammy coming out of her room.

"I was hoping to see you," Rona said. She quickly told Tammy about taking the watch in for repair. "The guy at the shop is supposed to call if the watch needs anything other than cleaning and an adjustment. If he calls while you're here, can you take a message and tell him I'll call him back the next day."

"Sure." She draped her arm over Rona's shoulders. "It was sweet of you to do that for her."

"I didn't know what else to give her for her birthday. Do you think it's enough?"

"Yes, but make sure you get her a card."

"I know that," Rona said as she made a mental note to buy a card during one of her lunch breaks.

On the way to work, Rona thought about the watch and the best way to present the gift to Anna. It seemed too personal to give it to her in front of her family. By the time she arrived at the music store, she had worked out a plan. The watch was supposed to be ready in a week, and Anna's birthday party would be the Saturday after that. She decided she would pick up the watch and then make a date with Anna for dinner. They could go somewhere nice and romantic. She would give her the watch then.

"You look awfully pleased with yourself," Verna said as she opened the door for Rona.

"That's because I have a suggestion I want to run by you," Rona replied. She saw Verna tense and rushed on. "Open the courtyard back up. Start the Saturday night jam sessions again."

Verna shook her head rapidly. "No. I can't. That was Sam's pride and joy."

"That's why you should keep it going, in honor of his memory."

"That's not possible." She quickly changed the subject. "We received a shipment of books late yesterday afternoon. I would appreciate it if you could verify the invoice and set up the display tower that was shipped with them. Get Jerry to help you set it up," she said before racing off to her office.

Rona kicked herself as she walked back to the storeroom. She should have approached the matter differently and given Verna a little time to adjust to the idea. As she inventoried the shipment of music books, she tried to come up with another strategy.

A steady stream of customers kept them all busy throughout the morning. At noon, she slipped into the back long enough to wolf down her sandwich and call Domingo at Taco Haven. There was still no word on Malcolm. During a lull after lunch, Jerry and Rona assembled the cardboard display tower. It was mindless work. She tuned out Jerry's gushing review of the new rock band he had seen the night before and thought about Anna. A shiver of excitement tickled her scalp as she thought about the planned night before them. The last couple of days had been so hectic;

they'd barely had time to talk. Verna was right. They shouldn't take their time together for granted.

"I'll let you enter the stock into the system while I set out the books," Jerry said as he handed her the invoice. "Let me know if you run into problems."

She nodded. The software system was straightforward. In fact, it was very similar to the program she had used while working at the auto parts warehouse. The next wave of customers struck as she was finishing the entries. Rona spent a great deal of time running to the storeroom to fill customer orders. It was late in the afternoon before she and Jerry were able to sit down behind the counter and take a breather. They were barely seated before a tall man with wide shoulders that filled the doorway came in. He was a silhouette against the glare of the large front window.

"That dude's big," Jerry whispered as he stood. "You've been running all afternoon. I'll take this one." He turned toward the customer and greeted him.

As the man walked toward them, Rona's heart missed a beat. She started toward him. "Lenny?"

He ran, grabbed her in a bear hug and lifted her from the floor. When he set her down, they both started talking at once.

"You first," he said in his booming voice.

She reached up and tugged at his beard. "When did you grow this thing? I thought you joined the Navy."

He ran his hand over his beard. "I did. After training, they assigned me to an aircraft carrier. I was a plane handler. I had been doing that for about three months when I started having problems with my ears. I think it probably started from all those years of standing in front of amplifiers," he said wryly. "Anyway, after about three miles of red tape, the Navy finally let me out."

"How did you end up in San Antonio?"

"I went back to Austin but couldn't find you guys. I drifted down here and hooked up with an old friend. The guy who owns Jansen's. He needed a sound tech."

"So you aren't with a group?"

"Nope."

She saw him glance at Jerry, who was practically jumping up and down. Rona quickly introduced them.

"I know you," Jerry replied. "You used to be with the Red Devils. I'd sneak into Jansen's on a fake ID and see you play. What happened? I went to see you guys one night and you were gone."

Lenny shook his head. "Man, now you're going way back. That was a bad scene, too many drugs. I may be deaf, but I ain't crazy."

"What are you doing now?" Lenny asked Rona.

"I work here."

He shook his head. "No. Don't tell me you had to get a day gig."

Rona glanced at Jerry, wishing he would go away, but it was obvious that he intended to stay.

"You're still with Eric and Zac, right? I mean, you guys started over, didn't you."

Rona swallowed the lump forming in her throat. "No. They left right after you did."

"Oh, jeez, you should've called me or something."

Rona shrugged. There didn't seem to be any point in reminding him that he hadn't left a forwarding address or phone number.

He tugged at his ear. "I'm really sorry about that. I never dreamed you guys wouldn't try again." An awkward silence fell between them. "What's brought you to San Antonio?"

To lighten the mood, Rona resorted to the punch line of an old joke. "My thumb."

Lenny smiled. "You never could tell a joke."

Jerry was moving ever closer, trying to get back into the conversation. "How do you two know each other?"

Lenny looked at Rona and smiled. "Did you ever hear of Leather and Lace?"

Jerry nodded. "Yeah, I read about them in the *Travis County Reporter*. They were a group out of Houston, I think."

"Austin," Lenny and Rona said together.

Jerry turned to Rona. "So you met him while he was with Leather and Lace?"

"No," Lenny said. "We met when she hired me as their lead guitarist."

Jerry's eyes grew round as he stared at Rona. "You were in a band?"

"Hell, man," Lenny thundered. "She was the band."

"Oh, this is too cool. Will you guys . . ." Jerry began to shuffle from foot-to-foot. "I mean, would it be okay if—"

"Christ, man, spit it out."

Jerry jumped back at the tone of Lenny's voice.

Rona couldn't help but laugh. People were always afraid of Lenny's size, but in truth he was a big pussycat.

"Can I jam with you guys?" Jerry stammered.

"No." Rona waved them off. "I don't play anymore. I'm all through with that."

Lenny looked at her and smiled. "You'll never be through. It was too deep in your blood."

"Not anymore," she said.

Jerry grabbed Lenny's arm. "We have a setup already," he said, nodding toward a display that looked like a miniature stage setup. "You just point to the guitar you want and I'll have it ready for you in"—he snapped his finger—"that quick."

Lenny looked around and pointed to an electric blue Fender. Jerry took off after it as if his shoes were on fire.

"Damn, I thought I was through with groupies," Rona said softly as Jerry raced around the showroom.

Lenny draped a massive arm over her shoulders. "I'm really sorry that we all deserted you."

His sudden tenderness made her eyes tear up. "You remember what Zac always said."

A deep rumble of laughter bubbled from him as he said, "What don't kill us will only make us more money."

They continued reminiscing about the old days but were careful not to mention Mary's name. When Jerry began to the tune the guitar, Lenny leaned down to Rona. "What do you think the kid plays?"

Rona glanced at him. "It has to be either rhythm guitar or the tambourine."

Lenny laughed. "I'd forgotten how cynical you are," he said. "But, Christ, I sure hope he ain't a wannabe drummer."

"It's ready," Jerry called out as he moved behind the drums.

"It doesn't look like it's going to be your lucky day," Rona said as she nodded toward Jerry.

"It's the best day I've had in a long time," he replied and gently squeezed her shoulder. "Come on. Let's show this little turd what a real band sounds like."

They took their places and agreed on an old standard that any musician worth his salt could play, "Proud Mary." Jerry surprised them both when he began to sing in a rich baritone. It quickly became obvious he was no slouch on the drums either. Rona closed her eyes and allowed her fingers to take over. How many dozens of times had she played this song? It was almost certain that before the band could call it a night, someone would request the John Fogerty classic. Zac and Mary had hated the song, but for some reason, she never minded it so much. She enjoyed the energy it always pumped into the audience. Before she knew it, Lenny brought the song to a close. When she opened her eyes, she found a small crowd of people standing just inside the door watching them. They began to clap as the notes died away.

Chapter Thirty

"That was awesome," Jerry shouted as he jumped up. "Did you hear them?" he hissed. "They loved us."

Lenny slapped his arm. "Chill, man, everyone loves that song."

Jerry's shoulders drooped as he turned to the crowd that was quickly dispersing now that the free show was over. "I thought we sounded pretty good."

Rona nudged Lenny. As she did, she noticed Verna standing at the doorway of the storeroom watching them.

"Yeah," Lenny relented. "We were rockin'. You're not bad with those sticks."

"I'll be right back," Rona said. "Don't leave, okay?"

Lenny nodded as Jerry pulled him aside.

Verna was moving to the sales counter. Rona joined her there.

"You never told me you were a musician," Verna started. "But I should have realized it by the way you played that first day."

211

Rona shrugged. "A lot people who aren't musicians play an instrument."

"Is that why you wanted me to open the courtyard again?" Verna asked. "So that you might meet someone who'll give you your big break."

"Playing in a band no longer interests me."

"What does?"

Rona thought about the question. "I used to write the band's music. I enjoy that, but I also think I'd like to get into the production side."

"You want to go where the real money is?" Verna sighed.

"It's not just about money. That's where the music comes alive. It takes more than good lyrics and skillful musicians to produce a great song."

"And you think you could do that?"

Rona looked at her. "Maybe not right now, but at the risk of sounding conceited, I think I could with the proper training."

Verna merely nodded before saying, "Your friend on the guitar is good. Is he working?"

Rona knew Verna was asking if Lenny was in a band. "I honestly don't know. We sort of lost touch over the last couple of years."

Verna nodded and glanced at her watch. "I noticed you didn't take much of a lunch today, so why don't you go ahead and leave. It looks like the rush is over for the day."

"Thanks. I'll see you tomorrow."

Verna nodded and walked away.

When Rona rejoined the guys, they were arguing over which company produced the better guitar. Lenny swore it was Fender, but Jerry insisted it was Gibson.

"Man, you're a drummer. What do you know about guitars, anyway?" Lenny asked.

Unfazed by the comment, Jerry opened his mouth to argue, but Rona quickly interrupted. "I'm through for the day," she told Lenny.

"Great, let's go grab a beer."

Poor Jerry looked so stricken, Rona almost offered to stay and work for him while he and Lenny grabbed the beer.

It took them a couple of minutes to extract themselves from Jerry's clutches, but they were finally able to make it outside.

"Where's you car?" Lenny asked.

"I don't have one."

He looked at her for a moment before nodding. "I'm parked down the street." They walked in silence until they reached the new white Chevy Impala. "This is it," he said.

"Wow. You've bought a Chevy Impala."

"Yeah. I always liked your old car."

"It's brand new. I guess the Navy pays well."

He blushed. "The pay was okay, but I managed to save a lot while we were together. I made some decent investments."

Rona started laughing.

"What's so funny?"

"I know someone who's going to absolutely love you." She could already picture him and Anna gushing over mutual funds and stock prices. "What are you doing tonight?"

"Nothing really. Just hanging out."

"Let's skip the beer and you come over to the house for dinner. There's someone I'd like you to meet."

His eyebrows shot up. "Would this someone be a woman?"

"Most definitely."

They got into the car before he asked, "How long have you been seeing her?"

"I haven't known her very long."

He nodded. "That's why you're smiling so much, and here I thought you were glad to see me."

"What about you? Is there anyone special in your life?"

He cranked the car and pulled out into traffic. "No, I can't seem to connect with anyone. It seems like all the women I know are happily married or lesbians."

Rona gave him directions to the interstate and they chatted about San Antonio and the Navy until they reached the house.

Tammy and the girls were walking up the driveway when

Lenny pulled into the driveway. Rona directed him to park to the side so that Anna could still get into the garage.

"Man, you didn't tell me she had kids," Lenny said. "Are they twins?"

"That's Tammy," Rona said. "She lives here also. Anna won't be home until later." She saw a look of fear pass over Tammy's face when she spotted the strange car. She rushed the kids inside the house.

"Do I look that scary?" Lenny asked.

"It's not you. She's running from an abusive husband. She's terrified he's going to show up here someday."

A low rumbling sounded in Lenny's chest. "Somebody ought to use the bastard as a punching bag and show him how it feels."

Rona saw a slight movement of the front blinds. "Come on." She stepped out of the car and waved at the house so that Tammy would know everything was all right.

"Maybe I should come some other time," Lenny said. "I don't want to upset her."

"She was only upset because she didn't recognize the car. Now come on." Rona leaned down and poked her head back into the car. "She's a great cook."

"Really?"

"You should taste her shrimp pasta. It's good enough to make a grown man cry."

Lenny unfolded his large frame from the car. "Well, what are you waiting for? You know how I love to eat."

As they walked to the house, Rona pushed away the memories of how the band members had once all gathered at her and Mary's apartment to talk over sets and eat. Lenny could eat a large pizza by himself and be looking for a snack in less than an hour.

Once inside, Rona quickly made the introductions. They soon had a pot of coffee brewing, and the remainder of the chocolate cake Tammy had baked the day before appeared on the table. It didn't take Lenny long to win over the girls. He was a natural-born storyteller and soon had them all laughing.

After one of his better tales, Rona dried her eyes and noticed Anna standing in the doorway leading to the hallway.

"You're home," she said, jumping up from the table. "I didn't hear you come in."

Anna set her briefcase on the counter. It was plain to see she wasn't happy. "It would've been pretty hard for you to hear anything over all that laughter. I could hear you all the out in the driveway."

"Lenny was just telling us about his days in the Navy," Rona explained as she tried to pinpoint what Anna was so angry about. "You didn't come in through the garage."

"No, I couldn't get my car into the garage."

Lenny jumped up. "I'm sorry. I thought I was over far enough. I'll go move."

"Don't bother," Anna replied sharply. "I parked on the street. If you'll excuse me." She turned and left.

"Anna," Rona called after her.

"Oh, man, I didn't mean to make her mad. I'm sorry, Rona. I swear I thought I was over far enough."

"You are," she replied and exchanged glances with Tammy, who shrugged slightly.

"I think I'd better go."

"No, wait," Rona said. "Let me go see what's going on. She's not angry because you're here. Something must have happened at work. Sit down. I'll be right back." Anna's bedroom door was shut. Rona tapped on the door before pushing it open. "Can I come in?" she asked.

"Looks like you already have." Anna was changing clothes.

"What's going on? You seem angry."

"Angry? Why would I be angry?"

"Anna, I'm not very good at guessing games. If you're pissed at me, I'd rather you just tell me."

Anna turned to her. "All right. I don't like coming home and finding strange men here. I've already told you that."

"Lenny isn't a strange man. You would have already known that

215

if you had given me time to introduce him. He was in Leather and Lace."

"Ah, yes," she said and nodded. "The band."

Rona closed the door. "Look, I don't know what the hell's wrong with you."

Anna took a step toward her and lowered her voice. "I came home expecting a nice quiet evening. I thought you and I had plans. You could have called me. I get here and a strange car is parked in my driveway. It sounds like a party is going on and I find a stranger sitting at my table. The same table, by the way, where I was expecting to find dinner."

"Well, fuck you very much," Rona spat as her fists flew to her hips. "Who the hell do you think you are?"

"I think I'm the owner of this house, or at least I was until it became a halfway house for vagrants."

Rona felt as if she had been slapped. She spun to leave, but Anna grabbed her arm.

"Rona, I'm sorry. Please . . . please, just please forgive me. Today has been—" Her voice broke as she began to sob.

Rona's anger vanished. "What's wrong?" Anna cried harder. "Anna, has something happened to your family?"

She shook her head.

"Then what's wrong?" Rona led her to the bed and helped her sit down. She tried to talk to her, but Anna was crying too hard to listen. Rona gave up talking and held her. Eventually the sobs began to lessen. "Can you tell me what's wrong now?" Rona asked cautiously.

"I can only tell you part of it. I have a client who owns a small company. I helped them set up their retirement plan. Anyway, this company went public last year. They recently found out that the item they manufacture is going to be used by the federal government. As soon as this is announced, this company's stock is going to skyrocket from its current price of about eight dollars a share to"—she waved her hands in the air. "It's impossible to say, but there's no reason why it shouldn't hit fifty dollars before it starts to level off. I was in the process of helping them expand their retirement plan to include profit-sharing." Anna stopped and took a deep breath. "Neal was at lunch and I really needed a file he has been working on. You know how we keep a spare key beneath our desks?"

Rona's cheeks burned when she recalled pilfering through the desks in Anna's office. She looked away and nodded.

"The file wasn't in the top side drawer where we usually keep the accounts we're working on," Anna said. "I checked the rest of his desk. In the back of the drawer I found a file." She paused again. "I found a confirmation statement showing that Neal had recently purchased over twenty thousand shares of this company's stock."

"I suppose that's considered insider trading," Rona said.

"It's not just that. Rona, he's a twenty-two-year-old college student who makes twenty thousand a year working for me. Where did he come up with one hundred and sixty thousand dollars?"

"What are you going to do?" Rona asked. She held her breath as a fresh stream of tears started sliding down Anna's cheeks.

"I've already done it. I fired him. Then I called the Securities and Exchange Commission and reported him."

Rona stared at her. "What's going to happen to him?"

"He's in jail." Anna sat down beside her. "If he's found guilty, and it's glaringly obvious that he is, he'll go to prison."

"What about you?" Rona's stomach twisted into a knot. "Can you get into trouble over this?"

"No, not me personally. I don't own any stock in the company, but I can't be sure how the publicity will affect us. I'm positive there will be a full-blown investigation."

"But surely people won't hold you accountable for what he did."

"He was an employee. It's bound to cause some backlash." She slid her arm around Rona. "God, I'm so sorry. I was such an ass to your friend."

"Don't worry about Lenny. He's cool."

"You can't tell anyone else what I've told you. I'm going to have to testify against Neal. I was told not to discuss the case with anyone."

Rona kissed her forehead. "Well, I'm not just anyone and I promise I won't talk about it."

"How do I explain my actions to Lenny?"

"Tell him the truth. You had to fire an employee. If anyone asks why you fired him, tell them he was stealing," Rona said as she pulled Anna to her feet. "Come on back and meet him. I think you'll like him."

They started to leave but Anna stopped her again. "I'm sorry about what I said about dinner and the halfway house. I don't know why I said it. Please, don't tell Tammy."

"I won't mention it, but since you brought it up, are you sure you don't resent having us here? We can talk about it later, but I've been thinking. Now that I have a job, maybe I should be looking for a place of my own."

"Don't leave because of what I said." She took Rona's hand. "It did bother me when I saw Lenny sitting at the table. I was jealous."

"Jealous," Rona asked, dumbfounded. "What could you possibly be jealous about?"

"The way he made you laugh. You've never laughed that way with me."

Rona pulled Anna into her arms and kissed her deeply. "And Lenny has never made me feel the way that you do." She looked into her eyes. "Okay?"

"Okay."

"Good, then let's get back out there."

Chapter Thirty-one

When they returned to the kitchen, it was empty. There was a note on the table from Tammy letting them know Lenny was taking her and the kids to dinner.

Anna read the note and moaned. "He must think I'm a first-class bitch."

"Don't worry about it. They probably just wanted to give us some time alone," Rona said as she pulled a chair away from the table and sat down.

"Let's go somewhere," Anna said.

"Where?"

"I don't care. Let's just drive."

Rona hopped up. "Can I drive?"

"Sure."

The phone rang as Anna was getting her keys. "That's probably Mom wanting to know if we'll be there Sunday." She grabbed the phone.

Rona was leaving the room until she realized that it wasn't Mrs. Pagonis on the phone. The look of concern on Anna's face stopped her.

"Can you tell me what he wants? . . . I understand, but it's rather hard for me to drop everything at a moment's notice . . . Yes, I understand that Mr. Tanner is an important client, but he needs to understand that he's not my only client . . . Yes . . ." Anna pressed the heel of her hand against her temple. "I understand but—" There was a long silence as Anna scribbled something on a pad. "Yes," she replied. "I'll be there. Of course, I understand." She hung up the phone.

"What's wrong?"

Anna ripped the page from the pad and crossed her arms. "That was Tanner's secretary. Tanner wants to see me first thing tomorrow morning. He's sending his private jet to pick me up."

"That's the guy from Midland right?"

"Yes." She ran her finger over her lip as she stared at the pad of paper. "Do you think he's already heard about Neal somehow?"

"I don't see how. What makes him think you'll hop on a plane anytime he wants?"

Anna gave a cynical smile and said, "Because he has a boatload of money that he has entrusted to me. He's well aware that I'll jump through hoops to keep his business."

"What do you think he wants?"

Anna's shoulders dropped. "Who knows? I just hope it's not about Neal."

"When do you have to leave?" Rona asked.

"As soon as I can get packed and get to the airport. The plane is already here waiting on me and a car is on its way to pick me up."

"He was pretty damn sure of himself," Rona said as she followed her to the bedroom. "It's eight o'clock at night." It irked her to sit idly by and watch Anna hurting while this Tanner guy ordered her around, but all she could do was watch her pack. "I wish there was something I could do," she said as Anna closed the suitcase.

"Just be here when I get back," Anna said.

"That you can depend on," Rona assured her as she pulled her into her arms and held her.

Anna stepped back when the doorbell rang. "That's probably the driver." She handed Rona her car keys. "Use the car while I'm gone. It'll give you a break from having to take the bus."

Rona took the keys and picked up the suitcase. "You call if you need me."

Anna smiled and kissed her again. "You know I love it when you get all butch like that."

Moments later, Rona stood in the living room alone. She finally went into the kitchen, made herself a salad and ate it while watching television.

It was after nine before Tammy came back. Rona met them when they came in. The girls were loaded down with stuffed animals.

"Where's Lenny?" she asked.

"He wasn't sure whether he should come in or not. He said to tell you he'd come by the store and see you tomorrow or Monday." Tammy was speaking low and looking over Rona's shoulder toward the den.

"She's not here," Rona said.

"Lenny won these for us," Katie announced.

Rona knelt down. "How did he win all these?"

"He picked them up with a big claw," Karla said.

Rona glanced at Tammy.

"I don't know what the thing is called. It's those machines they have all over the place, where you crank this claw around and try to pick up toys."

Rona grinned. "Well, it looks like he's found his calling in life."

"I finally had to make him stop," Tammy said as she ran her hand over the head of a bear Katie was holding.

Rona did a double take when she noticed the smile on Tammy's face. "It doesn't look like the kids were the only ones impressed with Mr. Leonard Wilkes."

"Go on up and get ready for bed," Tammy instructed the girls.

221

"I'll be up in a minute." As soon as they were out of sight, she turned back to Rona. "What's going on with Anna?"

"There was a situation at work and she had to fire the guy who worked for her."

Tammy's eyebrows arched in surprise. "What did he do?"

"I don't really know, but there are legal implications and he's in jail. She's worried about how her other clients are going to react when they hear about the incident."

Tammy nodded. "Where is she now?"

"On her way to Midland, or rather, I guess she's already in Midland. Some rich old fart wanted her there for a meeting first thing tomorrow morning. She was worried he'd already heard about the problems at work."

"If it just happened today I don't see how he could have heard about it so quickly." Tammy ran her hand over her neck. There was a series of loud squeals and laughter from upstairs. "I have to go settle them down. It may take a while with all the sodas and candy he fed them."

Rona smiled and started toward the stairs with her. "That's okay. I'm beat. It sounds like you had a nice time."

Tammy looked at her sharply. "Don't start that."

"What?" Rona tried to look innocent.

"It was just dinner," Tammy assured her.

"Hey, I didn't say anything."

"Yeah, well, you were thinking it."

Rona said good night and went to the room she hadn't slept in since those first few nights here. It had seemed so comforting and warm then. Tonight it seemed cold and lonely. After a few minutes, she tiptoed back downstairs, stretched out on the couch in the den. Too worried about Anna to sleep, she finally gave up and turned on the television. She was trying to concentrate on the movie she was watching when the phone rang. It was Anna.

"How are you?" she asked as soon as she heard Anna's voice.

"Okay, I'm just tired. I've definitely decided I don't like flying on small planes."

"I wish I could be there with you."

222

"I'm sorry our plans for tonight fell through," Anna said.

Rona heard her yawn. "Don't worry about that. There will be plenty of other nights. You should try to sleep. You sound exhausted."

"I am, but I wanted to talk to you and make sure you were all right. We didn't have much time to talk before they called."

"Everything is fine here. I told Tammy you had a problem at work and had to fire Neal. She understood that you were upset."

"I'll make it up to you," Anna promised.

"You just take care of yourself and get home as quickly as you can."

After Anna hung up, Rona couldn't get back into the movie. She finally gave up and turned the television off.

Tammy shook her awake the following morning. "Go get ready for work," she said as Rona swung her feet to the floor. "I'll start the coffee."

As Rona stepped into the shower, she promised herself that she would sleep late tomorrow and Sunday. She hoped Anna would be back by the time she came home from work. Tammy was humming when Rona walked into the kitchen.

"Someone's awfully cheerful this morning," Rona remarked as she poured coffee into the mug by the pot.

"It's Friday," Tammy reminded her.

"Do you have plans for the weekend?"

There seemed to be a slight hesitation before she answered. "No. I thought if the nice weather holds, I might take the girls to the zoo. They've never been. Would you like to go with us?"

Rona shook her head. "No, thanks. I always have this urge to let all the animals loose."

Tammy looked at her and frowned. "In that case, maybe you shouldn't go."

"I'll bet Lenny would love to go to the zoo," Rona said, unable to resist teasing her.

"On second thought, maybe you should go. I could accidentally bump you into the lion's pit around feeding time," Tammy said as she tossed a wadded paper towel at her.

Rona rode the bus to work that morning. She didn't feel comfortable driving Anna's car downtown. As she looked blindly out the window, she wondered how Anna was doing. She had sounded exhausted when she called from the hotel last night. Rona told herself to stop worrying. Anna could handle whatever Tanner threw her way. Rona's thoughts turned to Lenny and Tammy. They would make a cute couple. It was too bad she was still married to Wayne.

The constant rocking of the bus was making her sleepy. She forced herself to clear her mind of everything except the bus's progress and the day ahead of her.

As she was every morning, Verna was there to let Rona in. There were dark circles beneath Verna's eyes. Apparently no one had slept well the previous night, Rona thought, but as she drew closer, she saw there was also a sense of peace, maybe even excitement, showing in her eyes.

"You gave me a lot to think about," Verna said as she led Rona back to the storeroom. "I've decided to start holding the Saturday night jam sessions in the courtyard again."

"That's great," Rona said. "What made you change your mind?"

Verna tilted her head. "I guess it was seeing how excited Jerry got over those people applauding for you all," she said as she handed Rona a cup of coffee. "After you left, that's all he could talk about. It made me realize how important it is for these kids to get a break. Somebody has to help them. Why shouldn't I be the one to do it?"

Rona nodded and sipped her coffee. "I think it's a wonderful idea."

"Good, I want you and your friend to be among my first guests. I'd like to hold the first session on the first Saturday in April."

Surprised, Rona stared at her for a moment. "Verna, that's wonderful. I'm sure Lenny will be thrilled, but I really don't want to perform anymore."

"Not even to showcase your own songs?"

That stopped Rona cold. It hadn't occurred to her that she

224

could play her own material. "Couldn't someone else perform the song?"

"No, that was one of Sam's only rules. If you wrote the song, you had to be part of the performance. If you can't carry a tune, that's fine, someone else can sing, but I know you can play a piano, so you will have to at least act as an accompaniment."

Rona didn't know what to say. She would be thrilled to be able to have her songs showcased, but she really didn't want to be pulled back into that part of the business. It was too demanding and she was at a point in her life where she was ready to settle down in one place and stay there. But if a single performance would give one of her songs a chance to be heard, she had to take it. "Okay, but just this one time."

"Great. If your stuff is any good, you'll only need the one time," Verna said. "Now, all I have to do is find a few more performers and clean the place up."

"I'll be happy to help you fix up the courtyard. I can help after work and on Saturdays," Rona said. "What about Jerry?" she asked.

Verna frowned. "I'm sure he'll volunteer to help."

"No, I mean performing."

"Do you think he's that good?" Verna asked, clearly surprised.

"I've heard worse. He needs some polishing but he has some talent. I think he could do fine working with a house band."

"If you both run off at the same time, I'm going to find myself short-handed."

Rona held up her hand. "Verna, I give you my solemn promise, I won't be running off anywhere. I'm very happy where I am in my life right now, and I plan on remaining there for many years." As soon as the words left her mouth, Rona wondered if she had tempted fate.

Chapter Thirty-two

Rona was in the storeroom filing a new shipment of sheet music when Jerry came back to tell her she had a phone call. Thinking it was Anna calling to let her know she was home, Rona ran to the phone.

The man's voice on the line threw her for a moment. "Malcolm is here. He needs to see you today," Domingo said.

"Is he all right?" she asked.

"Yes and no. He had trouble with some bad *hombres*. He's not hurt," he replied.

"I can't get there until around six this afternoon," she said. Her lunch hour was too short to get there and back. "Ask him if that's soon enough." Going to see him would mean she would miss her bus and have to take the later one, but if he was asking to see her something was wrong. There was a muttered exchange before Domingo came back on the line.

"He can hide here till you come."

"What do you mean, hide?" she asked, but he had already hung up. Before going back to work, she tried calling the house, but no one answered. She hung up and called Anna's office. Sharon told her that Anna had called and said she would be spending another night in Midland. When Rona pressed her for details, she grew vague and told her she had another line ringing.

Business picked up and she was too busy to worry about anything. She was ten minutes late in leaving the music store and was forced to jog most of the fifteen or so blocks to the Taco Haven.

When she finally arrived she was so winded she could barely speak. Domingo saw her and nodded to the back of the room. Malcolm's beard and hair were longer and more unkempt than she ever remembered seeing them. His long legs stretched out across the aisle. She slapped him on the shoulder before sliding into a chair across from him.

"Where have you been? I've been worried about you."

He was staring at her.

"What?" she asked.

"You're looking good," he said in his slow measured cadence. "I hear you have a real job."

She grinned and nodded.

"I am glad for you."

Domingo came back with two coffees. "Are you hungry?"

"Yeah," Rona said even though she really wasn't. "I'll have a couple of the *carne guisada* tacos."

"Why do I even ask? You always order the same thing?" Domingo replied.

"What about you, Malcolm, what do you want?" she asked.

He looked at her before he ordered. "The same for me please."

Rona tried not to notice how badly his hand shook as he picked up the cup of coffee. They sat in silence until Domingo arrived with the food and it was all consumed. Rona gave her second taco to Malcolm and he finished it without effort.

When Domingo refilled their cups and left, Rona leaned forward. "Okay, Malcolm, what gives?"

"I'm in plenty of trouble."

"Are the cops after you?"

227

"No. It's not that kind of trouble." He settled in to tell his story. "On the day after that last time I saw you, I went over to the Ministry to see if the men in trucks need workers, but no one picks me. After they leave I wait around thinking maybe someone else will come. It gets late. Then Roach and Harper come with No Talk Willie and Mr. Lincoln. Then Soldier Man comes and we talk until it gets near dark."

No Talk Willie was a mousey little man who either couldn't or wouldn't speak. She usually tried to avoid him because he gave her the creeps. Mr. Lincoln was a tall gaunt man who could have easily passed as the original Mr. Lincoln's brother. Soldier Man was a quiet guy who wore a Purple Heart pinned to his lapel. She didn't know if the medal belonged to him or not.

"While we talk a truck comes with two men. We are surprised. Trucks do not come so late. The big man with scar"—he drew his finger horizontally across his chin—"he tells us he needs men for two maybe three weeks to go to Floresville and he promises us much money. We all go. To work that long is good and to make that much money." He held his hands up as if in prayer.

"Where's Floresville?" she asked.

He drew a little circle on the table and pointed at it. "It is a little hamlet maybe eighteen kilometers to the south of here. Soldier Man said there was much farming there and I think this is what we will be doing. However, when we arrive we were put inside a very big building with no windows. There are men who do nothing but walk around with guns watching us. When Roach sees these men he gets scared, but the man who hired us tells us these guns are for security. Then he says if the guns bother us, he will take us back to city and hire men who are not afraid. We only work at night with many other men I did not know. Men like us." He gestured to his shabby clothes.

"They live on the streets too," Rona clarified.

"Yes. We work with the men, but we cannot talk to them. All night, many trucks come and go. When they come we unload boxes from this side of the building," he explained and placed his right hand on the table. "Before they leave we must load box from this side of the building." He used his left hand to indicate the opposite side.

"What was in the boxes?" she asked.

He turned his hands palms up. "We did not know. All we knew was the boxes on the trucks that came in were very, very heavy. The boxes that went out were not so heavy." Rona started to speak, but he held up a hand and stopped her. "There is more I must tell you."

"Okay." She sat back with her coffee.

"We only worked at night. During the day we were taken to an empty house where we slept on bedrolls on the floor. One day Soldier Man tells us he is going to leave, because he thinks we are working for drug men and he does not want to do this. If police find them, we will all go to jail. No Talk Willie agrees. That night when truck comes to take us back to the building to work, Soldier Man tells the men that he and No Talk wants not to work anymore. The man says he will take them back to city."

Rona was dying to ask questions, but Malcolm pressed on.

"I too think about leaving, but I was greedy for the money they say they will pay us." He stopped and shook his head sadly. "I never learn. I am always greedy for money."

"What happened?" Rona prompted, unable to remain silent any longer.

"The truck takes us to building and the man asks if we also wish to leave. I almost say yes, but I am very greedy, only Soldier Man and No Talk Willie leave. When the truck comes back in the morning to get us, one of the men is wearing Solider Man's medal." His hands began to shake so badly he had to set his coffee cup down.

Rona took his hands as tears began to roll down his haggard face. "What happened then, Malcolm?"

"The man with the medal had blood on his pants."

"Are you sure it was blood?" Rona asked as her gut clenched.

He nodded vigorously. "I know what blood looks like. I have seen much blood."

"I believe you." She handed him a napkin to dry his tears. "What happened next?"

"After that I get very scared. I think something bad happened and these men did not take Soldier Man and No Talk back to city. When they take us back to house in the morning, I tell others what I think happened. Harper hits me very hard and tells to me keep quiet. As soon as we get our money we will leave, but I do not think they will pay us. I wait until everyone is asleep and I sneak away. I walk through fields for many days taking food wherever I can find it, until I make it back here to the city. I feel safe again. Then people tell me a big man with a scar on his chin is asking for me. I am afraid these men will find me. I try to find you, but you are gone. I am very scared."

Rona squeezed his hand. "You don't have to be scared. We'll figure out something. Do you think you could find your way back to this building where you worked?"

His eyes grew round. "Yes, I watched the road very closely, but I do not wish to go back there."

She shook her head. "I don't want you to go back, but if you could tell the police where it was, they could arrest these men."

Malcolm fingered his grizzled beard as he lowered his head. "I cannot go to see the police."

"Why not?"

"If I do, it is me they will put in jail."

"No, they won't. You didn't know you were doing anything illegal and when you started to suspect something was wrong, you left."

"The police look for me for many years, now. I did a bad thing many years ago."

Domingo started toward them with the coffeepot, but Rona shook her head to stop him. He gave an elaborate shrug and went back to reading his paper.

"What did you do, Malcolm?"

He folded his massive hands on the table. "I came to this country thirty years ago, when I was a young man."

"How old are you?" Rona asked.

"I am fifty-two, I think," he added with a frown.

Rona tried to hide her shock. He looked much older. She had assumed he was closer to seventy. "I'm sorry, I interrupted you. Please finish your story."

He nodded slightly. "I was at the university and a white man came. This man, Mr. Douglas, told me he would pay me much money if I would come to America and learn to play basketball. I think this man is daft to want to pay me so much money." He pointed to his head. "I tell him yes, but only if my sister Njeri can come with me. We were alone, our parents were dead." He smiled and glanced at Rona. "My sister Njeri is one year younger but much smarter than me. She says Kepha—" He stopped. "That is my real name Kepha Ooko."

Stunned, Rona didn't know what to say, so she simply nodded and waited for him to continue.

"Njeri says I am greedy to want so much money." He opened his hands. "She was correct. I read about American cars that go very fast and many things that I could never have in Kenya. Njeri did not want to come to America. I tell her I am the man and she will do what I say. That was very big mistake." He shook his head sadly.

"What happened?"

"I did not learn to play basketball like the white man wanted. I could not bounce the ball and run. Although I practice many hours, I could not learn." He gave a great sigh. "I wanted to be a teacher of art. When I could not learn basketball Mr. Douglas told me I must leave. I asked for my money. He laughed at me and told me I had no money. I must get a job and work. Then he called me a very bad name and I hurt him. I hit him very hard, many times. There was much blood and he said the police would get me. I ran home. Njeri told me I must turn myself in, but I could not. I ran away," he whispered as tears filled his eyes again. "I left little Njeri alone."

"Malcolm—or Kepha—" Rona began.

"I am Malcolm now," he told her.

She nodded. "Okay, Malcolm, this man, Mr. Douglas, cheated

231

you and was trying to scare you. I don't think the police are look-ing for you." She tried to convince him to go to the police but he wouldn't listen. Finally, she gave up and tried a different approach. "Will you tell me how to get there? I can call the police and leave an anonymous tip. I'll call them from a pay phone and they won't know who I am."

"What about the big man with the scar? He will find me."

Rona looked at him. Even if the police followed up on the tip and raided the place, they wouldn't catch everyone involved. If those trucks were coming and going, then obviously there was someone on the other end of their route. She knew there was only one solution for Malcolm. "I think you're going to have to leave San Antonio." The fear in his eyes hurt her. "I'll help you," she promised. "I have a job. I can help you go somewhere else. Where do you want to go?"

He fingered his beard again. "I want to find Njeri," he replied.

She nodded. "Okay. Where does she live? I'll buy you a bus ticket tonight."

"I do not know where she is. I never talked to her after I ran away. I was too ashamed."

Rona tried to keep the shock out of her voice. "You don't know where your sister is?"

"No."

"You've not talked to her in thirty years."

"That is true. All I have is this."

He reached beneath the many sweaters he was wearing and pulled out a cheap plastic kid's purse. As he slid back the zipper, Rona saw the faded image of Strawberry Shortcake. From the purse, he carefully extracted a worn piece of paper. With infinite care, he unfolded it and smoothed it out before handing it to her.

It looked like a photocopy of a newspaper article stating that Professor Njeri Ooko was leaving Columbia University to return to her native homeland of Kenya.

Rona stared at the article. How could she possibly find this woman if she was living in Kenya? She had no idea where to start.

232

"You are very smart like Njeri. With this"—he pointed to the paper—"you can find her?" His eyes searched her face, pleading.

"How did you get this?" she asked, holding up the paper.

"At the library, a very nice woman taught me to use the Internet. Everyday, I would go and search for my Njeri. This is all I ever find."

Rona searched the article again. There was no date to indicate when the article had been published. She handed it back to him and watched as he carefully refolded it before placing it back inside the small purse.

"You will find her for me?" he asked as he hid the purse beneath the bulk of sweaters.

"I don't know how, but we'll find her," she promised. She felt horrible for lying to him. How could she possibly find his sister? The brilliant smile on his face only made her feel worse.

The yellowed Nehi clock behind the counter indicated it was a little after eight. Surprised by the amount of time that had slipped away, she stood up.

"Wait here. I need to make a phone call." She wanted to let Tammy know she would be home late. As she walked toward the front, she realized that it was well beyond closing time for Domingo. She apologized for keeping him.

He stopped reading long enough to wave off her apology. "I live in the back," he said. "I'm always home."

"Can I borrow your phone?"

He nodded, pointed to it and went back to his paper.

She dialed Anna's number. When there was no answer, she hung up before the machine could kick on. She tried to decide what to do. Malcolm had to be kept somewhere safe. It wouldn't be easy for a man as tall as Malcolm was to go unnoticed. If the man with the scar was still looking for him, he would be searching the streets. For now, she needed to find him a safe place to stay while she searched for his sister.

Chapter Thirty-three

An hour later, Rona and Malcolm were in a cheap motel room located at the edge of downtown. She had rented the room under her name while Malcolm remained hidden outside. As tall as he was, he would be certain to be remembered if anyone came around asking about him.

"I'll try to find you something better tomorrow," she promised as she looked around the dingy room.

He poked the bed with his finger. "This is a very good bed. I will be fine. When will you find my sister?"

"I don't know," she admitted as she searched for a delicate way to say what she needed to tell him. "Malcolm, we need to change the way you look."

He smiled a wide smile. "You give me a disguise, like on the television."

She laughed. "I don't know if I could do a disguise, but I think we can change the way you look by cutting your hair and shaving off your beard."

He looked horrified. "Then my face will get cold."

"You won't have to worry about being cold anymore. I'm going to help you." Somehow, she added to herself.

After making him promise he wouldn't leave the room for any reason, Rona headed home. By the time she arrived, it was after eleven. Tired to the bone, she checked the answering machine, hoping Anna had called and left a message. The electronic voice advised her there were no new messages. She went upstairs and knocked softly on Tammy's door.

Tammy opened the door right away, still fully dressed. "Are you just coming in?" she asked.

Rona smiled. "Yes, Mother, and how long have you been home? You weren't home when I called earlier." The deep pink that tinted Tammy's cheeks gratified her. "I need to talk to you."

Tammy nodded and followed her downstairs.

They sat at the kitchen table while Rona quickly repeated Malcolm's story. When she reached the point about the man returning wearing Soldier Man's Purple Heart, tears formed in Tammy's eyes. "Did you know him?" Rona asked.

Tammy nodded. "He used to give the girls fresh fruit. I never knew where he got it. He would just show up at that old warehouse we stayed in for a while and bring them a bag of apples or oranges, or some other type of fruit."

"I never really talked to him," Rona admitted.

"He didn't talk much, but one night he was drunk and told me he had been a tunnel rat in Vietnam. After that one night he never mentioned it again."

They fell silent for a moment before Rona continued with Malcolm's story.

"What are you going to do?" Tammy asked when Rona finished.

"I can't afford to keep him in a motel for long. I thought I'd ask Lenny if he could stay with him for a while. The problem is, I don't know if he lives in an apartment or a house. He may not have room for him."

"He lives in a small house, but there's a spare bedroom,"

Tammy replied. The kitchen grew quiet as they stared at each other. "Today was the first time I've been there. He invited us over for a barbecue," she said defensively.

"Does he know about Wayne?"

Tammy nodded. "I told him everything. Besides, there's nothing going on between us. We're just friends."

Rona held up her hand. "I don't need to know."

"There's nothing to know."

"I suppose he's at work now," Rona said.

"Yes, but he's picking me and the girls up at ten tomorrow. We're going to the zoo."

Rona stretched. "There's nothing else I can do tonight. I'm going to bed." Long after she went to bed, she lay staring at the ceiling wondering why Anna was still in Midland and why she hadn't called.

A knock on her door woke her the next morning. Tammy poked her head in.

"I just talked to Lenny. He said Malcolm can stay with him until we find his sister or make other arrangements for him."

Rona sat up in bed. "Great. Just give me the address and I'll get him over there sometime after you guys get back from the zoo."

"It's raining. We aren't going."

"Oh. Sorry."

"I told him we would bring Malcolm over," Tammy said. "Lenny said he might be able to help locate Malcolm's sister. I didn't remember her name, but he said he could search the Internet and see what he can find, once we get there."

Rona rubbed her face to hide her smile.

Three hours later, they were all at Lenny's house. Rona had decided to take up Anna's offer to use her car and drove it downtown to pick up Malcolm.

After they arrived at Lenny's, Tammy got busy trimming

Malcolm's hair while Rona and Lenny began searching the Internet. After an hour with nothing to show for their efforts, Rona went to see how the barbering was going. As she walked through the living room, she found the twins completely engrossed in some cartoon.

In the kitchen, she found a freshly clipped and shaved Malcolm sitting at the kitchen table wrapped in a blanket. "Wow, you look different," she said.

"I feel very different," he agreed and smiled.

"I'm washing his clothes," Tammy called out.

Rona went toward the voice and found her in a small utility room.

"They're almost dry." Tammy lowered her voice and added, "They're in pretty bad shape."

"Do the best you can. I'll take him to Goodwill this afternoon and find him a couple of decent outfits."

"Yo, man. I almost didn't recognize you," Lenny said.

Tammy and Rona left the utility room in time to see Lenny waving a sheet of paper at them. "What's that?" Rona asked.

"It's a marriage announcement from nineteen eighty-three for one Miss Njeri Ooko to Mr. Edward Beasley of Philadelphia."

Malcolm began to laugh and clap. "I have a family."

Rona punched the air with her fist. "Yes. You are the man, Leonard Wilkes," she said as she grabbed him and gave him a hug.

"Watch it with the Leonard," he warned.

"All we have to do now is to see if we can find a number for Edward Beasley of Philadelphia," Rona said.

Lenny removed a sheet of paper from behind the one he had been waving. "As usual, I'm way ahead of you. I received eight hits. All we need to do is start calling."

Their elation gave way to disappointment as the names on the list began to be eliminated. Only two of the phone numbers couldn't be verified. One was no longer in service. No one answered at the other one.

"I'll go back and start looking again," Lenny said. "Now that I have a city, I can check the Philadelphia papers. I might be able to find birth announcements or something else. If nothing turns up there, I'll check the colleges. You said she was a professor, right?" he asked and looked at Rona.

"Yes," she replied as she watched Malcolm's earlier joy melt away. "She was at Columbia University."

Lenny clasped Malcolm's shoulder. "Don't give up. I have a friend who's still in the Navy. He's a genius on anything dealing with the Internet. I'll send him an e-mail and ask him to work his magic."

"Thank you, Lenny," he replied.

The hours ticked away. Rona wanted to call home to see if Anna had made it in, but the phone line was tied up with the computer. It was after six when she stretched out on the couch and fell asleep. She was in the middle of a wonderful dream about Anna when Tammy shook her awake.

"What?" she asked as she sat up.

"Lenny's friend found her," Tammy said as she danced a little jig of excitement.

"Are you sure? I mean, is he sure it's really her?"

"We called and Malcolm talked to her already. She left Kenya five years ago and is now living in Philadelphia."

Rona felt a twinge of disappointment that she had been left out of the monumental moment. "How did it go?"

"She wants him to come live with them. Oh, Rona, he was so happy."

"Why didn't you wake me up?" she asked peevishly.

"It all happened so fast. I'm sorry."

"Don't be. I'm just whining. The important thing is he found her," Rona said. "What time is it?"

"It's a little after ten," Tammy said as she sat down on the couch beside Rona.

"I can't believe I slept for four hours," She rubbed her eyes. "I guess I should call the bus station and see if there's a bus out of here tonight that I can put him on."

"That's not necessary," Lenny replied as he and Malcolm came into the room.

"Did you hear, Rona? My sister has been found in Philadelphia. She is working at a school for special children." He leaned over and gave her an awkward hug. "You said you would find her."

"Lenny found her," Rona said.

"Yes, but you found Lenny."

They all laughed, then Rona turned to Lenny. "Why isn't it necessary to call the bus station?"

"Njeri has arranged to have a ticket waiting for Malcolm at the airport. His flight leaves at five-thirty tomorrow morning." He showed her the e-mailed confirmation for the ticket Njeri had purchased.

Malcolm was smiling so, Rona was certain his jaws were aching. She stood up. "Come on, Malcolm. We have a couple of more things to do before you leave."

He tilted his head. "What more do I need to do?"

"It's time to go shopping," Rona insisted.

Malcolm looked at Lenny. "Sorry, man," Lenny said. "You're on your own with this one. Once women get you in the store you're stuck there for hours."

Before they left the house, Rona called Domingo to let him know Malcolm was somewhere safe. She didn't mention where Malcolm was, and Domingo was smart enough not to ask.

An hour later, Rona and Malcolm were at a twenty-four-hour Wal-Mart. They found him two pair of pants, along with shirts, shoes, socks and underwear as well as some personal hygiene items. On the way to the register, they found him a small carry-on bag. Rona tried not to cringe as the clerk rang up the purchases and gave her the total.

"I will pay you back," he insisted as they made their way to the parking lot.

"Don't worry about it." She stopped to look up at him. "You know, I'm not sure I would have made it out there on the streets without your help." She waited until they got into the car. "You know, there's one more thing we have to do before you leave." In the reflection of the parking lot lights, she could see the fear in his eyes.

"Yes," he agreed.

They drove to a nearby convenience store. From the pay phone, Malcolm called 911 and gave them directions to the building where he had been working. While he was calling, Rona went to a nearby ATM and withdrew more of her precious savings.

After they returned to Lenny's house, they agreed that because of the flight's early departure time, Lenny would take Malcolm to the airport. Rona hung back as Tammy said good-bye to Malcolm before helping Lenny get the sleeping twins into the car.

When they were alone, Rona pressed the folded bills into Malcolm's hand. "This is two hundred dollars to help you get started," she told him.

"I cannot take your money," he said as he tried to give her the bills back.

"Please, take it. You'll need a little something until you can find a job."

"Thank you." His eyes filled with tears and he hugged her tightly. "I shall never forget you, Miss Rona Kirby."

"Nor I you, Mr. Malcolm . . . Kepha Ooko."

He bowed slightly and smiled.

Rona rushed out before he could see her tears.

Tammy and Rona were silent as they drove back to Anna's house. Rona wondered if the police would take Malcolm's call seriously and check into it or if they'd think it was a prank. She didn't like Roach or Harper, but she didn't want to think about someone killing them either.

"Did you leave the kitchen light on?" Tammy asked as they pulled into the driveway.

"I don't think so," Rona said as a spark of excitement ran through her. "Maybe Anna came home."

"Look at you," Tammy teased.

"What?" Rona protested as she pulled the car into the garage.

"You're like a kid on Christmas morning. You can't wait to get into that house."

"You're so full of it," Rona scoffed. She jumped out of the car

240

and threw open the back door to get Katie. It had been a while since she had lifted either child. "Crap," she grunted as she picked her up. "What have you been feeding this kid?"

Tammy looked at her from the other side of the car. "Three meals a day, thanks to you and Anna."

"Did I hear my name?"

They turned to find Anna holding the kitchen door open for them.

"I was beginning to think everyone had moved away and left me," she said with a smile, her eyes following Rona.

"It's been a busy couple of days," Tammy replied as they trudged into the house.

"I just opened a bottle of wine," Anna said as she gently squeezed Rona's arm. "Shall I get out extra glasses while you two put the twins to bed?"

"May as well," Tammy said. "I'm too revved up to sleep anyway."

Anna winked at Rona as they headed up the stairs. Rona was relieved. Anna's meeting with Tanner must have gone all right.

After they put the girls to bed, Tammy stopped Rona in the hallway. "If you'd rather be alone, you can tell her one of the girls woke up and I decided to stay up here with them."

Rona took her by the arm. "Come on down. I want to hear all about you and Lenny."

"There's nothing between us," Tammy protested.

"Excuse me, but I've known Lenny for a long time and he spent the entire day watching every step you made."

Tammy smiled. "Well, he is very nice."

When they reached the kitchen, Anna poured the wine and they gathered around the kitchen table. "What happened with Tanner?" Rona asked before Anna sat down.

"He wanted me to sit in on a meeting with a group that was wanting him to invest in a particular venture, and then afterward he asked if I would review the portfolio of an old friend of his."

"Wow. Does any of this mean extra business for you?" Rona

asked. Anna appeared relaxed. Rona suspected the meeting with Tanner had kept Anna too busy to worry herself sick over Neal. "Yes," Anna replied. "His friend is going to become a client." She smiled and rubbed her forehead. "I told him all about the problems with Neal. I didn't want to take a chance of him hearing about it elsewhere. He said he understood and he appreciated the way I was upfront with him." She looked at them. "Now, tell me about your day."

Epilogue

Four Weeks Later

Rona walked around the courtyard for one final inspection. Two long tables loaded with barbecue and side dishes sat off to the side. A dozen picnic tables were arranged in the center. White twinkle lights were strung across the area and secured to wooden poles that had been bolted into the brick walls of the buildings. At the front stood the stage, with equipment ready for guitars to be plugged in.

During the past three weeks, she and Jerry had rebuilt the stage and repaired and painted the wooden benches and tables. Verna had pulled weeds and cleaned the area.

Verna called several club owners she knew and gathered names of new musicians who possessed enough talent to warrant the attention of music scouts. Then she began putting out the word to those who were looking for new acts.

"I believe you're more nervous that I am," Verna said as Rona stepped back inside.

"I just wanted to make sure everything was as it should be," Rona said.

"Are you ready?" Verna asked.

"As much as I'll ever be."

"Good. Then go find Anna and go for a walk. I'll handle everything from here on out. You concentrate on selling that song of yours."

"Are you sure? What if something goes wrong?"

"Then it'll get fixed."

Rona nodded and reluctantly left. She found Anna talking to Tammy and Lenny. When she joined them she was pleased to see that Anna was wearing the pendant watch she'd had repaired for her birthday.

Anna slipped an arm around her. "Are you all right?"

"Why does everyone keep asking that?"

"Because you look like you're about to heave," Lenny said as he rocked back and forth on his heels.

"And you're driving us all nuts with that rocking," Tammy told him.

"Maybe we should all go for a walk." Rona nodded toward the door.

The warm April air felt good when she stepped out. The fragrant smell of mountain laurel drifted on the breeze. Tammy and Lenny walked ahead of them. As they strolled, she and Anna gradually slipped farther behind.

"I'm scared," Rona admitted.

"I know you are, but you shouldn't be. I've heard the song. It's wonderful. You're going to be great."

"What if no one wants it?"

"Then you'll write another song and another for as long as it takes. If you want it bad enough, you know it will eventually happen."

She took a deep breath and slowly released it. "Maybe that scares me too."

Anna squeezed her arm. "What, you're afraid of being successful?"

"It's just that the more I have, the more I could lose."

"Rona, you aren't going to end up back on the streets. I promise you that. Tell me what I have to do to make you feel safe."

Rona didn't have the heart to tell her that she would never again have that fragile sense of security. She had seen how quickly it could all fall apart. She leaned over and kissed Anna's cheek. "Don't listen to me. I'm just whining to keep from worrying about screwing up tonight."

They walked for a while in silence. Rona stopped when she realized she was in a familiar area. As she looked around she thought about the past few weeks. So much had happened in such a short time. A billboard advertising a bank product made her think of Neal. "Did you ever find out where Neal got all that money?" she asked.

Anna sighed. "I don't know too much about it, but it seems he borrowed the bulk of it from his parents and grandparents."

"What a waste. He had so much going for him," Rona said.

"He got greedy."

Rona spotted a familiar landmark. "See that vacant building over there." She pointed to a three-story brick building that had large sheets of plywood secured over its windows.

Anna nodded.

"That's where I first met Tammy. There used to be a door to the alley that wouldn't lock and a bunch of us would slip in after dark. Malcolm and I went in one night and there Tammy was with those two kids. I don't know how she survived." A silence fell between them again as Rona continued to stare at the building. She had been checking the newspapers daily, but so far, there had been no mention of a drug bust or any other type of major police action in Floresville. Maybe the police had blown off Malcolm's call. She said as much to Anna.

"Oh, I almost forgot. I have something for you." Anna reached into her pocket. "A letter came for you today."

Rona looked at her and frowned. "A letter? Who would be sending me a letter?"

Anna smiled. "The return address was for Kepha Ooko of Philadelphia."

"Malcolm."

"Yes. I saved it until now, hoping it would help distract you."

Anna handed her the letter as they stepped into the bright glow of a street lamp.

Rona opened the letter. Inside she found a single sheet of paper carefully wrapped around a check. She skimmed the note. "He's working at an arts center," she said. "And he's painting again. He's still living with his sister and her husband, but he's hoping to find his own place soon." She glanced at the check before slipping it into her pocket. He had reimbursed her for the clothing and the cash she had given him.

"You're a good person," Anna said suddenly.

"I didn't do nearly as much as you did," Rona reminded her. "You took Tammy and me into your home. I'm not sure I could have done that." They turned the corner in time to see Tammy and Lenny steal a quick kiss. "It was nice of your mom to watch Tammy's girls tonight."

"She loves those kids. They're like her own now." Anna nodded toward Tammy and Lenny. "What do you think they're going to do?"

"I don't know, but Tammy actually mentioned the D word the other day."

"D word?" Anna asked, clearly confused.

"Divorce. I got the impression she's starting to think about looking into divorcing Wayne."

"I don't think he would have much of a chance in getting custody of the girls. I'm sure he'll think twice about harassing her if he has to contend with Lenny."

Rona stopped and pulled Anna into the shadows of a building. "There's something I want you to know. No matter what happens tonight, I love you. I have loved you for so long, but I was afraid to admit it." She leaned in and kissed Anna.

"I love you, too," Anna whispered as they embraced.

246

"Hey, guys, we need to head back," Lenny yelled from somewhere nearby.

Anna gave her another quick kiss and they started back.

Rona sat at the keyboard and stared out over the crowd. Verna was introducing her to the crowd and telling them how Rona had convinced her to start holding the Saturday night jam sessions again. As she looked around, she found herself thinking about Malcolm and how he had found his sister, and in a different way, she and Tammy had found a family too. In her heart, she knew that if she didn't sell the song tonight everything would still be all right with her.

She took a deep breath as Verna turned to her and announced to the crowd, "I'll let Rona introduce the song to you."

To stem her nervousness, Rona lightly fingered a few chords as she once more looked out over the crowd. "I'd like to welcome everyone tonight," she began. "This song was written for the person I love most in life. It's entitled, 'When Love Finds A Home.'"

Publications from
BELLA BOOKS, INC.
The best in contemporary lesbian fiction

P.O. Box 10543, Tallahassee, FL 32302
Phone: 800-729-4992
www.bellabooks.com

WHEN LOVE FINDS A HOME by Megan Carter. 280 pp. What will it take for Anna and
Rona to find their way back to each other again?   1-59493-041-4 $12.95

MEMORIES TO DIE FOR by Adrian Gold. 240 pp. Rachel Katz, a forensic psychologist,
attempts to avoid her attraction to the charms of Anna Sigurdson. Will Anna's persistence and
patience get her past Rachel's fears of a broken heart?   1-59493-038-4 $12.95

SILENT HEART by Claire McNab. 280 pp. Exotic lesbian romance.
                                                          1-59493-044-9 $12.95

MIDNIGHT RAIN by Peggy J. Herring. 240 pp. Bridget McBee is determined to find the
woman who saved her life.   1-59493-021-X $12.95

THE MISSING PAGE A Brenda Strange Mystery by Patty G. Henderson. 240 pp. Brenda
investigates her client's murder . . .   1-59493-004-X $12.95

WHISPERS ON THE WIND by Frankie J. Jones. 240 pp. Dixon thinks she and her best
friend, Elizabeth Colter, would make the perfect couple . . .   1-59493-037-6 $12.95

CALL OF THE DARK: EROTIC LESBIAN TALES OF THE SUPERNATURAL edited
by Therese Szymanski—from Bella After Dark. 320 pp.   1-59493-040-6 $14.95

A TIME TO CAST AWAY A Helen Black Mystery by Pat Welch. 240 pp. Helen stops by
Alice's apartment—only to find the woman dead . . .   1-59493-036-8 $12.95

DESERT OF THE HEART by Jane Rule. 224 pp. The book that launched the most popu-
lar lesbian movie of all time is back.   1-1-59493-035-X $12.95

THE NEXT WORLD by Ursula Steck. 240 pp. Anna's friend Mido is threatened and eventually disappears . . .   1-59493-024-4 $12.95

CALL SHOTGUN by Jaime Clevenger. 240 pp. Kelly gets pulled back into the world of
private investigation . . .   1-59493-016-3 $12.95

52 PICKUP by Bonnie J. Morris and E.B. Casey. 240 pp. 52 hot, romantic tales—one for
every Saturday night of the year.   1-59493-026-0 $12.95

GOLD FEVER by Lyn Denison. 240 pp. Kate's first love, Ashley, returns to their home
town, where Kate now lives . . .   1-1-59493-039-2 $12.95

RISKY INVESTMENT by Beth Moore. 240 pp. Lynn's best friend and roommate needs her
to pretend Chris is his fiancé. But nothing is ever easy.   1-59493-019-8 $12.95

HUNTER'S WAY by Gerri Hill. 240 pp. Homicide detective Tori Hunter is forced to team
up with the hot-tempered Samantha Kennedy.   1-59493-018-X $12.95

CAR POOL by Karin Kallmaker. 240 pp. Soft shoulders, merging traffic and slippery when wet . . . Anthea and Shay find love in the car pool.   1-59493-013-9 $12.95

NO SISTER OF MINE by Jeanne G'Fellers. 240 pp. Telepathic women fight to coexist with a patriarchal society that wishes their eradication.   ISBN 1-59493-017-1 $12.95

ON THE WINGS OF LOVE by Megan Carter. 240 pp. Stacie's reporting career is on the rocks. She has to interview bestselling author Cheryl, or else! ISBN 1-59493-027-9 $12.95

WICKED GOOD TIME by Diana Tremain Braund. 224 pp. Does Christina need Miki as a protector . . . or want her as a lover?   ISBN 1-59493-031-7 $12.95

THOSE WHO WAIT by Peggy J. Herring. 240 pp. Two brilliant sisters—in love with the same woman!   ISBN 1-59493-032-5 $12.95

ABBY'S PASSION by Jackie Calhoun. 240 pp. Abby's bipolar sister helps turn her world upside down, so she must decide what's most important.   ISBN 1-59493-014-7 $12.95

PICTURE PERFECT by Jane Vollbrecht. 240 pp. Kate is reintroduced to Casey, the daughter of an old friend. Can they withstand Kate's career?   ISBN 1-59493-015-5 $12.95

PAPERBACK ROMANCE by Karin Kallmaker. 240 pp. Carolyn falls for tall, dark and . . . female . . . in this classic lesbian romance.   ISBN 1-59493-033-3 $12.95

DAWN OF CHANGE by Gerri Hill. 240 pp. Susan ran away to find peace in remote Kings Canyon—then she met Shawn . . .   ISBN 1-59493-011-2 $12.95

DOWN THE RABBIT HOLE by Lynne Jamneck. 240 pp. Is a killer holding a grudge against FBI Agent Samantha Skellar?   ISBN 1-59493-012-0 $12.95

SEASONS OF THE HEART by Jackie Calhoun. 240 pp. Overwhelmed, Sara saw only one way out—leaving . . .   ISBN 1-59493-030-9 $12.95

TURNING THE TABLES by Jessica Thomas. 240 pp. The 2nd Alex Peres Mystery. *From ghosties and ghoulies and long leggity beasties* . . .   ISBN 1-59493-009-0 $12.95

FOR EVERY SEASON by Frankie Jones. 240 pp. Andi, who is investigating a 65-year-old murder, meets Janice, a charming district attorney . . .   ISBN 1-59493-010-4 $12.95

LOVE ON THE LINE by Laura DeHart Young. 240 pp. Kay leaves a younger woman behind to go on a mission to Alaska . . . will she regret it?   ISBN 1-59493-008-2 $12.95

UNDER THE SOUTHERN CROSS by Claire McNab. 200 pp. Lee, an American travel agent, goes down under and meets Australian Alex, and the sparks fly under the Southern Cross.   ISBN 1-59493-029-5 $12.95

SUGAR by Karin Kallmaker. 240 pp. Three women want sugar from Sugar, who can't make up her mind.   ISBN 1-59493-001-5 $12.95

FALL GUY by Claire McNab. 200 pp. 16th Detective Inspector Carol Ashton Mystery.
ISBN 1-59493-000-7 $12.95

ONE SUMMER NIGHT by Gerri Hill. 232 pp. Johanna swore to never fall in love again—but then she met the charming Kelly . . .   ISBN 1-59493-007-4 $12.95

TALK OF THE TOWN TOO by Saxon Bennett. 181 pp. Second in the series about wild and fun loving friends.   ISBN 1-931513-77-5 $12.95

LOVE SPEAKS HER NAME by Laura DeHart Young. 170 pp. Love and friendship, desire and intrigue, spark this exciting sequel to *Forever and the Night*.
ISBN 1-59493-002-3 $12.95

TO HAVE AND TO HOLD by Peggy J. Herring. 184 pp. By finally letting down her defenses, will Dorian be opening herself to a devastating betrayal?
ISBN 1-59493-005-8 $12.95

WILD THINGS by Karin Kallmaker. 228 pp. Dutiful daughter Faith has met the perfect man. There's just one problem: she's in love with his sister. ISBN 1-931513-64-3 $12.95

SHARED WINDS by Kenna White. 216 pp. Can Emma rebuild more than just Lanny's marina?
ISBN 1-59493-006-6 $12.95

THE UNKNOWN MILE by Jaime Clevenger. 253 pp. Kelly's world is getting more and more complicated every moment.
ISBN 1-931513-57-0 $12.95

TREASURED PAST by Linda Hill. 189 pp. A shared passion for antiques leads to love.
ISBN 1-59493-003-1 $12.95

SIERRA CITY by Gerri Hill. 284 pp. Chris and Jesse cannot deny their growing attraction . . .
ISBN 1-931513-98-8 $12.95

ALL THE WRONG PLACES by Karin Kallmaker. 174 pp. Sex and the single girl—Brandy is looking for love and usually she finds it. Karin Kallmaker's first *After Dark* erotic novel.
ISBN 1-931513-76-7 $12.95

WHEN THE CORPSE LIES A Motor City Thriller by Therese Szymanski. 328 pp. Butch bad-girl Brett Higgins is used to waking up next to beautiful women she hardly knows. Problem is, this one's dead.
ISBN 1-931513-74-0 $12.95

GUARDED HEARTS by Hannah Rickard. 240 pp. Someone's reminding Alyssa about her secret past, and then she becomes the suspect in a series of burglaries.
ISBN 1-931513-99-6 $12.95

ONCE MORE WITH FEELING by Peggy J. Herring. 184 pp. Lighthearted, loving, romantic adventure.
ISBN 1-931513-60-0 $12.95

TANGLED AND DARK A Brenda Strange Mystery by Patty G. Henderson. 240 pp. When investigating a local death, Brenda finds two possible killers—one diagnosed with Multiple Personality Disorder.
ISBN 1-931513-75-9 $12.95

WHITE LACE AND PROMISES by Peggy J. Herring. 240 pp. Maxine and Betina realize sex may not be the most important thing in their lives.
ISBN 1-931513-73-2 $12.95

UNFORGETTABLE by Karin Kallmaker. 288 pp. Can Rett find love with the cheerleader who broke her heart so many years ago?
ISBN 1-931513-63-5 $12.95

HIGHER GROUND by Saxon Bennett. 280 pp. A delightfully complex reflection of the successful, high society lives of a small group of women.
ISBN 1-931513-69-4 $12.95

LAST CALL A Detective Franco Mystery by Baxter Clare. 240 pp. Frank overlooks all else to try to solve a cold case of two murdered children . . .
ISBN 1-931513-70-8 $12.95

ONCE UPON A DYKE: NEW EXPLOITS OF FAIRY-TALE LESBIANS by Karin Kallmaker, Julia Watts, Barbara Johnson & Therese Szymanski. 320 pp. You've never read fairy tales like these before! From Bella After Dark.
ISBN 1-931513-71-6 $14.95

FINEST KIND OF LOVE by Diana Tremain Braund. 224 pp. Can Molly and Carolyn stop clashing long enough to see beyond their differences?
ISBN 1-931513-68-6 $12.95

DREAM LOVER by Lyn Denison. 188 pp. A soft, sensuous, romantic fantasy.
ISBN 1-931513-96-1 $12.95

NEVER SAY NEVER by Linda Hill. 224 pp. A classic love story . . . where rules aren't the only things broken.
ISBN 1-931513-67-8 $12.95